D1313324

We hope you enjoy this book. Please return or
renew it by the due date.

You can renew it at www.norfolk.gov.uk/libraries o
by using our free library app.

Otherwise you can phone 0344 800 8020 -
please have your library card and PIN ready.

You can sign up for email reminders too.

NORFOLK ITEM
30129 087 675 816

NORFOLK COUNTY COUNCIL
LIBRARY AND INFORMATION SERVICE

BOOKS BY EMMA TALLON

Runaway Girl
Dangerous Girl
Boss Girl
Fierce Girl
Reckless Girl

FEARLESS GIRL

EMMA TALLON

bookouture

Published by Bookouture in 2020

An imprint of Storyfire Ltd.
Carmelite House
50 Victoria Embankment
London EC4Y 0DZ
www.bookouture.com

ISBN: 978-1-83888-140-5
eBook ISBN: 978-1-83888-139-9

For my beautiful boy, Christian, and his soon-to-be-born sister. You are both the most precious gifts I've ever been blessed with.

And in memory of Julie Andrew, a very special reader who will live on through these pages forever.

PROLOGUE

The weight of whatever was to come next seemed to hang in the stale air of the courtroom, as Freddie and Paul were bought back in for the last time. They had been back and forth time and again as the Tylers' lawyer fought hard from every angle he could, but now a verdict had been reached and everyone in the room was waiting to find out what it was.

Anna felt Tanya's hand slip into hers and squeeze it in support. Mollie sat on the other side of her, crying softly into a tissue, a beaten shell of the strong woman she had been only weeks before. She had just lost her only daughter and was about to potentially lose her sons too. Freddie's son, Ethan, was not present, Anna having decided it was best for him not to witness this.

Freddie looked over and locked eyes with her, and Anna saw the tension she felt mirrored in them. There was no reassurance in his expression, no secret message for her this time. Which way this would go was anyone's guess, and for once Freddie was not able to control the outcome. Next to him, Paul, the younger of the two brothers, stood tall and stared at the wall, his jaw locked tight.

Aside from their lawyer and the three women, there was no one else present to support the Tylers. Freddie had asked his men to stay away, knowing the police would be watching out for known associates. He didn't want to give them any excuse to further link anyone to the firm's crimes. Whatever happened today, the business needed to continue thriving.

The judge cleared his throat and shuffled his papers, indicating that he was ready to deliver his verdict. Freddie looked back towards his desk and Anna's eyes followed his gaze. The tension in the room grew until it was almost tangible and Anna's heart began to race. She swallowed the dry lump in her throat and wished that he would just hurry up and get on with it.

Looking up, the judge cast a hard eye around the room, his bushy salt-and-pepper eyebrows furrowing into a serious frown.

'These cases are usually fairly cut and dry, but I have never before been faced with these sorts of charges against someone of your particular standing in the community.'

Anna held her breath. *What did that mean?* She glanced at Freddie but his carefully neutral expression held no answers.

'You have been caught with a large quantity of cocaine in your possession – this much is undeniable. The question of whether or not you intended to supply is a grey area. Indeed, the police have put forward their case for believing this to be so, however there has been no actual proof. With this in mind and considering that this is your first offence, in a normal situation I would be inclined to let you go home with a conditional discharge and a significant fine. However,' he continued heavily, 'despite the lack of solid proof of intent to supply, the sheer quantity found, the fact there was no cocaine found in your own blood and the way the product was packaged and moved leads me to believe that it is almost certainly a professional venture. And this gives me great cause for concern.'

Anna heard herself gasp and felt her blood turn to ice in her veins as she realised where the judge was going.

'No,' she whispered, covering her hand with her mouth.

'Having taken this into consideration, whilst I can only charge each of you with possession of a Class A drug, I am imposing the strongest sentence for this crime of five years' imprisonment, with the recommendation that you serve at least three.'

'No, you can't,' Anna cried out in horror, standing up and grasping the back of the bench in front. Tanya gripped her arm and tried to pull her back.

The judge continued, ignoring the outburst. 'There are good reasons why these drugs are illegal. The damage caused to people – to families and children – can be devastating. I suggest that you both take this time to think about your life choices and consider how you might change things for the better, in regard to both yourselves and society, upon your release.' He stood up. 'Court dismissed.'

'No!' Anna shook Tanya off and pushed past her towards the centre aisle. 'No, you can't do this,' she yelled. 'It was just possession!'

Freddie locked eyes with her, a clear hardness behind them that pulled her up short. He gave her a curt nod, his gaze intense, and she suddenly realised he had been expecting it. He wasn't shocked and he wasn't fighting. He was telling her to stop.

As they led the brothers away, Anna blinked, momentarily lost. She turned around and shook her head in denial.

'No,' she said to Tanya, who was now holding a wailing Mollie in her arms. 'No.' Her expression turned hard. 'This isn't happening.'

'Anna—' Tanya started.

'No.' Anna cut her off and marched out the door, still shaking her head vehemently. 'It's not happening. Not to Freddie and Paul. We're going to get them out.'

CHAPTER ONE

2019

Anna sat in the office of Club CoCo, tapping her pen on the blank notebook in front of her. She stared at the wall in front of her, not really seeing it. Not seeing anything but the courtroom they'd all sat in two and a half years before. In her mind she watched Freddie and Paul being led away; away from their family, away from their lives and their freedom. She closed her eyes and exhaled slowly, as the weight of what that day had done to them all sat heavily on her shoulders.

A lot had changed since the Tyler brothers had been sent down. London had changed. She had changed. Everyone and everything linked to the empire Freddie had built with his own two hands had changed. And now as the weather turned warm and the days grew longer, they all had to start preparing for another big change once more.

Most people were excited for the infamous brothers' return. Bill and Sammy and all the other men within the firm were buzzing to see their friends out of prison. Mollie had been organising a party for weeks, dreaming up and continuously changing a large menu of home-cooked food for the small army of people who would be there to celebrate Freddie and Paul's release.

For Anna it wasn't so straightforward. Her life had been thrown into complete turmoil the day the judge had sent them down, and for a while she had floundered. The situation had been dire and her heart had been broken by the distance placed between them, but Anna was a fighter, and so she had stepped up and done what needed to be done.

True to her word she had raised Freddie's son Ethan as her own and sheltered the boy as much as she could from the finer details of his father's imprisonment. And with Freddie's men by her side, she had taken over the reins of his businesses and kept them afloat.

It had been hard. There had been times she had not been sure she could do what needed to be done, but she'd persevered. Without Freddie and Paul's fearsome reputation keeping them at bay, the sharks had moved in. Competitors from all over the city began pushing at the boundaries and had tried to intimidate her into falling back. But she had held her ground, and had learned quickly that she needed to change if she was going to survive in the world Freddie had built.

It hadn't been an easy decision, to make those changes. There had been times when she had considered turning her back on the business completely, living life like a normal person. But turning her back on Freddie's business meant turning her back on Freddie, and whilst she wasn't sure what they even were to each other anymore, she still loved him deep down in her heart. For that reason she knew she could never turn away. This was her life now, whatever the circumstances that had put her here. And so she had committed to it.

The dark threats from outsiders taking their chances had been countered with dark deeds: the Anna Davis who had so blindly taken the reins was soon replaced by a harder, colder woman. Someone who people learned not to cross. When liberties were taken, she adopted Freddie's playbook. Using Freddie's men as her instruments, people were threatened, traitors were hurt and Anna's heart slowly toughened. Competitors began to retreat, no longer willing to cross the woman who was now running the Central London belt – or most of them, at least.

There were still a few thorns in her side that Anna had not quite been able to fully remove. As accepting as she had become of violence and intimidation, Anna drew the line at murder and there were people who knew it. There had been a few battles and some ground lost, which would not go down well with Freddie once he was out.

Anna rubbed her head, then opened the top drawer of the mahogany desk and pulled out a slim silver case. She slipped out one of the long, thin menthol cigarettes inside and lit it. Taking a deep drag, she relished the warmth as it filled her lungs, before blowing out a long plume of smoke.

There was a knock at the door, and it immediately opened as Seamus let himself in. He paused as he clocked the cigarette in her hand.

'I didn't know you smoked,' he said, his tone tinged with surprise and disapproval.

'I don't,' Anna said, taking one more long drag before regretfully stubbing it out. 'It's just something I do now and then when I'm extremely stressed. Don't tell Ethan.'

Seamus nodded. He didn't ask what was stressing her out – he figured he could already guess. 'I've collected the protection payments,' he said, shrugging the full backpack off his shoulder. 'Mr Latif has had some trouble with kids the last few nights. He's had a window put in, some thefts and threats.'

'Tell him we'll station one of our security guys there for the next week or so until it's calmed down. Hopefully the kids will come back and they can get taught a lesson, get scared off for good. Also get his window fixed – we'll cover that cost. Not much point him paying for protection if it doesn't do anything for him,' Anna said tiredly.

'Will do,' Seamus replied. Pressing one of the wooden panels in the wall, he stepped back as it opened up to reveal a safe behind. He began emptying the money into it.

'I need to arrange a meeting with Roman. Can you have an invitation sent to him, to come to the club tomorrow night?' Anna watched Seamus's jaw tighten. She knew he didn't like Roman, but she had never been able to understand why. The man had proved to be a valuable ally over the last year or so and was one of the few people she genuinely trusted.

'Sure,' Seamus replied, not turning around. 'Which club?'

Anna considered her options for a moment. 'Let's say Club Anya. I haven't been able to make it over all week. I can kill two birds with one stone.'

'OK. I've got to get back out; I'll catch you later.' Seamus locked the safe and shot her a tight smile before leaving the office.

Anna watched as the door closed and then sighed, picking the pen back up. There was just one short week to go until Freddie and Paul were back out, and she had to work out what needed to be done before then. The trouble was, Anna had no idea what to expect.

Would they be pleased with the progress she'd made with the businesses? Were they going to adapt to the changes, or expect her to roll over and disappear, business-wise, once they resurfaced? Because that was something that wasn't going to happen. Whilst Anna accepted that these were their businesses and that she was only looking after them temporarily, she was involved now. She couldn't just go back to how things were before. She'd changed. This was now her world too.

She sighed heavily, trying to imagine Freddie's reaction to everything – and to her. It had been two and a half years and both of them had been thrown into new worlds that had changed who they were forever. She doubted that either of them would even recognise who the other was anymore.

CHAPTER TWO

Tanya walked up to the red double front doors of the tall cream building and paused, looking at her watch. She was a couple of minutes early. Crossing the busy Central London road to the small green opposite, she found a bench and sat down to wait.

Looking up at the imposing building once more and at the small flock of parents and nannies gathering outside, she shook her head slightly. She could never understand why Anna felt the need to send Ethan to this posh private school. The local one would have been fine. The boy could have played in the mud and got up to mischief like every other kid. But this, of course, was what Anna was afraid of. She was terrified that the events of his past had damaged Ethan and that this would lead to bad life choices. She wanted to limit the poor choices he could make by surrounding him with all the sheltered rich kids who were already going somewhere in life before they'd even tried.

Ethan was a good kid though. If he'd been given the chance, he still would have made good choices – Tanya was sure of it. She'd seen enough damaged souls to know the ones who would turn into something good, rather than self-destruct. But there was no telling Anna that.

The door opened and a teacher appeared, ready to hand over each child as he recognised their responsible adult. Standing up, Tanya walked back across the road as Ethan came into view. The teacher clocked her and waved Ethan on, giving her an appreciative look as he did so. She ignored this and smiled broadly as the boy she'd come to love more than anything in the world came back into her day.

She hugged him quickly before he squirmed away, as she'd known he would.

'Tanya,' he laughed. 'Get off – people will see.'

'What's the matter? Am I too old and ugly to be seen with you these days, eh?' she joked, ruffling his golden-brown hair affectionately.

'No, 'course not,' he replied, as they turned to walk back to her car. 'But you're a *girl*.'

He said it with such disgust that Tanya burst out laughing. 'Well, Christ, I hadn't realised that,' she exclaimed in mock horror. 'How do I rid myself of this illness?'

Ethan rolled his eyes and giggled as they reached her shiny black Mercedes. Tanya opened the passenger door for him and then walked around to the driver's side. She slid her fingers along the paintwork, still marvelling at the fact it was hers. Up until just over a year ago she had never learned to drive, so this was her first-ever car and it was her pride and joy.

Until Freddie and Paul had gone away she'd never had reason to learn. It was only after Anna took over the businesses, and began to struggle with juggling everything she needed to do, that Tanya realised she needed to step up. She began to help raise Ethan, but that came with a lot of running around – football club, play dates with friends, the school run and all sorts of other things – so Tanya booked lessons so that she was able to take some of those responsibilities from Anna's shoulders.

They pulled off down the busy London street towards home. Home was now much closer to the school than it used to be. Anna had sold their flat, with Freddie's approval, not long after he went away. The task force had turned the place upside down searching for more evidence, the day they'd arrested him. Anna had come home to complete chaos, which was the last thing she and Ethan had needed on the day they'd buried Thea and lost Freddie and Paul to the police.

Tanya still couldn't believe they had been so callous as to swoop in with the SWAT team that day. Freddie and Paul had just lost their only sister. Thea had been caught in the middle of a badly handled stand-off between the brothers and a desperate drug dealer. They'd almost got her out; they had been so close. But a surprise bid for freedom on her part had caused the man holding her to panic and slit her throat. She had died in Freddie's arms, unable to even take one last breath. It was something the brothers would never forgive themselves for – that Thea had ended up leaving the world caught up in their mess like that. The funeral had been hard for everyone, but especially them.

Coming home after this, to find their home in complete chaos, had been the final straw for Anna. There were too many bad memories there, with that and some of the darker moments of their past. She had wanted to start afresh with Ethan in a new home.

When a large three-bedroomed flat above Tanya's came up for sale, she'd jumped at the opportunity. Then, more than ever, she had needed to be close to her best friend.

'So, how was school?' Tanya asked, waiting for the traffic lights ahead to turn green.

'It was OK,' Ethan said with a shrug. 'I got ninety per cent on my maths test.'

'That's brilli— Oi! Watch where you're going, arsehole! Sorry, Ethan.' Tanya glanced at him then back to the car that had just cut her up, shooting it a scathing look. 'That's brilliant, babe. You're a right little genius you, aren't ya? Just like your dad.'

Ethan went quiet and looked out of the window at the hustle and bustle of the city around them.

'You looking forward to him coming out next week?' she asked.

'I guess,' he answered, his young voice unsure.

Tanya's heart filled with pity for the boy. At nine years old he had seen and experienced far more than he should have in his lifetime already.

'You can talk to me about it, you know,' Tanya offered. 'I'm always here to listen.'

They had formed a deep bond over the last couple of years, since Ethan's mother had sold him off to Freddie for a fresh start in life. Jules had been a selfish, cruel woman who had taken out her frustrations on the poor boy time and again. Neglected and malnourished to a heartbreaking level when Freddie first found out about him, Ethan had been a completely different kid to the one he was today.

Now, Ethan looked healthy and happy, and the older he got, the more he looked like Freddie. Aside from the same hazel-green eyes, they had the same intensity in their expressions and the same definitive jawline. As young as he was, under the pale, rosy complexion, he had the distinctive Tyler look about him.

Tanya thanked the heavens for this whenever she rested her eyes on his face. It had been hard enough for Anna to come to terms with the situation when Ethan had first arrived on the scene – especially after finding out that she couldn't have children herself. If Ethan had looked like his mother, Tanya wasn't sure Anna could have taken to him the way she eventually had. She wouldn't have been able to look into his face each day if what stared back at her was a constant reminder that he was another woman's.

Ethan twisted in his seat, his expression troubled. 'I don't really know how I feel about Dad and Uncle Paul coming home,' he admitted. 'Nan keeps telling me I should be excited and that we have loads to catch up on…' He pulled a face. 'But what am I supposed to say? I only really knew Dad for a few weeks and then he went away. It's Anna who looks after me now. And you,' he added. 'I don't actually know him.'

Tanya drew in a deep breath and exhaled slowly. 'That's true,' she conceded. 'But you know, no one is expecting anything of you. You don't need to worry about the right thing to say or what it's going to be like. Your dad is still the same person you spent those few weeks with.' As she said it, Tanya silently prayed that she was right. 'I wouldn't overthink it. If I were you, I'd just go with the flow, talk when you want, retreat when you don't. And I'll be right there with you the whole time. And you know if you feel funny about anything you can always just jump downstairs to me.'

'Yes, I suppose,' Ethan replied, looking a little more hopeful.

'It's going to be fine, I promise you. OK?' She watched him nod then glanced at her watch. 'OK, so let's go get you some tea and we'll watch a film before your stepmum gets home. She'll be late, so you can pick one of the ones she never lets you watch.'

'OK.' Ethan grinned and Tanya returned an affectionate smile.

She hid the feeling of worry she felt underneath her calm exterior. Freddie had been away for a long time and him coming out was going to change life again, for all of them. Was he going to be the dad that Ethan remembered from those few short weeks? What was he going to think of the young boy they had been raising without him? She and Anna had both parented him together, these past couple of years. But now Ethan's father was going to be back on the scene, the missing piece of the family set.

She let the question she didn't dare voice out loud creep back into her mind. What would Freddie's return now mean for *her* role in Ethan's life?

CHAPTER THREE

Bill Hanlon hid his irritation as the prison guard took his time patting him down at the security station. Every now and then, the guard gave him a suspicious look before carrying on his methodical search. This guy was very obviously new to the job and clearly hadn't made it onto Freddie's payroll yet. One of the more familiar guards caught his eye across the room and shot him a look of apology. Bill shrugged in response. It didn't matter. It wasn't like he was smuggling anything in. Any contraband that made its way to the Tylers came in via the guards. It was a far easier method of delivery.

Finally satisfied that Bill wasn't trying to get anything past him, the guard allowed him to continue through. He picked up his jacket from the end of the security scanner belt and walked through the double doors towards the next guard, who would accompany him through to whatever room Freddie was waiting for him in. It had long been arranged that their meetings were held in a private room, rather than the visiting hall. That was one of the perks the Tylers had organised the second they arrived.

As he walked, Officer Akenhead fell in beside him. 'Sorry about that,' he muttered, glancing over his shoulder.

'No worries. Newbie, I take it?'

'Yeah, fresh down from somewhere up north.' He paused to unlock one of the security doors. 'Bit wet behind the ears.'

Walking on, they turned a corner and Officer Akenhead sped up to open one of the many doors ahead. He stepped aside to let Bill pass.

'I'll be just out here, when you're done.'

Bill nodded and closed the door behind him. Freddie sat on one side of a small table in the sparse room, staring out of the window over the fields beyond. Smoke curled up from the lit cigarette in his hand and he absentmindedly tapped the ash into an ashtray on the table.

'Not a bad view, this,' he remarked as Bill sat down opposite him. He stubbed the cigarette out and twisted back around, away from the window. 'But I won't miss it,' he added. 'This will be the last time you have to visit me in here. I bet you won't miss it either.'

'I certainly won't,' Bill replied with feeling. He hated coming here. Every time he stepped through the front doors, it was a small reminder of what his life would be like if he was caught out again. He'd done time himself, years before, and didn't intend on repeating it.

'So, what's happening? What's new?' Freddie asked.

'Nothing new to report really – most of the stuff we'll need to go through on the other side,' Bill said with a meaningful look. Freddie nodded. Even with the freedom his position allowed him inside prison, it wasn't wise to go into too much detail. 'Your mum's been organising a welcome-home party for you both.'

Freddie groaned.

'I know it ain't exactly what you want, but Anna says it's been keeping Mollie sane. It's all she can focus on.'

'Yeah, of course. Wouldn't expect anything less,' Freddie replied.

He looked down, a small wave of grief rippling over him at the thought of going home. He hadn't been home since the day of his sister's funeral. The police had descended just after they'd laid her in the ground, before the reception. He had never been able to properly grieve or help his mother through that heartbreaking time.

'How is she, me mum? She doing OK still?'

Mollie visited both her boys often, but she kept a brave face on each visit and refused to talk about anything that might upset or frustrate them whilst they were inside. Freddie knew she would be finding everything a lot harder than she let on.

'Ah, she's alright.' Bill shifted awkwardly in his seat. 'She's a right brahma, your mum – you know she is.'

In truth Mollie hadn't dealt with the loss of three of her children at once well at all. As someone who lived and breathed for her family, she hadn't known what to do with herself. They had all stuck together to look after her, after Freddie and Paul went away, the same way they knew would be done for their own mothers, had the situations been reversed. But it had still been hard.

For a while Mollie had poured all her efforts into tracking down her youngest son, who Freddie had told her was living out a new life under a different name in South America. It had briefly distracted her from her overwhelming sense of loss. She had no clue that Michael was actually dead and buried in a cemetery only an hour down the road. Everyone had kept this truth from her in the hope it would save her unnecessary heartache, but in doing that they had given her false hope and led her to begin a search. Bill had had to be careful, steering her away from finding anything out whilst Freddie and Paul were locked up. He hadn't told Freddie any of this, not wanting to cause any frustration while the brothers weren't at liberty to do anything about it.

'And Anna?' Freddie asked. 'How's she been?' It was a loaded question and Bill noted the tension that gathered in his shoulders as he waited for the response.

Anna had taken Ethan on, and the businesses, to her credit, but relations between the two of them were deeply fractured. Anna no longer visited unless she had no choice, and when she did, Bill had heard that she was cold and to the point. It was all business. Despite this, though, their lives were still heavily entwined, and underneath the strain and separation that the current situation had forced upon them, he was pretty sure the love they once shared was still there. He hoped it was anyway.

'She's alright. Same old, really. She suggested once you're back and settled in that we all get together for a meeting.' Bill felt awkward inviting Freddie to a meeting with his own men, but times had changed and Anna had been running the show for a while now. 'So we can all get up to speed.'

Freddie nodded and lit another cigarette. 'Yeah, of course.'

Anna's suggestion of a meeting wasn't a surprise; he would need an extensive handover from her. It was best if everyone was together for this. From what he'd heard, she'd done a good job of keeping the firm afloat whilst he'd been away. He was eternally grateful to her for this – amongst many other things. He owed her a lot.

Freddie considered probing further and bit his bottom lip as he pondered. It wasn't so much the business side of things he wanted to know about. He trusted Anna – she was one of the sharpest people he'd ever met. But not once in the two and a half years that he'd been away had he heard any mention of her dating someone else.

Part of him clung to the possibility that even though prison had officially separated them, she had stayed single and was waiting for him to return. Not that he had asked her to wait for him; he hadn't wanted to place that burden on her alongside everything else. Instead he had given her the space to decide for herself. It had only been fair.

The realist in him was convinced that two and a half years was too long to wait for anyone, and that she would have definitely moved on. And a shrewd voice in his head told him that if she had moved on, his men would protect him by keeping back this information. But still he held on to a small sliver of hope.

Freddie pushed these thoughts away and turned his attention back to business. 'I'll need to see Ralph, too, once I'm out. See how the land lies, there.' Ralph had been Freddie's business partner in several building ventures that had been mainly legitimate so far. He wasn't involved in any of the firm's general activities and therefore would not be invited to the meeting.

'I believe Anna was going to set up a lunch with Ralph separately,' Bill said.

Freddie frowned. 'I wasn't aware she was involved with Ralph.'

'From what I understand Ralph came by about six months ago with an opportunity, looking for investment. Anna invested. I don't know more than that.'

'I see,' Freddie replied. He sat back. 'Interesting. She's never mentioned it.'

Why was that? he wondered, a trickle of cold suspicion creeping up his spine.

Bill looked at his watch. 'Listen, I've got to shoot. Just wanted to let you know you'll be picked up Saturday lunchtime when they let you out, and I'll have fresh clothes and everything sent ahead of that for you both. Everything else can be caught up on after the party. All good?'

'All good,' Freddie said with a nod. 'You've been a true diamond through all this, Bill. I won't forget that.'

'I know you won't,' Bill replied with a grin. 'I'm looking forward to having you back on the outside. It's been far too long.'

Freddie stood up and walked his old friend to the door. 'Just a few more days,' he said, slapping Bill on the shoulder. 'A few more days and I'll be back on top. And then everything will go back to normal,' he said, a determined glint in his eye. 'Just like it was before.'

CHAPTER FOUR

Mollie sat on the perfectly made double bed in the back bedroom of her house and stared off into the distance, carefully cradling a worn-looking teddy bear with one eye missing. She stroked the top of its soft head and half a smile tugged briefly at the corner of her mouth as a happy memory played out inside her mind.

It was Thea's room. It still looked exactly the same as it had the day her daughter had died. Necklaces still hung from a jewellery tree on the dressing table and all her clothes still waited in the closet. Her pictures of friends and family were still Blu-Tacked to the mirror. The only time Mollie moved anything was to clean and dust. The room still looked as though Thea might return to it at any moment. And whilst she kept it like this, sometimes when she sat here, she could fool herself that this could happen. Just for a moment.

A knock at the door sounded through the empty house and roused Mollie from her reverie. She placed the teddy back in its spot on the pillow and rubbed her tired eyes, before standing up and heading downstairs.

Opening the front door, she smiled as Ethan walked in, with Anna right behind him.

'Hello, Nan,' he said, wrapping his arms around her in a big hug.

'Hello, young man,' she greeted him fondly and ruffled his hair before they all walked through to the big kitchen at the back of the house.

'Here's all his stuff,' Anna said, placing an overnight bag on the kitchen table. 'He's got rugby tomorrow, but his boots are still at school because he keeps forgetting to bring them home.'

'Oh, you're as bad as your dad,' Mollie said with a chuckle. 'He always used to forget his too.'

Ethan stayed over at Mollie's a couple of nights a week. Officially this was to help Anna out as a lot of her business was conducted late at night. She didn't really need the help with Tanya always available to tag team, but it was nice for Ethan to be able to spend time with his grandmother and it gave Mollie some purpose.

'Have you got everything you need for him?' Anna asked, more out of courtesy than necessity, as she knew Mollie was always prepared.

'Oh yes, all sorted. We've got roast beef for dinner tonight. You like my roast beef, don't you, Ethan? Are *you* able to stop for dinner?' Mollie asked Anna, peering into the oven to check the meat was getting on as expected.

'I can't tonight, sorry, Mollie.'

Mollie glanced over towards the woman who she had, for years, seen as her daughter-in-law. Indeed, Anna was still the closest thing to a mother that Ethan had, but she had no idea where things stood between Anna and her son these days. Whenever she asked, no one would give her a straight answer.

'You look nice,' Mollie commented, appraising her. 'You going somewhere special?'

Anna always made an effort with her appearance, wearing fitted dresses and walking around with ease in heels that would destroy Mollie's back if she tried them for even five minutes, but today she looked particularly dressed up.

Anna blushed slightly through her perfectly applied make-up under Mollie's scrutiny. 'Just work,' she said, with a dismissive shrug. 'I have a couple of meetings tonight at the club. Might have a drink with Tanya afterwards if there's time.'

'Oh, OK.' Mollie raised her eyebrows and turned back towards her oven. 'Well, have fun.'

'Will do,' Anna replied. She pulled Ethan in for a hug and kissed the top of his head. 'Be good for Nan. I'll see you tomorrow night.' Giving him a wink, she set off, already switching her mind back to business mode as she walked out of the house.

Mollie watched her go with troubled eyes. Her boys were out in less than a week. What was going to happen between Anna and Freddie? Had it been too long? Anna was definitely not the girl he had left behind. There was a coldness about her these days that he wouldn't recognise. Mollie wasn't sure how well their reunion was going to go. Glancing at Ethan as he pulled his homework out of his bag, she sent up a silent prayer that they could find some common ground still, for his sake.

*

Anna walked into Club Anya with her head held high and her spirits raised for the first time in days. She always enjoyed her meetings with Roman Gains. Carl, her loyal friend and dependable general manager of the club, smiled as he saw her enter and greeted her as she passed the bar.

'How's things? You look nice,' he said pleasantly.

'Thanks. I'm good. Is Roman here?' She looked around.

'He is – he's in the VIP area. It was free, so I sent him over to wait for you there.'

'Oh great.' Anna glanced over and caught sight of the smoothly handsome man sitting casually on one of the leather sofas in the VIP area. 'Has he got a drink?'

'He does, and he has your favourite wine over there in a chiller too.' He shrugged when she gave him a look. 'He said you wouldn't be long; I figured I'd get ahead of myself.'

'OK,' Anna said, with a nod.

Smoothing her dress down, she walked over and smiled as he stood to greet her.

'Anna, how are you?' he asked, his deep velvety voice making her feel warm inside. He always seemed to have that effect on her.

She smiled. 'I'm great, thanks for asking. And yourself? How is everything?'

They sat down opposite each other and Roman set about pouring her a drink.

'Everything is going well. We found a new route around the coast guard, since they changed their shifts. Which means we can potentially open up another regular shipment line.'

'Interesting,' Anna mused, taking a sip of her wine.

Not long after Freddie went down, they'd lost their regular shipment space on the containers that came into the docks. Their main contact retired, and unable to turn his replacement, their supply line of illicit alcohol had suffered. Anna was a sharp businesswoman though, and it hadn't taken her long to source an alternative.

Roman Gains was a freelance smuggler with a small fleet of pleasure boats. He legally ran this business in the daytime, then used the boats to transport his clients' wares under the radar through the night. He was more expensive than the containers, but not by too much, and there was significantly less risk involved. They had to dodge the coast guard, but they had access to their patrol routes, and at least with Roman all the crew were in on the operation. They didn't have to worry about any do-good officials walking round the corner at the wrong time and seeing something they shouldn't.

Anna crossed her slim legs and leaned her arm across the back of the sofa. Her dark blue eyes narrowed in thought. 'How easy would it be for me to get a small package down to Gibraltar?'

Roman's eyebrows rose up in surprise. 'It would depend on how small we're talking.'

'The contents would fit into an A5 envelope.'

It was Roman's turn to narrow his gaze. 'What's in the package?'

Anna smiled, the warmth not quite reaching her eyes. 'Now that would be telling. It's not legal, I can confirm that much. But other than that, the less you know, the better.'

'That's true,' Roman conceded. If he didn't know what he was carrying, he could legitimately claim ignorance should anything go wrong. 'Still,' he said, grinning, 'I am intrigued. You have many strings to your bow, Anna Davis, and every time I turn around it seems you're adding one more.'

The respect and admiration he felt for her shone through his deep brown eyes. She was a beautiful woman and an accomplished one at that. He knew, of course, that she had taken over the day-to-day running of the Tyler empire when they got sent down – everybody knew that – but she had already been running her own successful businesses way before, and instead of sitting around babysitting the Tylers' operations, it seemed she had jumped on every opportunity she could to grow it. There were not many women in the world with that level of gumption about them.

'If it can be hidden to the point it can get through a port undetected, I could get it to Gibraltar directly. But the way it's stashed must be completely foolproof.'

Anna nodded, twisting her mouth to one side as she thought through how she could do this.

'Otherwise, I can smuggle it to the north coast of Spain – Santander or A Coruña, maybe – and have it driven down across the border. It's a soft border; it wouldn't be an issue, but this would take longer. What's your time scale?'

'Fairly flexible, but the sooner the better.' The goods Anna was trying to move were hot property and she wanted them as far away from her as possible. 'I think we'll be safer smuggling through Spain than trying to conceal them through the port. It's too much of a risk if they're discovered.'

'OK, give me a few days – I'll sort something out,' Roman replied. 'And now that business has been conducted…' He leaned forward and topped up her wine from the bottle in the chiller. 'Let's get back to enjoying our evening.' He smiled. 'I feel like I haven't seen you for ages; we need to catch up. How's that crazy business partner of yours doing?'

Anna laughed, her eyes crinkling prettily at the sides. She knew Roman found Tanya's exploits entertaining. Most people did. 'She's very well, thank you. In fact she asked me to tell you that if you ever decide to smuggle anything to the Bahamas, she'd be more than happy to come along as an extra pair of hands.'

Roman threw his head back and laughed. 'I bet she would. I've never known anyone so desperate for a holiday. When is that girl going to actually get herself a passport?'

'God only knows,' Anna replied with a chuckle. 'She's been meaning to do it since the day I met her and, so far, I haven't even seen an application form.'

'She's a corker, that one,' Roman said, shaking his head with a fond smile. 'Anyway, do you fancy grabbing some dinner? I made reservations at Nobu, on the off chance you were free? I know how much you enjoyed it the last time we went.'

Anna considered it. She would have loved to go, but there was a lot of business she still had to attend to tonight, and she was already short on time. She bit her lip as she warred with herself. Dinner with Roman would be relaxing and fun and take her away from her troubles for a while. No matter where they went, he was always fabulous company, and he was right – she did enjoy the food at Nobu. But unwinding and forgetting her cares was not on the cards tonight.

She sighed with regret. 'I wish I could, really I do,' she said sincerely, 'but there's so much to do and I'm already chasing my tail. Rain check?'

'Of course,' he replied graciously.

He put his glass down and stood up, smoothing the front of his suit. Several of the women nearby gazed appreciatively at the dark, handsome man and the muscular body that showed clearly through his fitted white shirt. It wasn't lost on Anna either, but used to Roman's handsome appearance she respectfully maintained eye contact as she stood to bid him farewell.

His gaze held hers, with a twinkling challenge for a moment, and she felt the usual intensity between them.

'I'll let you get on then,' Roman said, leaning forward to kiss her on the cheek.

Anna breathed in the musky scent of cinnamon and cedar wood that Roman always seemed to carry with him and kissed him lightly on his smoothly shaven cheek.

'It was a pleasure to see you, as always,' Anna said warmly. 'Give me a call in the week – let me know how things are going.'

She watched as Roman left the club, then picked up her purse and walked over to the bar, waiting until Carl had finished serving a customer.

'If Tanya comes in looking for me, tell her I'm over at The Sinners' Lounge. I've got some business to sort out.'

With a steely glint in her eye, she walked out with purpose.

CHAPTER FIVE

The Sinners' Lounge was just around the corner from Club Anya, two floors hidden away above a little Italian restaurant. Two years previously, around the same time the Tylers got sent down, Anna and Tanya had set it up as a whorehouse – a spin-off from the club.

The club had many acts for the customers to enjoy: burlesque, girls performing high up on rings and ropes, choreographed dances and, of course, all the girls were dressed in outfits that left very little to the imagination. But despite these tantalising teasers, the club was fully above board and Anna had wanted to keep it this way. Rather than have the girls committing seedy acts in the back alley with overexcited punters, they now had somewhere safe and comfortable to go once their shifts were over. A discreet agreement on the club floor was all it took and the dark deeds that followed were no longer associated with the club itself.

When the popularity of the whorehouse grew, Anna took a leaf out of Freddie's book, incorporating a bar area and making it a place where they could enjoy more than just a quick bang before heading home. Business had flourished, and a year or so before, she had finally hired a full-time manager, Josephine. This was who she was on her way to see now.

Opening the door, Anna climbed the stairs to the first floor and entered the large main room. Dim lighting around the bar in the centre of the room gave punters the freedom to feel up the half-naked women sat on their laps in dark corners. One of these women stood up and began to lead her client off towards a bedroom. Anna ignored them and made a beeline for the tall woman dramatically draped across a small sofa at the side of the room, fanning herself.

'Anna, my dearest,' Josephine greeted her, in the deep, masculine voice that she couldn't quite hide. 'It's so good to see you.'

'And you, Josephine.' Anna sat down next to her and waited as her friend poured her a tea from the tray ready in front of her.

Josephine's long, claw-like nails were painted the same bright red as the silk kimono she was wearing and the shiny lipstick she'd applied. Her hair was curled and piled up high on her head, held in with two chopsticks. There was clearly a traditional Asian theme running through her overall look this evening, Anna surmised with a small smile. She rather enjoyed Josephine's theatrical tendencies.

'This tea,' Josephine began, as Anna took her cup with a nod of thanks, 'comes from a mountainside in China, where the leaves have been picked by the mouths of virgins.'

'What?' Anna asked, with a small laugh.

'Oh, it's true, darling. It's tradition, you see. They believe that this special tea ends up with added health and well-being, after soaking up the energy from the virgins.' She closed her darkly lined eyes and took a deep sip, before making a sound of appreciation. 'Oh yes, I feel the energy of the virgins running through my veins already.'

Shaking her head with a smile of amusement, Anna took a sip from her own cup. 'It is very nice,' she agreed. 'So' – she glanced down at Josephine's outfit once more – 'are you visualising yourself as a Chinese virgin this evening?' she asked.

'Me? Oh, Christ no,' Josephine laughed, her Adam's apple bobbing up and down. 'Aside from the fact that I can't even remember the days I was a virgin myself, these particular virgins also have to have natural C cups, and let's face it, mine are nothing but silicone.' She glanced down at her bosom. 'Still, they are rather fabulous, even if I wasn't born with them.'

Anna just nodded, used to Josephine's ways. 'So, how is everything?'

Josephine switched into work mode instantly, sitting upright and crossing her long, muscular legs as she twisted to face Anna.

'Our income has risen significantly since adding the twins to that back room. They draw a lot of interest, and the clients never last long between them. They're a complete goldmine. The viewing room has proved popular too. That was a very good idea. Now the clients who are waiting for their girl can pay us extra to stand and watch whoever's in there, making us more money for the same amount of work. It's surprising how many clients are up for being the one on show too. There are some proper dirty perverts in here, I tell you.' Josephine grinned, the action lighting up her broad face. She fiddled with one of the heavy gold earrings hanging from her ears and gazed at Anna thoughtfully. 'You didn't come here just to hear that though. I already told Tanya all this last night.'

'You're right, I didn't.' Anna leaned forward, double-checking first that they weren't being listened in on. 'I've sorted a route out for the diamonds. In a few days the package will be taken by boat to the north coast of Spain and smuggled in. Then it will be driven down and over the border into Gibraltar. I'll have to give you the exact timings later, but the point is, we can get it there.'

A look of excitement flashed through Josephine's dark eyes. 'And you completely trust the carrier?'

'Completely,' Anna confirmed.

'Well, this is news to be celebrated,' she replied, pulling a slim cigarette out of the packet on the table in front of her and lighting it.

'Not yet,' Anna said with a shake of the head. 'Let's just make sure it all runs smoothly before getting too excited. If it works' – she swayed her head to the side – 'this could be the start of a regular thing. But let's not count our chickens just yet.'

She watched as Josephine nodded and blew smoke up into the air. If she was being truthful, Anna was nervous about the whole deal. There were so many risks at so many points. But there was also great reward, and if they didn't use the opportunity that had presented itself, eventually someone else would.

It had been Josephine's idea to begin with. For many years, before she had decided to discard her socially acceptable mask and become who she really was, Josephine had lived and worked as a young man named Joseph in her father's shop in Hatton Garden. Josephine had been miserable every day, living an empty life, pretending she was somebody she wasn't. She'd hated living as a man – wearing suits and having to endure the nice, young Jewish women her mother would push in front of her, as she tried to turn her into a dutiful husband. No one understood that she didn't like women in that way, nor that she saw himself as a woman.

It wasn't her fault she'd been born into the wrong body. But in her parents' culture it was not acceptable to be anything other than what you are born as. And so she had suffered for many years, in misery. The one thing that did make her happy though were diamonds. Beautiful, unique, sparkling diamonds. They could be turned into whatever someone wanted them to be. A necklace, a ring, a number on a watch. It was admired by all, no matter what form it took.

When Josephine could no longer continue living the lie, she told her family who and what she really was. She began dressing in female clothes and wearing make-up, and used her savings to put herself through different surgeries to help transform her into the young woman she was born to be. In return she had been shunned and bullied by both her family and the close-knit community they lived in. Friends became enemies and places she used to frequent began turning her away.

Josephine had tried to hold on to the parts of her life that she could, hoping that with time people might become more tolerant. But after a year of loneliness and condemnation, and after a traumatic incident where she was dragged into an alley and beaten by people she had grown up with, the depression she'd been fighting finally took over completely and she was ready to give up on life.

Battered, bruised and feeling like the light inside had finally gone out, Josephine had put on her favourite clothes and painfully dragged herself to the Golden Jubilee bridge in the middle of the night. She couldn't go back to living her life as Joseph and nobody in her world was willing to let her live as Josephine. Stuck in this lonely limbo, she hadn't wanted to keep fighting through every day. There was no place for her in the world. She craved the peace that would come with ending her painful existence.

The bridge was a favourite place of hers, somewhere with beautiful views of the South Bank and a place she'd always considered to be the very heart of the city. It was as good a place as any to go. This way she could find her peace and lie quietly at rest in the centre of the city she called home forever.

But she had not been the only person there that night. Another young woman had gone for a late-night walk, to clear her head. Anna.

When Anna had come across someone so distressed, she'd stopped to talk. Surprising herself, Josephine had told Anna her woes, and by the time they'd finished talking, Anna had led her away from the bridge and offered her a place in her world. A real place, where she could work among people who didn't judge and where she could be whoever she wanted to be. That was the night Anna Davis had saved her life and given her a reason to live. And that was the night Josephine felt she had truly been born.

Initially she had worked in The Sinners' Lounge as a general assistant. She welcomed clients as they entered and poured their drinks. She helped with the schedule and changed the sheets between punters. She was little more than a skivvy, but she was grateful to be somewhere she was allowed to live freely and be herself.

Determined to prove her worth to the woman who had saved her, she soon started implementing small changes that helped smooth and speed up the efficiency of the operation. Impressed, Anna had promoted her to manager after just a few short months, and not long after that, Josephine had approached her with an idea.

Josephine was a shrewd woman who missed nothing. As if the shining beacon of the illicit whorehouse wasn't already enough, she could see that Anna had her fingers in several other not-so-legitimate pies and this had given her the idea.

During her time in Hatton Garden, plenty of people had approached her family's business with stolen or unmarked diamonds. They had been offered at ridiculously low prices as they were hot property, and Josephine had been sorely tempted to buy them, but her father had been strictly against anything that wasn't fully above board. He sent them away, time and again.

As time had gone on, Josephine had begun getting to know some of these people and had even helped a few of them make other connections. She still had their details now. Sharing all this with Anna, she had suggested that they go into business together, buying and selling the diamonds on to a contact she had in Gibraltar, who could mark any unmarked diamonds himself and turn them into jewellery to sell on again. She had the knowledge and the diamond connections, and Anna had the money and the transport connections. It was a match made in heaven.

Over the last month or so, they had carefully selected which pieces to buy and now had the first load ready to go. This would be their first transaction and Josephine was beyond excited.

'We need to think about how we're going to package them,' Anna said, sitting back in her chair and sipping her tea once more. 'I said it would be something no bigger than an A5 envelope, but I think perhaps it would be worth maybe sewing them into the lining of something the carrier could wear, in case they got searched.'

Josephine shook her head. 'If they were in the lining of a jacket or something, they might not be seen, but they could still be felt. Plus, if they got put through a scanner…' She pulled a face. 'Perhaps rather than hide it, we should leave them in plain view.'

'What do you mean?' Anna asked with a frown.

'Well, perhaps attach them as studs on a handbag. No one would suspect they were real – they'd be assumed to be decorative crystals. Or,' she continued, leaning forward to flick her ash into the ashtray, 'have them knocked up into wearable everyday jewellery this end and have them worn across.' She shrugged. 'I know a guy – he works with silver. It's pretty cheap.'

Anna thought about it for a moment, casting her dark blue eyes around the room as she mulled it over. 'If they do get stopped it will be for the illegal crossing. I don't think we need to worry so much about clothing going through a scanner. What we should do is place something else on the boat as a decoy smuggle load. Nothing serious – something they'd only get a slap on the wrist for.'

'Cheese would be a good idea. Dairy products aren't allowed into the country unless they're vacuum-packed and documented. Perhaps stick a box full of stinky blue on there. If they're caught, the Spaniards will be so outraged at that, they won't think to look for anything else.'

Anna grinned. 'Good idea. I'll speak to Roman about it.'

'Ahh, Roman,' Josephine replied. Her lips curled up into a smile and her eyes sparkled knowingly. 'So that's who you've been arranging this all with. Well, good.' She stubbed out her cigarette. 'That man would do anything for you. I've never seen anyone so devoted.'

Anna felt her cheeks warm and she sat upright. 'I don't know what you mean, Josephine. He's just a good friend and a loyal associate.'

'Mhm,' Josephine murmured sarcastically. ''Course you don't.'

Anna's phone beeped and she looked down to read the text. With a sigh she stood up. 'I have to go. I'll pop in later in the week, but text me if you need anything.'

'More to do tonight?' Josephine asked with a tinge of concern as her boss made to leave. 'It's so late, I assumed I'd be your last stop.'

Anna grinned back at her over her shoulder. 'You know what they say, Josephine. There's no rest for the wicked.'

CHAPTER SIX

Making her way across the busy dance floor, Anna marched towards the stairs that led up to Club CoCo's office. The music throbbed loudly and the dancers lost in their revelry littered her path, but she wound round them as quickly as she could. Sammy's message had sounded urgent, which was unusual. He was the calmest of all the men around her usually, even in difficult circumstances.

Taking the steps two at a time in her high heels, she entered the office to find Sammy, Seamus and Seamus's father Craig already waiting for her. Back when this had been Freddie's main office, he had never let a soul pass through these doors unless he was present, not even the cleaner. But Anna had found it more practical to give those in his inner circle – whom she trusted with her life, as did Freddie – a key of their own.

As she closed the door her eyes slipped down to Seamus's hand, which was bleeding profusely. Craig was attending to it, an open first aid kit on the floor where he knelt.

'What happened?' she asked, looking to Sammy.

'We were in the holding warehouse in Soho picking up a couple of booze orders. I was carrying a load out to the van when I heard a crashing sound inside. As I went to see what was going on, two men ran out past me. They'd waited until Seamus was in the back corner then pushed the top crates over on top of him. Luckily, he happened to step back so they didn't hit him full on, but they've still crushed his hand.'

'What the hell!' Anna exclaimed in horror. 'Why would they do that? Who were they? Did you see?'

Sammy's expression was grim. 'I don't know their names, but I've seen them before. They're Russian. Aleksei's men.'

'Fuck,' she cursed, under her breath.

Aleksei was a Russian mobster who had come to town looking for an area to stake his claim just after the Tylers had gone away. He had no previous ground in London at all, as his thriving underground business had been based in Russia until that point. But something had forced him to leave his country and move his operations elsewhere. He had money, men and a well-established business. All he'd needed was somewhere to call home.

'Seamus, how bad is it?' Anna walked over to him and crouched next to Craig, trying to assess the damage.

'I won't lie, Anna. It's more painful that sitting through a two-hour sermon with the Reverend Miller,' he joked bravely, trying to mask the severity of the situation.

'Eh,' Craig tutted and swiped his son around the head. 'Now ye don't go around talking about the priest that way. I don't care how badly you're hurting.'

Seamus winked up at Anna with a small grin. 'Jokes aside' – the grin faded – 'it's completely bust. I can't flex it; there's bones broken. Argh!' He cried out and bit down on his lip as Craig reset another finger.

'I'm sorry, lad,' he said quietly. 'Nearly done.'

'Shouldn't we take him to hospital?' Anna asked, her frown deepening.

Craig and Sammy both shook their heads.

'If it goes on his medical record, he'll be out of the game for a year,' Sammy replied. 'It will also highlight to every other boxer that this is his weak spot. They'll target it. We can't let anyone know. Craig is setting the bones and wrapping them here. That way once they're healed, we can try and get him back in quicker.'

'Well, Christ, that isn't everything, Sammy,' Anna snapped. 'Surely his health is more important.'

'It's what I want,' Seamus cut in. 'Anna, I don't want to be out of the game any longer than I have to be. It's what I live for. You know that. Plus, there's nothing more a hospital can do than my da can.'

She sighed and nodded reluctantly. 'OK.' She took a deep breath. 'What does this mean for the matches that have already been set?' she asked Sammy.

'It means we're set to lose a lot of money. Like, a *lot*,' he stressed, looking her in the eye. 'This weekend he was up against Joe Hunter; it was sold out weeks ago. It was rigged for Seamus to win, whilst the odds showed Joe as the favourite. Even with the game off, a lot of the bets against him win by default. It's going to set us back nearly fifty grand.'

'*Fifty grand!*' Anna's mouth shot open in shock. 'You can't be serious?'

'Deadly,' Sammy replied. 'We can take it, but it's a huge hit when we weren't expecting it. And it's not great timing with Freddie and Paul coming out on the same day.'

There was a protracted silence and Anna blew out a long, slow breath. She moved around the desk and sat down in the large leather chair.

Sammy changed the subject. 'We can't overlook the fact that Aleksei is messing with people in the firm now. Something needs to be done about it.'

'What would you suggest?'

'Retribution. We can have the men found and dealt with.'

Anna shook her head. 'That would start an all-out war, which we definitely don't need right now. It's too precarious a time.' She bit her lip. 'You're sure it was them?'

'I'm sure.' Sammy heaved a great frustrated breath. 'We can't let this go, Anna. They're trying to show us that we don't scare them. That they're not going anywhere, even with the Tylers coming back.'

'Hmph,' Anna snorted and raised her eyebrows. 'They've been a thorn in my side since the day they arrived,' she said resentfully.

Not long after Freddie and Paul were sent down, all the firms who wanted to try their luck with pushing boundaries had started to creep in. Anna and the rest of them had worked hard using threats, deals and negotiations to make sure they all understood that the business was running as usual. They had all retreated gracefully. All except this one.

When Aleksei had arrived in London and heard the whispers that the current kings had fallen and the area was being watched over by a girlfriend with no real experience in their world, he'd felt as though all his Christmases had come at once. It was an area primed for the taking. Charging into Soho with his Russian girls, heroin and guns, he had tried to overthrow them and take control. But Anna and the network around her hadn't been that easy to overthrow.

It had been a lengthy battle, and at times Anna had been sorely tempted to allow Sammy and the rest of them to take care of him once and for all. But whilst she was perfectly OK with violence these days, she stuck steadfastly to ordering only the odd beating or broken arm. She could never quite bring herself to order someone's death, whatever the rules of the world she now inhabited.

No matter how hard she had become, the memory of the life she had taken a few years before still haunted her. It had never quite gone away, and she had learned to live with the fact that it probably never would. She couldn't bear the thought of having a second person's blood on her hands – of the sleepless nights and the guilt that would sit in the bottom of her stomach like a stone. She would never be able to order that in cold blood.

Instead the battle waged on and the Tyler firm had managed to push Aleksei back to one small corner of Soho, with threats of destruction to his businesses if he tried to take any more ground. It was not quite the win the men had hoped for, as now their businesses faced competition on territory that was supposed to be their own. If Freddie and Paul had been around, it would never have been allowed. But they weren't, and the men had sworn to follow Anna's lead whilst their bosses were away.

Anna wasn't happy with it either, but it had served to keep them all on a fragile truce for the time being until the brothers were back on the scene. Then, she reasoned, it was up to them what they did about it. Any blood spilt would not be on her conscience.

But now it seemed Aleksei was flexing his muscles again. And Sammy was right: something did need to be done about it.

'I'll visit Aleksei tomorrow,' she said finally. 'Warn him and insist on retribution for these two men.'

Sammy barked a humourless laugh. 'You really think that's going to do anything? Anna, it's gone way beyond that point.'

'I'm aware of that,' she snapped at him, then took a step back and a calming breath. It wasn't Sammy's fault. 'I'm aware of that,' she repeated in a softer tone. 'But considering the timing, I think it would be wise to give him a warning and wait to see what Freddie and Paul would like to do.' Much as she worried about their return, this was one situation that would greatly benefit from the Tylers being around.

Sammy nodded, visibly perking up at the mention of the brothers. He tactfully chose not to reply, sensing his current boss's stress; surprised at the fact she had even mentioned Freddie's name. Their release seemed to be a sore subject around Anna at the moment, and he could understand why, to a degree. There was going to be a lot of change and it was going to affect her more than anyone. At this point it was anybody's guess how.

'I'll drop by his strip club after it opens at lunchtime,' Anna continued. 'Deliver the message then.'

'I'll come with you,' Sammy replied automatically.

Anna nodded. 'Seamus, is there anything I can do for you? I'll have the boys split your routes between them until you're feeling more able. And I'll cancel your sessions at the gym.'

Seamus looked up at her, sadness etched deep into his face. 'You can make sure those bastards are taught a lesson.' His face clouded over. 'I don't need much in life. The air in me lungs, a bed to sleep on and me hands to box with.' He looked down at the bloody mess his father was now wrapping up. 'They've taken the one thing I love away from me for a long time.'

Anna nodded solemnly. 'I know,' she said. 'And I promise you, those men and their boss are going to rue the day they did that. I wouldn't allow anyone to get away with what they've done to you, Seamus.' Anna felt the anger build up inside of her and carefully packed it away to be used at the appropriate moment. 'But if we're going to do it properly, we need the whole arsenal.'

'Well, let's hope the big guns come out of prison loaded. Because I'm a peaceful man, Anna,' Seamus said, giving her a hard look. 'But this is one fight that I won't turn me back on.'

CHAPTER SEVEN

Freddie reached under his bunk and pulled out the shoebox he kept there. Discarding the lid, he spread the contents out on the bed beside him, turning on the small hand torch he kept for nights like these when he couldn't sleep. There were a few photos of Anna and Ethan scattered among a pile of letters which were all dated at the top. Freddie ran his fingers over these, picking one up from just a few months after they were sent down.

It was from Anna, updating him on how they were doing, telling him all about Ethan's new school. He didn't have to actually read them anymore to know which ones held what information. He'd read them so many times he knew them almost by heart. Pulling them into date order, his gaze flickered down the line of numbers. At first Anna had written regularly, but over time, as things became more strained between them, she'd slowed down and eventually stopped completely.

Next his fingers rested on a thick pile of sealed letters at the back. These were the ones he had continued to write to her but had never sent. Through the long nights when his brain refused to switch off and he was missing her, he'd written down everything he had always wanted to say but knew he never would. Now that his time here was coming to a close, these were items he no longer wanted to keep hold of. Whilst they had been a comfort to him until now, all they would bring him on the outside was bad memories.

Reaching over, Freddie pulled the small metal bin that sat beside the bed over towards him, and with one long, final look at the letters he dumped them in. Picking up his matches – an item that for most inmates would be banned from their cells, but for the Tylers was just one more of the many luxuries they'd paid for – he lit one and held it to a corner of one of the letters. Freddie watched as the small flame curled the paper and turned its white edges brown before catching on the other letters.

The sound of another match being struck broke the silence and Paul's legs swung over the top bunk. A hand appeared holding an open pack of cigarettes in offering. Freddie took one. He rolled it in his fingers before lighting it and glanced up at the makeshift smoke alarm cover they'd maintained for the last two and a half years. He wouldn't miss this, always feeling on edge in case they set it off.

The guards on cell rotation were all on their payroll and therefore no threat. They turned a blind eye to the smoking and other luxuries the brothers had arranged. They smuggled the cigarettes in and even emptied the ashtray each day. But if the alarm system was triggered and an investigation was undertaken it could go much higher up the chain – and damage their chances of getting out this week.

'Did I wake you?' Freddie asked quietly as he watched the letters burn down into nothing in the small metal bin.

'Nah,' Paul replied in his deep, craggy voice. 'Just thinking about what there is to do when we get out. It don't feel real somehow, that it's so close now. Another few days and all this is history.' He took a deep drag and exhaled the smoke as he continued. 'I keep thinking I'm gonna wake up and be back where we were a year ago, freedom just some fantasy in the distance, you know? Time stretching on like some never-ending story.'

Freddie nodded in the darkness. 'Yeah, I know what you mean. But it's here now. And there's a lot to do when we get out.'

'Mm,' Paul grunted, uneasily. 'Ain't there just.'

The last letter shrivelled down to ash, and the weak glow coming from the small fire died out. Freddie felt a fleeting moment of emptiness, as his main link to his past life was suddenly gone, but he pushed it aside. Soon his life would begin again and it would be refilled with real substance, not just a few old words on a page. What that substance would be yet, he didn't know. Coming out was going to be like running round a blind corner headlong into the rest of your life. He felt the pressure press down on him and mentally held himself up higher. Nothing had defeated him yet, not even prison. Whatever life had in store, he could take it.

His mind wandered to Mollie. They still spoke to her most days, though all they really discussed was the weather and what her neighbours had been up to. It was meaningless small talk, but Freddie knew that keeping that link open and hearing her sons' voices was what kept her going. Even through her forced joviality he could hear the weak brokenness in her soul underneath. Mollie lived for her family and it had killed her losing her children the way she had.

A familiar stab of fury burned through Freddie's chest as he cast his mind back to his sister's funeral. The police had shown no mercy, no decency, not even waiting until the funeral was over before they rushed in with a full SWAT team and dragged them off to prison. He would never forgive that, and one day Ben Hargreaves, the Secretary of State for Justice, was going to get his comeuppance for ordering it. Swallowing his resentment, Freddie pushed the memories aside. There would be a time and place for that, but not yet. Right now they had to focus on what was imminently ahead of them.

'We need to be careful, when we get back out there,' he said. 'Hargreaves might have got his conviction, but I wouldn't put it past him to keep a tail on us for something more.'

'You spoken to Riley yet?' Paul asked.

Freddie's expression darkened. 'No,' he said. 'She can't come here, you know that. Wherever the land now lies, we can't have her cover blown. Not yet anyway.'

Sarah Riley was the DCI in charge of the team who had made the case to have them sent down. She was also on Freddie's payroll and had been tasked with making sure that this never actually happened. They had nearly been home and dry – the task force had nothing on them thanks to Riley's constant stream of insider information, and they'd been ordered to shut the case. But at the eleventh hour one of the officers had pulled a surprise piece of evidence out of the bag and it had been enough to secure a conviction. Riley swore blind that this had been collected behind her back and that she'd done all she could to avoid it, but as far as fuck-ups went, this one was colossal. Freddie wasn't sure yet whether or not he accepted her version of events.

He took a drag on his own cigarette and flicked the ash into the bin, his hazel-green eyes turning hard. 'I need to see her in person, read her. Only then will I be able to tell what really went down. And then' – he looked up at his brother – 'then I'll decide whether she's still one of us, or whether she's owed a one-way ticket to the afterlife.'

CHAPTER EIGHT

Anna came to a stop halfway down the busy London street and narrowed her eyes hatefully at the glaring neon sign above the strip club across the road. Sammy stood behind her and waited. This was where Aleksei had opened his first and the largest of his enterprises. Anna had heard that this was also where he held the guns he imported – and had been tempted on more than one occasion to give the police an anonymous tip-off. But this was completely against the rules of the underworld, and whilst Aleksei was an enemy, she still had to abide by these.

This was one of the first things Freddie had instilled in her when he handed over the reins. In her first meeting with him in prison, he had stressed the importance of never, ever flouting the rules. No matter what. Because once it became acceptable for one person to do it, others could retaliate in the same fashion and the London underworld would come crashing down upon them all.

The memory of that meeting flickered through her mind, and she felt a tug of residual pain in her chest. Sitting there that day in front of the man she had loved for so long, she had finally realised for the first time that he wasn't coming home. There was no fall-back plan, no plot to break him out, no loophole to slip through. He was there for at least half of his sentence. Which meant that life as she had known it was gone.

Closing her eyes momentarily, Anna pushed this painful memory aside and focused on the task at hand. Waiting for a black cab to pass out of her way, she marched across the road with purpose, Sammy matching his stride beside her.

Pushing open the door, they entered the dark building and let their eyes adjust as it closed again behind them. A scantily dressed young woman sashayed past and blew vape smoke into their faces, narrowing her eyes in distrust as she sat on a stool at the small bar to the side. Anna pointedly ignored the unfriendly reception and made her way across the floor of empty tables and past the runway where two tired-looking women were slinking around the poles for the small smattering of clients who had arrived for the lunchtime show.

In a red leather booth at the end of the room sat Aleksei, surrounded by a handful of his men. One of them touched the inside of his jacket meaningfully as they approached and two more stood up. Sammy opened up his own jacket to show them he was unarmed and Aleksei nodded to allow them through.

'Anna Davis.' His thick Russian accent curled around his words as he looked up at her mockingly. 'To what do we owe this pleasure?'

'You know exactly why I'm here,' Anna replied, her tone sharp.

Aleksei twisted to make himself more comfortable and appraised her with a cold smile. 'Well, that's where you're wrong, sweet girl,' he mocked, knowing his endearment would serve only to anger her further. 'For it could be a number of things. But I'm going to let you tell me which one of them it is today. I don't want to ruin any surprises.'

Anna studied his face for a moment. She had no doubt that there were things Aleksei had running that she wasn't aware of yet. Every time they turned around, there seemed to be another issue involving him. She made a mental note to ask Bill to dig around, but for now she let it go.

'Two of your men were sniffing around one of my warehouses last night and caused considerable damage to one of my men's hands. They broke several bones, which have had to be reset and will take time to heal. I want to know why,' Anna said, cutting to the point. She hated being in this seedy excuse for a club.

'Yes, I heard there was a misunderstanding,' Aleksei replied casually, not breaking eye contact.

'A misunderstanding?' Anna asked, her eyebrows shooting up in disbelief. 'If you think I'm buying that for one moment, you are sorely mistaken.' She eyed the men around him coldly, wondering if it was any of them Sammy had seen leaving the warehouse. 'Was it just playground bullshit?' she asked witheringly. 'Or was it something more?' Raising one eyebrow, she waited for the response.

Aleksei sat back and lifted his cup of coffee with a half-smile and a hard glint in his eye. 'I hear Joe Hunter is set to win each match all the way to the top of the league, now that Seamus won't be able to compete,' Aleksei said pointedly, meaning dripping off every syllable.

Anna's fury erupted inside as he confirmed what she had suspected, and it took all her self-control to contain it. She saw Sammy's knuckles whiten as his hand balled into a fist beside her.

'So, you're working with the Hunters?' she questioned, her tone cool but level.

'Oh no, I'm not working with anybody. I just made sure to square some big bets on Joe. I stand to make a killing over the next few weeks. Though, from what I understand, you have not been so lucky.' He pulled a dramatically sympathetic face. 'My condolences, Miss Davis. It is a travesty for such a pretty young woman to find herself at such a loss…'

'Cut the crap, Aleksei,' Anna snapped. She detested being spoken to like she was some pathetic, empty-headed girl. It riled her more than anything else. She was Anna Davis, underworld baroness and someone who'd earned a damn sight more respect than she was currently being shown. But, of course, Aleksei knew this, which was why he was going to such trouble to talk down to her.

She stepped forward, her dark blue eyes boring into his. 'You can't seriously think that we're going to take what you've done lying down – no, for all your faults you're too intelligent for that.' Anna gritted her teeth as her fury threatened to erupt. 'I allowed you this corner of Soho. I pulled back when I could have pushed you out completely, and we came to an agreement that meant we could all live and work in peace. But it seems that not a month goes by where I don't hear you're pushing the boundaries, edging in or just plain taking the piss.' Anna's voice grew louder with every sentence. 'And now this.' She fanned her arms out. 'You hurt one of my men.' She eyed him hard and felt herself grow deadly calm. 'And I want one of yours in return.'

'What?' Aleksei blinked in surprise, not expecting this.

Even Sammy turned to Anna with a look of surprise, before swiftly hiding it. She hadn't told anyone about this plan, though Sammy had to admit, he admired her for it. It was very Old Testament – an eye for an eye.

Anna smiled coldly, the action not reaching her eyes. 'You heard me. I want one of your men – in return – to do with as I please. Preferably the one who pushed the boxes down on Seamus last night, but it doesn't really matter,' she added dismissively. 'So long as they work for you, that will suffice. Call it retribution. Your payment for what you've done here. Part payment anyway. You'll also hand over the fifty grand you lost us, so that we're fully even.'

Aleksei stood up with a frown, all pretence of friendly banter gone. 'I will not hand over one penny to you, nor one of my men, today or any other day,' he spat. 'They're people, not coins to make payment with.'

'Oh, but you will, Aleksei,' Anna replied with confidence. 'You have one week to deliver the money and whoever you feel should pay the price for Seamus's hand, or one will be taken from you.'

She turned and walked away with her head held high. Sammy tore his eyes away from Aleksei, whose jaw had nearly dropped to the floor, and followed her out, hiding a grin of amused admiration.

'One week,' Anna repeated without turning around. 'Time to start repaying your debts and to remember whose city this is in the first place.'

CHAPTER NINE

Josephine was completely lost in thought, staring down through the window at the smoky streets of Soho when Tanya's jovial voice pulled her back into the room.

'Daydreaming about lover boy, are you?' Tanya teased. She smiled as Josephine blushed. She'd heard rumour that her friend had a new lover, though she had yet to find out any detail, as Josephine's love life was the one thing she seemed to keep notoriously close to her chest.

'Not at all,' she replied tartly. 'I was just wondering what a lady of the night from the eighties would wear.' She looked Tanya up and down pointedly. 'But now I know.'

Tanya chuckled. 'Ooh, I hit a nerve.' She leaned in as Josephine kissed her on each cheek in greeting. 'But actually, this skirt would be far too long.' Tanya's dark leopard-print dress clung flatteringly to her curves all the way down to the knee.

'True,' Josephine conceded with a warm smile.

They walked over to the small bar in the middle of The Sinners' Lounge and sat down. The place was dead, still being a little early for clients. Opening the plastic bag Tanya had brought in with her, she pulled out a thin, plain zip-up hoody and handed it to Josephine.

Josephine turned up her nose as she viewed the shapeless garment. 'Thanks, but you shouldn't have,' she said in a flat, sarcastic tone.

'It's not for you,' Tanya replied. 'It's what the carrier is going to wear from the boat down to Gibraltar.'

'Ah, I see.' Josephine nodded her understanding and pulled the material through her hands, pausing to look closely at the seams.

'Anna wants you to have them sewn into the waistband. See here,' she pointed. 'It's double layered around the bottom. Sew them into a thin pouch, then sew the pouch into the middle.'

'OK, if she's sure that this is safe enough.' Josephine didn't look convinced. 'I still think we can come up with a better way.'

'You already did. The cheese. They won't be looking at some fisherman's jumper if they get caught bringing in dairy.'

'OK.' Josephine folded the garment back into the bag and crossed her long legs.

'So, what *were* you thinking about when I came in?' Tanya changed the subject with a cheeky smile and a twinkle in her bright green eyes.

Josephine pulled a face at her. 'Oh, you know exactly what I was thinking about, you pushy mare.'

'So, are we ever going to meet him then? From what I hear from the girls, your late-night booty call is coming more and more often these days.'

Josephine felt her skin grow cold. 'They've seen him?' He didn't want to be seen – that was the whole point of his sneaking around. As much as she hated it, she respected his reasoning.

'No,' Tanya said with a slight tone of regret. 'They haven't seen anything but his shadow in the background after he's gone. They've had no juicy gossip for me about him at all. Why is that anyway?' she asked curiously.

Josephine pulled a cigarette out of the packet of Vogues on the side, irritated. Tanya was her friend and a close one at that; it was natural that she would want to know what was happening in her love life. But this wasn't a normal situation, and instead of being excited for her, Josephine's friends were definitely going to disapprove.

Looking up into Tanya's face as she blew out her first full breath of smoke, she could see there was no point putting it off any longer. She had dodged scrutiny for this long, but it was never something she was going to be able to avoid forever.

'It wasn't something we planned, this thing between us,' she started. 'It just happened.'

'That's how all the best stories start,' Tanya replied, leaning her weight onto the bar beside her.

Josephine smiled sadly. 'He's married,' she said bluntly.

Tanya nodded, no surprise on her face. 'I figured. Why else would he be sneaking around?' There was a short silence. 'Listen, you clearly care about him,' she said carefully. 'But relationships that start this way, they never end well.' She watched as Josephine's face seemed to shut down in front of her. 'I'm not judging you – or him,' she continued hurriedly. 'Every situation is different, and I don't know yours. But what I do know is that there are only so many ways it can go. Either he breaks it off to go back to his wife, or she finds out and you get blamed, or maybe he even leaves her for you.'

She ran her hands through her long red hair, worried for her friend. 'But whichever way it goes, you *will* get hurt, or at least go through some really bad shit. And even if you do end up together, you'll never be able to truly trust him. Not really. Not deep down.' She bit her lip, wondering if she'd said too much. Josephine was looking away, no expression on her face. Tanya shook her head sadly. 'Look, whatever you do, I'm just saying I'm here for you if you want to talk about it. OK?'

Josephine turned back to her with a bright smile. 'Sure. Now, are you staying for some drinks before the punters start arriving, or do you need to go?'

'I wish I could, but I need to meet Anna.' She slipped off the bar stool and grabbed Josephine into a swift hug. 'Next time for definite. Look after yourself, OK?'

Josephine watched her go and then looked down to her phone. She wanted to text him – her married man – to touch base and talk about trivial, unimportant things, like how his day had been. But she couldn't. It wasn't allowed.

Reaching over the bar, Josephine grasped a tumbler and a bottle of vodka. Pouring herself a generous measure, she smiled bitterly. At least she could always count on the comfort a few vodkas would bring.

CHAPTER TEN

Letting herself into the flat above her own, where Anna now lived with Ethan, Tanya chucked the keys into the bowl on the side and walked through to the lounge. There was no one there. Searching down the hallway, she saw a light on in the office and made her way through. Anna was seated behind the desk with a large glass of wine in her hand, staring at the wall.

'Well, it seems I'm interrupting everybody's private thoughts tonight,' she said with a short laugh.

'Hm?' Anna looked up at her in question.

'Oh, nothing,' Tanya said, waving her hand dismissively. She took a seat across the room in the comfortable Sherlock armchair and kicked off her shoes, tucking her feet up under her. 'You OK?' she asked.

'Yeah, I'm fine,' Anna replied, though her expression didn't quite match her words.

'Really?'

Anna stared at Tanya for a moment. 'No, not really.'

'Want to talk about it?'

There was a long silence. Anna ran her hands through her long, dark hair and rubbed her forehead wearily. 'I'm having a bed delivered tomorrow, for this room. Finally turning it into the third bedroom it was supposed to be. I don't really need an office here anyway.'

'For Freddie?' Tanya asked.

'Yes,' Anna replied. She took a sip of her wine. 'I mean, this flat is just as much his as it is mine and Ethan's. This will be his home, whether we're together or not.'

'And you're not?' Tanya questioned. It was such a sore subject around Anna that they had barely talked about it in all the time Freddie had been in prison. But no one was really sure where the pair stood these days.

'Well, no,' Anna replied. 'I mean, we haven't seen each other, save for the odd business meeting, in two and a half years. I wouldn't call that a relationship of any kind.' Her voice had a hard edge and Tanya nodded, choosing not to reply.

Anna sighed. 'It's not that that's worrying me though. So much has changed in that time. Our whole world was turned upside down in an instant. Not only did Freddie leave Ethan and I alone, but *you and I* – she pointed to Tanya and then herself – 'we got thrown into this crazy underground world of his.' Anna opened her arms wide. 'And we did it. We took it on. We made it work and made it our own. For Freddie.'

'For the family,' Tanya corrected.

'Everything just…' Anna tried to find the right words. 'We changed, you know? And this is our life now. But the day after tomorrow Freddie and Paul are coming back. And I would imagine they think they're coming back to the world they left, but that world doesn't exist anymore. Even the people they left behind, they don't exist either. The Anna, Tanya, Ethan they knew…' She stared at Tanya. 'We're completely different people now. And I just don't know how we're going to cope with everything changing again.'

'We just will,' Tanya replied with a shrug. 'That's what we do, isn't it? We survive, we adjust. We did it before – we can do it again.'

'But what if I don't want to, Tan?' Anna asked quietly. 'What if I can't go back to how things were?' She let out a long breath. It felt good to finally say it aloud. 'I didn't choose this, but it's part of me now. I know that this is Freddie's business; I'm not disputing that. And I'll help him get up to speed and settle back in. But I'm not prepared to just hand back the reins and retreat to being good little Anna in the background.'

The two women stared at each other across the room for several minutes, each thinking back over the battles they had been through and the hardships they had faced. Anna was right, Tanya realised – it wasn't going to be easy to back down after fighting so hard for so long.

'Well then, Freddie is going to have to come to terms with that,' she replied heavily. 'Whether he likes it or not.'

CHAPTER ELEVEN

After buttoning up the cuff of the crisp white shirt Bill had delivered to the prison for him, Freddie shrugged on the suit jacket and ran his hands down the front to smooth it. He closed his eyes for a moment, savouring the feel of the tailored jacket. It had been such a long time since he had worn anything so decent. The last time had been in court, when the judge delivered his verdict with a blow of the hammer. He opened his eyes and took a deep breath, pushing the memory away. Today was a good day, a cause for celebration, not reflection on past battles lost. It was the day that he and Paul were finally getting out.

Next to him, Paul straightened his own suit jacket and they gave each other a nod of approval. There were two bunks to a cell in this prison without exception and it had been at maximum capacity when they arrived, so although they hadn't managed to wrangle private cells, they were glad they'd been able to at least arrange being put together.

The cell door opened and the brothers walked out and down the long hallway past the closed doors of all the other cells. As they walked, the hard soles of their smart shoes clanged on the metal hallway floors and a cheer broke out through the prison. Whistles and well wishes surrounded them as they made their way towards freedom. Just as they had been on the outside, the Tylers were well respected in here. Underworld royalty held its status amongst criminals everywhere.

Neither of them spoke as they were read their release conditions for the last time and handed back their bags of personal items at the front desk. They signed their names on the dotted lines of the prison paperwork and with purpose walked out of the front door and into the prison car park.

The electric gates rolled back, groaning in protest, finally allowing them the freedom they had been granted, and as the gates shut tight behind them Freddie turned to Paul and grinned, breathing in deeply.

'Do you smell that, brother? That's the smell of fucking freedom.'

'It's certainly the smell of something,' Paul replied, staring at the overflowing bins just upwind. He glanced down the street and saw Bill coming around the corner towards them. 'Here's our ride.'

Freddie looked about, taking in the first new sight in two and a half years. It wasn't much, the area outside the prison – just a dead-end road with more potholes than actual tarmac. But it was more than they had been staring at inside, and it was just the beginning of the journey they had ahead of them. He felt a renewed energy flow through his veins like fire. It had been far too long since he had overseen his kingdom, and now that it was so close, he could barely wait to be back at the helm. Old habits died hard, and Freddie had never been one to sit idly by whilst there was business to be done.

Bill greeted them warmly as they jumped in, then swiftly turned the car around, not wanting to spend any more time there than he had to.

'God, it's good to see you both on the right side of those bloody gates,' he said with feeling.

'Tell us about it,' Freddie replied.

Bill glanced sideways at Freddie and in the mirror at Paul. 'I've been told to take you to Mollie's – they're all waiting to celebrate your return – but if there's somewhere else you'd rather be...'

'Nah, it's OK,' Freddie said, shaking his head. 'Don't want to keep her waiting. Let's go.'

He stared out of the window, drinking in the passing sights of cars and buildings. Two and a half years was a long time for everyone, not just for them. What was he going to find when he got home? There were some tough times ahead, of that he had no doubt. But how tough exactly? And who, or what, was going to be the most difficult challenge to overcome?

CHAPTER TWELVE

Anna watched Dean light up his cigarette in Mollie's back garden, where they were all milling around waiting, and felt the urge to light one up herself. She was nervous. More than nervous. But Ethan was here, and she didn't want him to know her dirty little secret.

She smirked at the thought. Here she was, running the largest underground firm in London, dealing in drugs, prostitution, illicit goods and racketeering, waiting for her prison-bird ex-boyfriend to come home – and the thing she most feared Ethan finding out was that she occasionally smoked. She shook her head, wondering if she really had lost the plot along the way after all.

Tanya sidled up and handed her a drink. Anna looked down into the dark liquid and raised an eyebrow.

'What is it?'

'Vodka and Coke. Mainly vodka. You look like you need it,' Tanya replied.

'Thanks.'

Anna's gaze wandered over to Ethan, who sat at one of the garden tables put out for the occasion, playing cards with Sammy. He looked calm on the outside, but Anna wasn't fooled. She knew he had been up late the night before, worrying about today. Eventually around midnight he had knocked on Anna's bedroom door, where she also lay awake worrying, and they'd had a heart to heart.

What if he's not who I remember? Ethan had asked, staring up at the ceiling in the dark next to her.

He won't be, Anna had replied, glad the darkness was hiding her own troubled expression. *We've all changed a lot since then. But the one thing that has always been true of your dad and will never change no matter what is that his family mean more to him than anything. And that's you, Ethan.*

And you, Ethan had replied.

Anna had stayed silent, unable to lie to the boy she loved as much as she ever could her own flesh and blood.

Coming back to the present, Anna lifted the glass Tanya had handed her and drank from it deeply. Cringing at the amount of vodka in it, she turned towards her friend.

'Like I said,' Tanya continued, 'you look like you need it.'

Anna gave a nod of grudging agreement.

A sudden shriek of excitement sounded from inside the house and Anna felt her blood turn to ice. The shriek had come from Mollie, which could only mean one thing. They were here.

Ethan's gaze shot over to her and she could see the naked uncertainty in his eyes. For his sake she hid her own feelings and gave him a reassuring smile. Tanya moved up closer beside her and she was glad of the support.

Watching Mollie usher everybody into the garden, as the lounge was too small to host all the well-wishers who had come to welcome the brothers home, Anna tried to relax. She was relieved she wasn't expected to walk inside, as she wasn't sure she could force her feet to take her forward right now if her life depended on it.

There was a loud cheer throughout the swollen crowd between her and the kitchen door. Anna watched Freddie and Paul step out into the bright summer sunshine. Her heart skipped a beat as Freddie's handsome face flashed into view between bodies. She took in his chiselled jawline and broad torso. He looked even more in shape than ever. Clearly, he had been working out. She supposed there was ample time for that when locked away behind bars. His smile lit up his face and his hazel-green eyes twinkled with life, the way they always used to. The way that had always melted her heart when they had been together. She swallowed the lump of pain that sat in her throat. It had been a long time since she had last seen Freddie like this, where he was truly himself again. She wanted to look away, to ease the discomfort she felt, but she forced herself to keep her attention forward and her head high. She was Anna Davis. She was not going to crumble at the first hurdle.

Freddie leaned forward and grasped Mollie in a huge bear hug, whilst Paul greeted some of their men with hearty pats on the back and a broad grin. They swapped over and everyone flocked around Freddie, congratulating him on his safe return. Anna watched as Ethan worked up the courage to move forward from his place on the sidelines towards his dad.

Freddie's expression lit up as he caught sight of his son for the first time since he'd been arrested. They had agreed that prison was no place for such a young boy to visit. Anna watched the myriad of emotions play out across his face; saw his eyes roam over Ethan and take in how tall he had grown, how much he had changed. Sadness and guilt mixed with happiness and wonder as he reached him and grasped the tops of his shoulders.

'Look at you,' Anna heard Freddie say, his voice filled with emotion.

Ethan's worry evaporated as he faced the man who had saved him from a loveless existence and set him on a better path, and he wrapped his arms around Freddie in an affectionate hug. The action filled Anna with warmth and relief. She had desperately hoped this wouldn't be too difficult for Ethan, even if it was hard for her.

Freddie's eyes searched around the garden as he held Ethan and stopped only when they locked with Anna's.

As their gazes connected, it was as though suddenly they were the only two people in existence, caught in a limbo that even they did not understand. The air between them felt charged with electricity, and Anna could not tear her eyes away. They solemnly stared at each other, a million emotions playing out behind each of their carefully constructed masks. The distance between them was no more than a few feet, but it could have been an ocean for the ability each of them had to cross it.

What's the next move? Anna wondered in despair. *Where do we even begin?*

Someone walked across their line of sight and the spell was broken. Anna blinked and took in a deep breath, tuning back into the sights and sounds around her. Freddie looked over at her once more and nodded a polite greeting, which she returned, before he turned away to answer a question.

The hollowness she felt as Freddie's attention moved on was unexpected, and she subconsciously put her hand to her chest.

'Why don't we see if we can go and help Mollie with anything?' Tanya suggested tactfully, having observed the strained exchange.

'Yes, good idea,' Anna replied, clearing her throat.

Walking through the crowd towards the kitchen, Anna smiled warmly at Paul and returned the bear-like hug he gave her as she passed him.

'Great to see you out, Paul,' she said.

'It's bloody good to be out,' he replied with a laugh. 'Ain't it, Fred?'

'It certainly is,' Freddie replied, turning to face them.

'It's good to see both of you out,' Anna said with a small smile.

There was an awkward silence, and Tanya stepped forward to give each of them a quick squeeze.

'Well, it's about time really, isn't it? You done with your little holiday now, are ya, boys? Eh?' she joked. 'Chilling out on your jacksies while everyone else does the hard work, I don't know...' She shook her head in mock disappointment then gave them a cheeky wink.

'Yeah, alright, you do the holiday next time then, you cheeky mare,' Paul replied with a deep chuckle.

'Nah, I'm good, thanks,' she replied, wrinkling her nose. 'Anyway, we were just on our way to see if your mum needs any help.' She ushered Anna forward, trying to dispel the tension that lay between her and Freddie. 'We'll catch you in a bit.'

As they walked away, Tanya sidled up next to Anna. 'There now, the ice is officially broken. That wasn't so bad, was it?'

'It's not the ice breaking that I'm worried about,' Anna replied darkly. 'It's what the hell happens next.'

CHAPTER THIRTEEN

The office door opened and bright red light flooded the dimly lit room. The deep techno beats from the strip club beyond became louder for a second, until the heavy door swung back closed behind the man who had just entered.

Aleksei looked up from his comfortable position behind his desk and blew out a thick plume of cigar smoke as he waited for the update.

'Well, Rohan?' His deep voice rumbled with impatience.

Rohan took a seat opposite his boss and leaned forward, placing his fingers carefully together on the desk.

'They were picked up by Bill Hanlon and delivered straight to their mother's house. There was a party to welcome them home, and after the guests left for the night, Freddie got into the car with Anna Davis and his son and they drove off in the direction of her flat. Paul stayed behind. That was twenty minutes ago.'

'A welcome-home party for the kings of the fucking castle,' Aleksei spat, his lip curling back in anger. He took a deep breath and tapped his thick fingers on the table next to the still-smoking cigar in the ashtray. 'Well, I hope they enjoyed themselves,' he continued, 'because they will not be laughing for very long. Times have changed and the city they ruled no longer exists. They are about to have a very rude awakening indeed.'

'You think you can force them to keep to the same arrangement as Anna Davis?' Rohan questioned.

'No.' Aleksei shook his head. 'The infamous Tylers would never allow that. And I've known that from the start.' He gave Rohan a hard stare. 'This is what I have been waiting for. Anna Davis, pushy though she may be, has only been babysitting their empire whilst they relaxed at Her Majesty's pleasure. The men around her have followed loyally and the other firms have stayed at bay because they all knew the Tylers were coming back.' He shrugged. 'So, we've taken our stake here and played our part in appearing to toe the line for all this time. But now' – a cold grin crept over his face – 'now it is time to take action.'

Rohan sat up straighter, an interested gleam in his eye. 'What are you thinking, boss?'

'I'm thinking it is time for a new king in town. One who is already here. One who has a foothold and an advantage above all the other pretenders.' He puffed on his cigar.

'If you're saying what I think you're saying, it could mean a war. They are highly protected, especially at the moment.'

'Yes, they are,' Aleksei conceded. 'Which is why we do this carefully. We shall wait for them to come to us. We shall pretend to fight our corner as if we are fighting *only* for our corner. And then, when they least suspect it and when their guard is down' – he stubbed the cigar out and watched the last dying embers burn out – 'then we kill them. We kill them, destroy any lasting belief the people of this city have in them, and as their firm falls apart, we take all four corners for ourselves.'

*

Anna pushed the front door wide open and stepped aside to allow Freddie to enter the spacious hallway and see his new home. It was the first time he had set foot in the place, after she'd sold their last flat and bought this one whilst he was still in prison. It had made sense at the time, to be close to Tanya and to have the extra space. Now more than ever, Anna was glad of the third bedroom.

Freddie stepped inside and looked around. The hallway gave off a cosy feel with hardwood floor and warm tones. An oversized lamp threw off dim light from an oak side table where Anna laid her keys in the bowl designed for that purpose. The bowl was the only thing he recognised in the hallway from their old home.

'This is the living room,' Anna said, gesturing through the archway to one side.

Freddie noted that she had at least kept their sofas and a few other pieces of furniture. This took away a bit of the tension he felt, knowing that Anna hadn't completely erased their history. It was still here, woven into their everyday life, even if most other things had changed.

'And the kitchen runs off the back of the lounge, there,' she continued.

Ethan turned from where he had been hanging up his coat. 'Um, I'm going to go to bed.' He glanced up between the two awkwardly tense adults. 'I'll see you guys in the morning.'

'Night, sweetheart,' Anna said with a tired smile. 'Tanya's going to take you to the park in the morning, OK?'

'Sure.'

'Oh,' Freddie sounded surprised.

'Oh, er—' Anna shifted her weight awkwardly. 'I didn't know what you were doing, or... I mean, I can cancel Tanya if you want to do something...'

'No, no.' Freddie shook his head with a strained smile. 'It's fine. I've got stuff to do anyway.' He felt disappointed, assuming he'd be able to spend time getting to know Ethan again straight away. But he didn't want to come charging in and mess up their routine. The last thing he wanted was to rock the boat when the boy was so settled.

'If you're sure...' Anna said.

'Yeah. We'll arrange something another time.' He smiled at Ethan. 'Goodnight, mate.'

''Night, Dad.'

They both watched as Ethan disappeared down the hall and into his bedroom, closing the door behind him. They turned back to each other almost reluctantly. It was still there, the tension, the unbridgeable gap between them. Each of them felt it pushing down on them like a ten-ton weight.

'So, that's Ethan's room,' Anna said with a tight smile. 'And um, mine is just next door to his. The bathroom is at the end there' – she pointed to it – 'and this is your room.'

Opening the door nearest to them, Anna led the way inside. Freddie followed and looked around. It had clearly been her office until recently, with a desk and chair moved up into one corner and a tall bookshelf in another next to her favourite Sherlock armchair.

The sight of the chair brought back memories of a thousand nights when he would come home to find her engrossed in yet another novel. He would sit and listen to her describe the storyline and talk about the author for hours, though he had no intention of ever reading them himself. It was moments like those that he had missed the most through the lonely nights in prison.

'I hope the room is OK.'

Anna's voice pulled him back to the present and he turned to her. 'Of course.'

The double bed was made up with fresh sheets, and on the pillow was a washbag overflowing with all the products he used to use. A thoughtful touch, he noted.

Anna made to move out of the room.

'Listen, Anna,' he said, wanting to stop her and talk things out. But he paused, not sure how or where to start. There was an awkward silence as he floundered, and he rubbed his forehead, agitated. 'Look, I just want to say' – he looked around – 'you've made a great home for Ethan. A great life. I don't know how to thank you for that. You were put in a hard position, and—'

'It's nothing,' Anna said curtly, cutting him off.

'It's not nothing,' Freddie replied.

Anna let out a long breath. 'Look, before any of this happened – you, prison – we made a deal. We made the decision to *both* be parents to Ethan. And from that moment, that was exactly what I did, full throttle. Whatever else was going on and whatever happened between you and me' – she shook her head – 'that didn't affect that decision. He is my son in almost every sense of the word, and I've come to love him as though he were my own flesh and blood.' Her dark blue eyes locked with Freddie's and he could see the wary defence behind them. 'So please don't come in here and thank me as though I'm an outsider. As though I'm a nanny who's due to clock off.'

This was one of the worries that had been haunting her recently, an underlying fear that wouldn't go away. Ethan was not hers by blood and the paperwork placing him in her care had been pretty shady. It'd been drawn together hastily and legal channels paid off under the radar to have it pushed through quickly, back when Freddie had been trying to get rid of Jules, Ethan's useless, abusive mother.

Now that she and Freddie were no longer together, if he wanted to take Ethan away from her, he could. And whilst the Freddie she had known and loved would never have done that, she had no idea how much prison had changed him. For all she knew, her demands to stay involved in the business could result in her being painted as the enemy. Things could get ugly and then where did she stand regarding the boy she loved so much?

Freddie frowned. 'Anna, that's not what I meant. I just meant…' He shook his head. 'I just wanted you to know I appreciate that you've been such a great parent to him. I'm glad, after the life he had before and after I went away that he had you.'

Anna nodded, not trusting herself to speak through the wave of emotions Freddie's words brought forth. There were going to be some difficult times ahead. She just hoped Freddie still felt that way then. She swallowed hard and pulled herself upright.

'I'll leave you to get settled in,' she said finally. 'It's been a long day and you must be exhausted.'

Freddie nodded, pushing down the emptiness that the invisible distance between them made him feel. He allowed his eyes to roam over her just once as she walked out the door, remembering the way her thick, dark hair used to feel between his fingers, and the smell of her breath mingling with his. But that had been in another life. And it was clear that too much had happened since then for them to ever be able to go back.

CHAPTER FOURTEEN

The wrought-iron gate closed with a resounding clang behind Freddie as he walked up the worn path towards the hill where they had laid his little sister Thea to rest, two and a half years before.

Freddie clenched his fist at the memory of the police storming her funeral and took a deep breath to calm himself. Now was not the time for anger. Now was the time to finally pay Thea his first, long overdue visit.

He reached the grave and, after staring at it for a moment, sat down on the grass beside it. Breathing in, he took in the beauty of the place. Just outside of London and on top of a hill, he could see countryside for miles. Thea would have loved it here. She would have said it was the perfect spot to take pictures. That's why they had chosen it.

'You weren't supposed to go,' Freddie said quietly, shaking his head. 'Me, perhaps. Maybe Paul. They were the risks we took. But not you. You should never have been caught up in all that.' He squeezed the bridge of his nose as tears threatened and swallowed down the lump that was forming in his throat.

The memories of that fateful night flashed through his mind. The dark hallway where Jacko held Thea, a knife to her throat. The look of strength and determination in Thea's eyes, even in the face of it all.

They'd almost had her. Jacko hadn't known there was someone creeping up behind, nearly close enough to grab the knife from his grip. But Thea, as headstrong as always, had been working on her own plan of escape. Only it hadn't worked, and before any of them could intervene, Jacko had ripped the blade through her throat.

She had died bleeding out on the floor, shock written all over her face as she was unable to draw in one last breath. He had held her, tried to stem the flow, but it had been no good. Freddie had watched as her eyes turned glassy and lifeless, no longer seeing his face, just staring straight through him.

His beautiful, talented, loving sister had slipped away from this Earth in just a matter of seconds, never to return again. It was something he still couldn't quite come to terms with. It didn't feel real, even after all this time. He guessed it probably never would.

Placing his hand over the ground where she lay, he closed his eyes for a few moments.

'Rest now, Thea,' he whispered.

Standing up, Freddie slowly walked back the way he came and out onto the street outside the cemetery. Pausing, he narrowed his eyes for a moment as he saw the tall figure leaning against the hood of his car, before making his way over.

'I thought I might find you here,' Sarah said, turning to face him and pushing her hands deeper into the pockets of her thin leather jacket. Her tone was wary, as she was unsure what sort of reception she was going to get.

Despite the fact she was on Freddie's payroll, Sarah had not been able to visit Freddie or Paul in prison at all, as she was a detective. It would have looked too strange. Especially as it was her own team who had taken him down. The brothers had been locked up and she had been forced to fake a smile for the world as she accepted praise and rewards for her team accomplishing the one thing she had been trying to avoid. As they had worked hard night and day to find solid evidence against the Tylers, DCI Sarah Riley had wiped details, forewarned Freddie of their traps and led them on as many wild goose chases as she could. But it had all been for nothing. In the end, one of the officers had created a solid case that even she couldn't do anything about.

Freddie eyed her hard and Sarah repressed a small shudder, reminded of just how dangerous a man he could be. It was why she had headed him off here, straight away. She couldn't have borne waiting in the shadows for him to turn up, not knowing where she stood. Not knowing whether she was still part of his world or whether she'd get a bullet in the head.

'What happened?' Freddie asked. He'd heard the details of the evidence in court and a third-hand account of Sarah's side through Bill, but he wanted to hear it first-hand, see her face as she spoke. It was the only way he could know for sure whether she was still trustworthy or whether she'd double-crossed them.

Sarah ran her hand through her short dark bob and checked over her shoulder out of habit.

'Everything was on track. I'd given you all the details of where the team was due to look, and thanks to your lawyers' harassment accusations, they'd been ordered to wind up at the end of the week. We were home and dry.'

'Clearly not.' Freddie's voice was clipped and his eyes flashed dangerously as he held back his anger. Two and a half years of hard time was not *home and dry*.

Sarah swallowed and lifted her chin. 'I honestly believed that we were,' she stressed, looking him in the eye. 'Adam Chambers had taken out a camera for a recce shoot. He was going to replace it the next day but forgot to bring it in. I checked in with him – he had nothing. But he must have gone back out.' She exhaled loudly. 'The next thing I knew, Ben Hargreaves burst in and had the SWAT team ready to go. Adam, in his eagerness, had gone straight to him over my head. I tried to call you. I tried to get them to wait until at least after…' Her eyes flickered towards the graveyard and then downward in shame.

Sarah hadn't got on well with Thea; in fact, the two had a prickly history, but the fact the SWAT team had burst in during the funeral had sat on her chest as a weight of guilt ever since. She didn't believe that anybody deserved that sort of callous treatment.

'I tried to make them wait a day,' she continued. 'But Ben has had it in for you since that business with Katherine.'

Freddie gave a slight nod of agreement. His youngest brother Michael had kidnapped the daughter of the Secretary of State for Justice outside one of his own clubs and had left her with lasting scars. Ben had held a grudge against the entire family ever since.

'Was it Miechowski? Did she plan this?' Freddie asked, moving away from the painful subject of the day he was arrested.

'No.' Sarah shook her head.

DI Holly Miechowski had been an undercover officer working in his club trying to gain evidence years before and had been exposed to Freddie by Sarah. When they confronted her, Freddie had threatened Holly with a slit throat in the night, should she ever reveal that Sarah was working for him at the same time as working on the force. Holly had been furious and frustrated when she found Sarah was to lead the team tasked with taking down the Tylers. She knew that Sarah's main objective would be to sabotage their efforts and that with Freddie's threat over her head there was nothing much she could do about it, but to their knowledge she had remained silent, sensibly valuing her life above her job.

'If she could have found a way around it, she would have. And she would have had me locked up too. But she was aware of how serious you were and I'm still here.' She shrugged. 'I couldn't find a link anywhere between her and the evidence, and although she was pleased with the result, there was no gloating afterwards. She's just kept her distance. I think we were genuinely just unlucky.'

'Unlucky?' Freddie gave a short, bitter laugh. 'Is that what you call the time we've spent behind bars?'

'Look, I'm one person, Freddie,' Sarah said, jumping to the point. 'I juggled putting out every fire that team lit. There were so many times they nearly had you and I stopped it. I did my job. But I'm only human and there was nothing I could have done when Chambers sidestepped me to the top.' She took a deep breath, her heart sinking as Freddie's cold expression didn't change. 'I was as loyal to you as I could have been. I still am. There was nothing more I could have done.'

There was a long silence as they stared at each other. Sarah was a strong, formidable woman, but even she had to stop herself from buckling under Freddie's cold, hard gaze. Her heart began beating faster as the fear started to set in. If Freddie had decided she wasn't being totally truthful, that she had something to do with them being sent down, she was done for.

'I know,' he said eventually, stepping down the intimidation.

He had needed to see her say it himself before he could truly believe this version of events. Because no matter how convincing a lie may seem, if you looked closely, you could see the truth hidden behind the eyes. And he could see that Sarah was telling the truth.

'That's why I'm putting you back to work, straight away.'

'What?' Sarah blinked, taken aback by the sudden change in Freddie's demeanour. She collected herself quickly. 'Of course, anything you say.'

Relief flooded through her, and the stress she had been holding on to for two and a half years finally trickled away. She smiled at Freddie gratefully.

'Do you still work under Ben?' he asked.

'Yes, though the task force was disbanded after they took you down,' she replied.

'That doesn't mean he won't be looking in our direction again, now that we're out.'

Sarah acknowledged this with a nod. 'No. He's got loose surveillance on you already. Though nothing major at the moment.'

'I would imagine he's wary of having more harassment accusations,' Freddie replied. 'I need you to keep me up to date on that and anything else I need to know. Ear to the ground. Because I am not going back inside.' He eyed her hard. 'Not for anyone.'

'Got it,' Sarah replied. She checked over her shoulder once more, glancing at the car which pulled up and parked just behind them. It was Paul. 'I'll be off then. I'll update you soon.'

'Do,' Freddie replied curtly.

He watched her walk back to her car, then turned to greet Paul. It had felt strange not waking up to Paul's snoring that morning. They had spent so long sharing the same cell, the silence was going to take some time to get used to.

'Brother,' he greeted him with a hug.

Paul stared past him at the gate to the cemetery, the grief clear on his face. Freddie cleared his throat. This visit was one Paul needed to do alone. He needed time with Thea, without anyone else watching or listening.

'Listen, I've already been in. You go ahead. I've got some calls to make from the car. We need to gather everyone together, get up to date on where everything is with the businesses. It's going to take some time.'

'Yeah, sure,' Paul replied, not taking his eyes off the gate. 'See you in a bit.'

Freddie patted his shoulder as he passed, knowing that this was going to be just as hard for his brother as it had been for him. Sliding into the car, he switched on the engine and used the car phone to call Bill's mobile. It was picked up in two rings.

'Bill, I need you to get everyone together at Club CoCo in an hour. We need to go over things; I need to be bought up to speed.'

There was a long pause and Freddie frowned, wondering why.

'Fred, we're already at CoCo,' Bill eventually replied, his tone awkward.

'What, everyone?' His frown deepened.

'Yeah. We're just in a meeting… with Anna.'

CHAPTER FIFTEEN

Taking the steps two at a time, Freddie stormed up to his office in Club CoCo, Paul hot on his heels. Pushing the door open, he entered to find Anna sat calmly behind his desk, her hands neatly clasped in front of her. In a circle around the room sat all his closest men – and Tanya. Bill rose to greet them respectfully, and Sammy, Dean, Simon and Seamus all followed suit. Tanya gave them a warm smile. Freddie swallowed some of his anger. He undid his jacket, then circled the room and hung it on the back of one of the vacant chairs.

Anna greeted them politely but did not move from her position. Noting this, Freddie assessed her thoughtfully. She had been running this firm for the last few years, and so, by rights, didn't need anyone's permission to use the office or call a meeting. But why now, when he was back? And why keep it from him?

'I don't recall you mentioning this meeting,' Freddie said, his level gaze boring into her.

Anna held his stare and lifted her chin a little higher. 'We meet here every week at this time to share updates. It's nothing of urgent importance. You only got out yesterday; I assumed you'd want time to settle back in before returning to the business.'

'*My* business, you mean,' Freddie shot. There was a short silence.

'There was no intention to leave you out of the meeting, Freddie,' Anna replied. 'It was just nothing important. And besides, you were still sleeping like the dead when we left this morning. I didn't want to wake you from what I'm sure was probably the best sleep you've had in a while.'

Freddie glanced around the room. Everyone looked tense and awkward. This was not how he had wanted to start things off. He rubbed his forehead. Perhaps he was reading too much into it all. It had been a long time since he had been in the game.

'Well, now I'm here, why don't you continue and I'll start catching up.'

'We've actually just finished, but if it's OK with you perhaps I can catch you both up myself?' Anna suggested.

Freddie bit back the retort on the tip of his tongue. He was beyond grateful to Anna for all she had done, he really was, but there was some sort of underlying fight for power going on in this room right now and that was unexpected. Part of him wanted to order his men to do something else, just to show Anna that he still held the cards, but the bigger part of him knew this was petty and stupid.

'Sure,' he said finally. 'You guys go, get on with what you need to.'

Everyone stood to leave.

'Catch you later,' Tanya said with a wink.

'Sammy.' Anna shot the man a look and he nodded and sat back down.

Freddie and Paul took seats by the desk as the door shut and Anna leaned forward on her forearms.

'I will catch you up on everything to do with the businesses, but there's something more urgent that needs to be dealt with first.'

Freddie frowned. 'Go on.'

She took a deep breath. 'When you both went down, the central belt was left wide open. People knew this firm was still running things, but they saw me as an easy target compared to you.'

Freddie nodded. This much was expected. He had not left her with an easy task.

'They all tried. We pushed back. I left them not willing to try and test me again.'

Anna saw a small flicker of surprise cross Freddie's face and her dark blue eyes turned hard. She had crossed a lot of lines back in those early days, for the first time. She had gone through a baptism of fire into the underworld and had come out on top. She'd had to – it was a case of survival. But Freddie didn't need to know the details of all that. This wasn't what was important right now.

'Most were established firms and they've retreated back to their territories. But one firm was new to London altogether. A Russian firm, headed by a man called Aleksei Ivanov.'

Freddie sat upright and exchanged glances with Paul. 'I've never heard of him.'

'No one had,' Anna replied with a sigh. 'He just turned up one day out of the blue like a bad penny. Apparently, he was some big gangster in Russia, ran a chain of strip clubs and the heroin distribution in his home city. But something happened. We don't know what, but whatever it was made him flee Russia pretty sharpish. All we could find out is that he can't go back.'

Anna pushed her hair back over her shoulder and took a deep breath. 'So, he came here, and after hearing about our situation he tried to take over, claim this area as his own. We fought back and a lot of people got hurt, but he wouldn't leave. I guess when you have nowhere else to go, you have nothing to lose.' She shrugged and shook her head. 'We pushed them right back until they were just in one small corner of Soho. He'd managed to bully his way into taking over premises there and turned it into a strip club. He based all his men there, all his Russian girls, stashed a shit-ton of weapons in the basement… It would have been suicide to try and overtake it. So we came to an agreement.'

'An agreement?' Freddie repeated, in disbelief.

'An agreement,' Anna confirmed, ignoring his tone. 'We would stop fighting him and allow him this one club and the local distribution of heroin, so long as he stopped fighting us and didn't overstep beyond the boundaries we'd given him.'

'You are joking, right?' Freddie and Paul looked at each other.

'No, I'm really not.' Anna felt her insides grow colder, despite the confidence in her tone. She had always known that Freddie wouldn't like this – it was why they had kept it from him. But now the time had come, and she had no choice but to tell him everything. 'There was only so far I was prepared to go, and an all-out armed war in Soho with the Russians was way beyond that.' Anna's voice had become icily clipped, but she softened it before continuing. 'I needed to contain the problem until it could be dealt with. Until you were back. And that's what I did.'

Freddie just stared at her, his face hard and expressionless as he processed the information. Paul shook his head and looked towards Sammy with a frown.

Sammy sat up and cleared his throat. 'Um, there's more. This truce seemed to hold things for a while. They tried their luck here and there but nothing massive. That is until this last week.'

'What happened?' Paul asked.

'Seamus and I were in the smallholding warehouse in Soho picking up some crates of product. They were due for delivery. Two of Aleksei's men were there waiting and pushed some crates down onto Seamus. If he hadn't seen and moved quick, he'd be in hospital at least, possibly worse. As it is, they broke his hand. Badly.'

'Shit,' Paul cursed.

Freddie narrowed his eyes. 'Who was he due to fight?'

'Exactly the right question,' Sammy answered with a grim expression. 'He was supposed to be up against Joe Hunter yesterday. It was rigged – we stood to make a lot of money.'

'How much did we lose?' Paul asked.

'Fifty grand.'

There was a long silence and eventually Freddie turned back to Anna, raising an eyebrow in question.

'I confronted him the next day.' Anna's eyes glinted with something Freddie couldn't quite place. 'I explained that he had one week to pay us back the fifty grand we lost and to hand over one of his men for us to mete out our own punishment.'

Freddie settled back in his chair and hid a small smile of respect and amusement. If his life had depended on it, Freddie would never have been able to predict Anna's response to Aleksei's actions. It surprised him immensely. It also served to remind him that he had no idea who Anna really was anymore. He wasn't sure whether to be proud or saddened by how far she had come in their world.

'That's an interesting response,' he said finally. 'But what do you plan to do when he refuses? Because he will.'

Freddie didn't know Aleksei, but he didn't need to. No man who had risen to such a position would just roll over and give in to a demand like that.

'Oh, I'm not going to do anything,' Anna replied. 'You are.'

'I am?' Freddie asked.

'Yes.' Anna sat back in her chair and allowed her mouth to curl up into a cold smile. 'You both are. You've been away a long time. The underworld needs reminding who you are and needs to be shown that you haven't softened in your years away.' She leaned forward and pulled a map from a pile of papers on the desk. 'I've got a plan that's going to deal with our little Aleksei problem and do just that, all in one fell swoop. It's time for London to know the Tylers are back.'

CHAPTER SIXTEEN

Anna clicked through to Club CoCo's online banking and sent a payment to another account. Checking that the invoice she had mocked up matched the amount one last time, she slipped this into a folder in the top drawer before sliding it shut. Logging out, she checked the VPN was turned on before logging in to a second account. The money she had just moved was already there, and without hesitation she forwarded it through to a third account number. Repeating the process several times, Anna then carefully wiped the browser history and turned off her laptop for the night.

It was an habitual process now, one she had been carrying out since she'd realised Freddie was not coming home. Every month she made payments from each of the many legal businesses under her control against false invoices, and sent them on through a string of offshore accounts until they could no longer be trace-able. It was a risk, but she'd made sure to get advice on how to leave the companies looking kosher before attempting it. Now, even if one of the accounts was investigated and the payment was flagged – which was unlikely – they'd never be able to find the money, or pair it against the end destination. By the time it reached the other side, it was perfectly clean and untouchable by any authority. And this was what she needed, if her plan was going to work.

Staring off into the distance, Anna fiddled with a button on her cream satin shirt, which was tucked into a pair of tight black trousers. High black patent heels tapped nervously on the floor as she pondered the new risks that came with Freddie and Paul being out. Perhaps she should make the payments less frequently for a while.

The door opened, letting in the upbeat music playing in Club Anya just beyond, and Tanya swept through with a bottle of wine and two glasses.

'We need a drink,' she stated, plonking the bottle down on the desk in front of Anna and standing the glasses next to it. Unscrewing the top, she poured them each a large measure. 'Here.' She handed one to Anna, who was busy trying to move the club's paperwork out of the way.

'Thanks.' Anna took the glass and relaxed back into her office chair as Tanya made herself comfortable on the small sofa against the wall opposite. 'Why is it we need a drink again?'

'Well, *I* need a drink. And *I* becomes *we*, when we're both in the office.'

'Makes sense,' Anna replied.

'So, how did Freddie take you telling him you still want to stay in the running of the business?' Tanya asked, before taking a deep drink.

'I haven't raised it yet.'

'Oh, Anna, come on,' Tanya scolded. 'The longer you leave it, the more awkward it will be.'

Before Anna could reply there was a small knock and the door opened. Carl's face peeped round. 'Sorry, girls, but Roman's here. Says you weren't expecting him but you'll want to see him.'

'Oh, yes.' Tanya sat up and grinned at Anna. 'Send him through, Carl.'

'Will do.'

The door closed and Tanya winked at Anna. 'Saved by the bell this time, Davis, but don't think we won't continue that discussion.' She pointed a long, polished, accusatory finger at her best friend.

Anna rolled her eyes and then quickly plastered a welcoming smile on her face as the door reopened and Roman walked in. She stood up and greeted him with a kiss on each cheek.

'Roman, so good to see you.' Once again, she breathed in his musky scent and was reminded just how good the man smelled. She stepped back and gestured for him to take the seat opposite hers at the desk. He did so, greeting Tanya and unbuttoning his jacket before shifting position slightly so that he was able to address both women at once.

'I've got good news. We're ready to move.'

'When?' Anna asked, taking her seat and leaning forward in interest.

'Tonight.'

'Tonight?' Anna repeated, her eyebrows shooting up in surprise. She turned to Tanya. 'Will it be ready?'

'Should be,' Tanya replied. 'I'll go check up on it now. Roman, I'll bring it to the boat. Where and what time?'

Reaching into his pocket, Roman pulled out a small piece of paper and handed it to her. 'Burn that before you come,' he warned.

Tanya nodded and set off to chase up Josephine. Roman twisted back to face Anna and smiled warmly.

'That was fast,' Anna remarked. 'Will it always be last minute?'

'Not once we get set into a routine, no. But I had to wait for a guy to be off a long job. He's back on it tomorrow so we only have one night.'

'Fair enough,' Anna conceded. 'Would you like a drink?' She gestured towards the open bottle.

'I can't, no,' Roman replied, his dark brown eyes narrowing slightly in challenge. 'But perhaps I can buy you one at dinner tonight, before the shipment leaves?'

Anna took a long, deep breath and smiled ruefully. She had Ethan this evening, and even if she didn't, it was an awkward time at the moment. Freddie's presence at home was something she was constantly and vividly aware of, and even though there was nothing going on between them romantically, going out with Roman that evening just didn't feel right. Old loyalties were hard to let go of.

'Rain check?' she asked. 'It's not the best time at the moment.'

Roman nodded, lowering his gaze in graceful defeat. He stood up and buttoned his smart black jacket once more, shooting her his most charming smile.

Anna couldn't help but respond warmly to it. Roman had a way about him that could charm the birds from the trees if he so wanted. But she had to think with her head at the moment. There was a bigger game at play, and it was one she had to focus on fully if she was going to win.

'I will just have to find a way around your schedule, Miss Davis,' he said smoothly. 'Because it's been too long.' Giving her one last intense look, he chuckled and sighed regretfully as he realised she wasn't going to give in this time. 'I'll send word that everything went OK in the morning.'

'Thank you,' Anna replied. She watched him leave and stared at the door thoughtfully as it closed. Her fingers drummed out a rhythm on the top of her laptop and eventually her eyes slid back to it.

Opening it up she checked the browser history one last time. Because now more than ever, she needed to make sure there was absolutely no trace of what she was doing with that money.

CHAPTER SEVENTEEN

Ignoring the half-dressed women grinding away and straddling clients in the lounge areas they passed through, Josephine led Tanya through the main building and up to her living quarters. Pulling the large, old-fashioned key from one of her many pockets, she unlocked the door and led the way in.

'Come through, darling – take a seat wherever.' She flapped her hand towards the sofa in the small living room and disappeared into the bedroom.

Tanya sat down and looked around, admiring the bursts of different colours and styles around the room. Chinese lanterns stood next to jade buddhas, Mexican death-day skulls hung from feather boas, Spanish fans were mounted next to artistic shots of the New York skyline and statues of camels stood beside sprays of fake poppies built into wooden clogs. Everywhere you looked there was a mark of a different country or culture. It shouldn't have worked, but strangely it did, as was Josephine's unique style. And as Tanya plumped a pillow underneath her arm with a picture of the Queen's corgis on, she allowed herself a small smile of amusement.

Josephine had never travelled beyond the M25, but she spent all her free time researching the world and soaking up all the romantic notions she came across. She collected adventures that she had yet to go on. Or at least that was what she told people when they asked.

'Here we go.' Josephine came back through with a waft of heavy perfume and the long black robe she wore over her dress flowing out dramatically behind her. 'Your ugly jumper with our dazzling diamonds securely hidden in the lining.' She threw it to Tanya with a look of distaste.

'It's not mine – I wouldn't be seen dead in it,' Tanya replied. She checked over the lining and felt around carefully until she found the subtle thickening she was looking for. When she tugged at the seam around it, the cotton held tight. She gave a little nod. 'Nice work.'

'Why thank you.' Josephine fluttered her long fake eyelashes and smiled broadly at the praise. 'Now, I'm glad you're here because I have something to share with you that I *know* you'll appreciate as much as I do.' She flounced over to the fridge in the small kitchenette and Tanya twisted round to see.

'If it's a man, I think we need to talk about how you're keeping them,' Tanya joked.

'Oh darling,' Josephine said, her tone dripping with disdain. 'I think we both know how different our tastes are in that department. No—' She pulled out a white porcelain jar, taking care to use both hands and move slowly, and her smile grew. 'This is much better than that. Look.'

Placing it down on the small kitchen table, she beckoned Tanya over. With a curious frown, Tanya joined her and read the front.

'Morus…' Her head shot round. 'Is this what I think it is?'

'Handcrafted gin made from the leaves of a single, one-hundred-year-old mulberry bush, aged for two years and bottled at sixty-four per cent proof,' she said reverently. 'Four thousand pounds a jar, with only twenty-five litres being released in the entire world. It is the gold dust of alcoholic royalty.'

Tanya's mouth dropped open. 'No way,' she gasped. 'I didn't think these were even out yet, though I read about them online. Where'd you get it?'

'My man knows a man,' Josephine said with a coy smile. 'And he managed to get one early. He gifted it to me last night. Said something so rare and beautifully crafted should feel right at home with me.' She blushed through the thickly applied make-up.

Tanya couldn't help but smile. Despite being worried about her friend's position as a secret mistress, she could also see how happy this man was making Josephine. And clearly the guy thought a lot of her to be making such grand gestures.

Josephine shrugged. 'I know what you think of him, and I know he's far from perfect. In many, many ways,' she added wryly. 'But you know what, he makes me feel…' She looked up as she searched for the words. 'He makes me feel like a real woman. He sees who I really am inside.' She tapped her fist to her chest. 'And more than that, he makes me feel elegant and classy and… I don't know. Proud? When he's here, this is a palace and I am his queen, even if it is for only a short time. And I'd rather take that for the few moments I get than live without it at all.'

Tanya smiled sadly. 'Well.' She picked up the jar and admired it. 'I can't say I've ever been anyone's queen. But I guess if I had, I'd probably want to keep it too. Whatever the cost.'

Josephine sniffed and changed the subject. 'Anyway, apparently the best way to appreciate this stuff is to add just a splash of water and sip it.'

'Is it nice?'

'I wouldn't know; I haven't tried it yet. It wouldn't be any fun trying something like this on my own, would it? It's something to be enjoyed with friends, so I've been waiting for you.' She grinned. 'Up for it?'

'Am I ever!' Tanya replied, her green eyes twinkling as she smiled back. 'Come on then, let's do it. I can't be long though. I have to get this to the dock before tonight. And I have a little extra surprise in store that I'm not sure Roman is going to like…'

CHAPTER EIGHTEEN

As the door to The Black Bear swung shut behind the Tyler brothers, the busy pub became quiet and still. Freddie looked around pointedly, noting who was there, before walking towards the bar. As they passed each table, those who had not been of enough importance to be invited to their welcome-home party – and had therefore not yet seen them since they got out – stood up and greeted them respectfully. They shook hands and nodded back to each man until they reached the bar and gradually the hum of activity started up to a low level once more. The brothers leaned on the warm mahogany bar top and faced each other, waiting for the manager to be done with the pint he was pouring.

'Where's Bill?' Freddie asked.

'Should be here any minute.' Paul glanced around, his weathered face unhappy and strained. He had looked like that ever since they'd walked back out into freedom and this fact wasn't lost on Freddie.

'What's going on with you?' he asked quietly.

'What do you mean?' Paul asked, glancing back at his brother.

'What can I get you boys?' The manager came over with a broad smile. 'Whisky or beer?'

'Alright, John?' Freddie greeted him with a brief smile. 'Think we'll go with whisky.'

John reached up to the top shelf and grabbed a bottle of what he knew to be their favourite. 'Here. It's on the house. Call it a welcome home present.'

'Ahh, that's good of ya,' Paul replied, 'but you know we never leave a tab unpaid. Have one yourself, yeah?'

'Thanks, Paul,' John said gratefully, before tactfully retreating to let them talk.

'You know what I mean,' Freddie continued quietly, as he poured them each a measure from the bottle John had left. 'You've had a face like a slapped arse since we caught fresh air. Want to talk about it?'

Paul took his glass and necked it in one, before holding it out for a refill. 'Nah, not really,' he replied.

Freddie nodded slowly and drank from his own glass, turning so that his back leaned against the bar. 'He stayed with Nathan and Sadie for a while, at first.' Freddie felt Paul tense up beside him as he talked openly about Paul's ex, James, for the first time since they got sent down. 'Then moved to a sleepy little town called West Wittering, on the coast. He's a general manager at a small pub restaurant. I got Bill to track down all the information you'll need.' He glanced sideways at his brother and for once couldn't read his face. He let out a long breath. 'You know he's going to need to be talked to. To make sure he understands what's expected of him.'

Paul nodded, then poured himself another drink. This was a hard conversation for him to be having and one he had been putting off for a while. But it was always there, hanging over him. James was an ex who knew too much and therefore had to be given a warning. Keep quiet and he could live in peace, but cross the brothers and he would be treated as any other enemy would.

It was not a pleasant task, but it had to be done. This was what had been playing on his mind since they'd got out. Not just this specific conversation, though – it was the thought of his ex in general. Wherever he went there were memories of his life with James, of the happiness he had finally found with someone for the first time in his life. Inside had been a different world, and although it had been hard, it was like reality had been suspended. He could almost pretend it wasn't real. It was only now that it was all coming back to him, as fresh as if it had happened yesterday.

'I can go, if you'd rather,' Freddie offered.

'Nah.' Paul shook his head. 'It needs to be me.' He took a deep breath in and sighed heavily. 'I'll go after we've sorted the Aleksei problem. Another few days won't make a difference.'

Freddie nodded and stood upright as Bill walked in. John wandered over and handed them a third glass, and they all headed towards the back booth of the pub where they could talk without being overheard.

They sat down and Bill took off his jacket, fanning himself with his hand. 'It's getting bloody hot around here, these days.'

'Don't worry, mate – it's England. Summer will be over in a few minutes,' Freddie joked.

'True story,' Bill muttered. 'Anyway, I've been talking to Ralph Hines today like you asked. Asked him about his meeting with Anna. Apparently, she gave him a tip-off about a bit of land outside London that was going cheap through auction. Said it would make a good area for luxury housing, that he'd stand to make a killing.'

'So, what, she invested?' Freddie asked with a frown.

'That's the thing – apparently not,' Bill replied with a frown of his own. 'Which is odd. It's not like they're big mates, so I'm not sure why she'd go out of her way to tip him off if she weren't interested.'

Freddie sat back and pondered this. It was an odd one indeed.

'Who did invest?' Paul asked.

'Ralph says it's a silent investor, some offshore company happy to shove in the money without so much as meeting.'

'Why on earth would they do that?' Freddie asked.

'Exactly,' Bill replied. 'So, either Ralph's lying to us, or Anna has something to do with this company and is going to great lengths to make sure no one knows about it.'

Freddie's insides grew cold as he thought over the possibility. Why would Anna need to go to such lengths to hide a business deal? He had handed his entire life over to her, had trusted her more than anyone else on the planet. Had he been wrong?

Would Anna turn out to be the enemy they never even had a chance to see coming?

CHAPTER NINETEEN

'No. It's not happening. Absolutely not.' Roman crossed his arms over his chest and stood firm.

'Yes, it is,' Tanya replied, crossing hers in an equally stubborn manner.

'Hell will freeze over and the devil will pop up to hand us all ice creams before I let you join a smuggling operation,' Roman replied. 'Not to mention the fact I'm pretty sure Anna would have my balls for putting you in that sort of danger.'

'Oh, get off your high horse, Lancelot, you ain't *putting* me in anything. I'm putting myself, thank you very much,' Tanya complained with a look of disgust. 'I'm responsible for me own decisions, and Anna would tell you that and all, whatever she thought of it.'

Standing tall, Tanya pushed her long red hair back over her shoulder and raised a defiant eyebrow at him. Roman sighed, exasperated, and looked her up and down.

'Even if I was up for you coming, you ain't exactly dressed for it. You do know it's freezing out there on the open sea at night?'

Tanya glanced down at her leather trousers and leopard-print shirt ensemble and frowned. 'What's wrong with this? I wore trousers.'

Roman stared pointedly at her heels and just shook his head before staring up at the heavens.

'Plus,' Tanya continued, 'I have a jumper. A very expensive one.' Pulling the hoody that held the diamonds out of her bag, she put it on and zipped it up. 'And it's now wrapped around me. So, unless you want to go all the way over to Spain empty-handed, I suggest you stop your bitching and let me on. I'm bored. I want to get going.'

'For crying out loud…' Roman mumbled in frustration. 'Fine. Get on. But on your head be it. These trips are far from risk-free.'

'Thank you,' Tanya replied, her tone sarcastic. Sweeping past him she boarded the small leisure boat and immediately began searching for something over the side.

Roman frowned. 'What are you looking for?' he called.

'That ice cream you promised me. Can't see the fucker any-where…' She smirked and continued on to find a perch near the front of the boat.

Narrowing his eyes and shaking his head, Roman stifled a smile of amusement. She had balls, that woman – he'd give her that.

An hour later, once the shore was just a glowing line in the distance and all that lit their way were the stars, Roman stepped out of the cockpit and took a seat next to Tanya. She was leaning back against the side of the boat, staring off into the distance, a small smile playing across her lips.

'You OK?' Roman asked, offering her a can of Coke. She declined and snuggled into the oversized jumper a little deeper.

'Yeah, I'm good. It's proper beautiful out here,' she mused.

'Even better in the day,' Roman replied. 'I've always loved being at sea. It's why I started this business. I can get out here whenever I want.'

'It must be really nice,' Tanya replied wistfully.

'Why did you want to come on this anyway? This ain't exactly the sort of trip you have fun on. I could have arranged you a proper trip, you know, if you'd asked.'

Tanya smiled and twisted her mouth as she contemplated telling him the truth. Glancing at his open face under the starlight she decided to be honest. 'Alright. I've never been to another country. Not even, like, Wales.'

'What?' Roman asked, with a small laugh. 'I knew you didn't have a passport, but I thought you'd at least have tramped about the UK a bit.'

'Yeah, I know – it's sad. But I've never got round to it, and the chances to go on holiday with people even if I did get one get fewer and farther between. Everyone has partners or kids or big groups of friends that go every year.' She smiled sadly. 'No one wants their single friend or that odd mate that's not part of the group hanging round. I figured this way, tomorrow I can say that I've been to Spain. That I've set foot in another land. Even if it is in the dark for just a moment. Even if I never go somewhere for real, I'll know I did this.'

Roman blinked and turned to her, his jaw dropping open. 'Are you actually serious?' he asked bluntly. 'Jesus. You fucking nutter.' He broke off into a laugh.

'Yeah, alright, no need to be a dick,' Tanya replied with a scowl.

'For God's sake, Tanya,' Roman continued still smiling in amusement. 'I'll go on holiday with ya. I'm always looking for travelling partners. Get your bloody passport and we can book something. Go do the tango and get pissed on sangria for real, instead of you dipping your toe in the Spanish sand in the middle of the night.' He glanced at her. 'As mates, I mean. I'm not propositioning you.'

Tanya snorted as she began to laugh herself. 'Oh, I know you're not!' she replied strongly. 'We all know there's only one woman *you've* got eyes for.'

Roman fell silent and cast his eyes back to the water.

Tanya paused and bit her lip. It was the truth – he couldn't deny it. Anyone who'd ever seen them together could see the chemistry sparking away.

'What happened between you two anyway?' she asked.

'Why are you asking me?' Roman answered carefully. 'Anna's your best friend.'

'She is,' Tanya agreed with a nod. 'But she's also notoriously good at keeping things close to her chest. Even with me sometimes.'

Roman didn't answer and the two fell into a long silence, the only sound the waves crashing against the hull of the boat as they powered forward through the sea.

'How has she been, since Freddie got out?' Roman asked eventually.

If Tanya was surprised by the question she didn't show it. 'Tense,' she replied. 'Very tense.'

Roman nodded. 'Things between them… They have a lot of history…' He trailed off, not sure exactly which question he was trying to ask.

Tanya sighed. 'They do.'

She thought back over the years and all the challenges Freddie and Anna had faced and overcome together, and once more felt a pang of sadness at the deflated ending that had befallen their relationship. She was a cynic when it came to love, but these were two people she really had thought would make it.

'Right from the start, there was this… intense bond they formed, that wasn't like anything else I've ever seen. Like they were just two halves of this unstoppable magnet. Perhaps it was because of the hardships they had to go through; perhaps it was something else – I don't know,' Tanya continued. 'But it was just this crazy, other-level thing that they had between them.'

Roman nodded. 'Sounds intense. But then sometimes it's the intense ones that burn out the quickest.'

'True,' Tanya replied. 'And it did. Or rather it was forced to.' Her expression turned sad. 'But whatever the future holds for them, I don't think either of them are over it yet. The wounds are still raw. Especially now they have to adjust to this new way of living around each other.' She looked up at Roman. 'I think you just need to give it time and let them work out how to get used to all these changes. Anna can't mentally juggle anything else right now.'

Roman let out a long breath and nodded reluctantly.

'You still never answered my question,' Tanya prompted, undeterred. 'What happened between you?'

The door to the small cabin opened behind them and Jason, one of Roman's men who had come along to drive and help with the drop, came hurrying out.

'Roman, we ain't alone,' he said urgently. 'I've just picked up coast guard on the radar and I'm pretty sure they've spotted us too. They're headed straight for us.'

'Fuck,' Roman spat, jumping up. 'Get inside, Tanya.'

The three of them ran into the small cabin and Roman leaned over the controls.

'There.' Jason pointed to the screen.

Tanya watched as a small dot started moving steadily towards the centre and her eyes widened in shock. Not once, when deciding to hijack this adventure, had it crossed her mind there would be any *real* danger. Roman had done this hundreds of times and never been caught. This couldn't be the time they finally cop it, the one time she had come aboard, surely?

Her heart began to race as the implications set in. She couldn't get caught out here. Aside from the fact they were all here illegally with a huge container of cheese, she was wearing thousands of pounds' worth of diamonds in her jumper and she didn't even own a passport. She could be thrown in jail for any one of those things. How could this be happening?

Roman looked up and squinted off into the horizon. Sure enough, there was a weak light in the distance growing steadily clearer as the coast guard moved in.

'Fuck,' he repeated, louder this time. 'Grab the sides, *now*. It's about to get messy.'

Jason immediately gripped on to one of the metal pipes running down the wall and braced himself. Her heart still hammering against her chest, Tanya twisted round and began searching for anything to grab hold of. There was a bracket on the wall next to her, holding some sort of equipment, and she reached for it.

She was a moment too late as Roman grabbed the wheel and swung the boat around with force. With a small cry she toppled over and landed with a crash on the floor.

'I said, grab something,' Roman yelled over his shoulder.

'I'm fine,' Tanya called back, gritting her teeth through the sharp pain that shot up the side of her leg. 'Just get us out of this.'

Pulling herself up, she wrapped her arm into the bracket and held on tight as Roman ramped up the speed to full power. Suddenly they were no longer bobbing smoothly up and down with the swell of the waves. Now they were violently crashing and thudding along so hard that Tanya wasn't sure she was going to be able to keep her grip. Roman had wrapped his legs around the bolted-down stool to keep himself in place as they went, and she momentarily marvelled at the skill it took him to stay upright.

As they ploughed through a particularly big wave, the boat shuddered sideways for a moment and Tanya's head smashed against the wall. She held back the cry, biting through her lip until she drew blood, not wanting to distract Roman at any cost.

The light grew stronger as the coast guard slowly drew closer.

'Their engine is more powerful – they're gaining,' Roman shouted back towards Jason.

'We can cloak, but we'll be down to the manual engine – we'll only be able to go half this speed,' he shouted back.

Tanya's eyes shot from one to the other, wide and alert, waiting for one of them to fix this. They had to.

'Shit,' Roman cursed once more as he warred with himself. 'I don't think they've laid eyes yet, we're small. If we do it... We could try. Maybe if we change direction…' He let out a strange sound of exasperation. 'Do it,' he said. 'Just do it.'

'OK.' Jason moved along the wall to the back, still holding on. 'Cut the power. Now.'

Roman flicked a switch and suddenly everything stopped. Tanya held her breath as the heavy silence around her began to fuel her panic even more.

'Roman? What's happening?'

The choking roar of an engine starting up sounded from behind her, and she glanced back into the darkness. They began moving again, this time slower, and Roman turned the boat in another direction once more.

'We were on their radar, but we're too small and dark to see by eye. Now we've gone blank online, so we'll have disappeared from their screens,' Roman explained with a grim tone. 'We've switched to a manual engine instead, which will move us but slowly. We've changed course and just have to pray that by the time they reach this spot, we'll be far enough away that they won't see us and won't have a clue what direction we've gone in.'

'What are our chances?' Tanya asked, moving up to stand next to him.

He glanced up at her and her hope died as she saw the truth in his eyes.

'Not brilliant.'

CHAPTER TWENTY

Freddie stared up at the ceiling in the darkness, listening to the sounds of the flat around him. The boiler ticked on as the water fell below temperature, and somewhere in the flat above a floorboard squeaked. Anna and Ethan had gone to bed hours ago, but he hadn't been able to drift off, too many questions running around in his head.

With a sigh of defeat, Freddie slipped out of bed and shrugged on a T-shirt with his boxers. Walking through to the kitchen, he eyed the whisky bottle on the side for a moment before pouring himself a glass of water instead. Whisky wasn't going to help him tonight.

A mixture of moonlight and street light flooded into the lounge through the windows, and as he leaned back against the kitchen counter his eyes were drawn towards the laptop bag Anna had left down the side of the sofa. He stared at it for a few moments, then glanced towards the dark hallway.

The clandestine meetings with Ralph and the strange tip-off were bothering him. Something didn't add up, and he needed to work out what that something was before she realised he had cottoned on.

Abandoning his drink and any hopes of sleep, Freddie picked up the bag and took it back to his room. Closing the door, he switched it on and began methodically searching through the files.

It was the accounts laptop, the one he'd arranged to be handed to Anna after Thea died. Thea's neat filing system and spreadsheets were still exactly where they used to be, and this brought forth a fresh wave of grief. Closing his eyes for a second he ran his fingers over the worn keys. How many times had his sister's fingers flown over them, as she sorted out their finances and found inventive new ways to launder money?

Pushing away the memories with difficulty, Freddie focused back on the task at hand. He didn't have long. He opened up the current spreadsheet for Club Ruby Ten, running his eyes down the figures and notes on the expenses page. Most of it looked pretty normal, the usual suppliers popping up every other line, with the day-to-day costs in between. Closing this, he moved to the scrapyard. This sheet was shorter, with more going in than out of this particular business. Screwing his mouth to one side in thought, he clicked into the Club CoCo spreadsheet.

Scrolling down the page he paused as he reached a large payment logged to a company called Medbourne Enterprises Ltd. The notes in the payment category section claimed this was against an ongoing payment plan for interior refurbishment. He frowned. There hadn't been any refurbishment in Club CoCo since he went down. It still looked the same as it had three years ago.

Opening up a new browser, Freddie googled the company name. Nothing came up that could be related to an interior design company. He exhaled slowly and narrowed his eyes. Typing in 'Companies House', he searched for the business there and clicked into it as soon as it came up.

The company had been up and running for over two years but when it came to the director, there was a second company in place of a name. Freddie swore under his breath. Clicking through to find the details of the second company, he swore again. The only available detail was the address, somewhere in the state of Oregon, USA. Noting this down on his phone, Freddie made sure to wipe the browser history before replacing the laptop in the bag and taking it back out to the lounge.

As he bent down to push the bag back along the side of the sofa, the sound of a door opening came from behind him. He shoved it in quickly and turned around, stepping away towards the kitchen area.

Anna appeared at the doorway with a small frown as she rubbed the sleep from her eyes. 'I thought I heard something. You OK?' she asked.

'Fine,' Freddie lied. 'Just needed a drink. Having trouble sleeping.'

Anna nodded and wrapped her arms around herself, feeling the chill of leaving warm bedclothes in a thin nightie. 'I guess it takes some getting used to, all the changes.'

'It does,' Freddie said levelly, holding eye contact intensely. 'More changes than I had initially realised.'

They stood there in the dark, staring at each other for a few long moments, the loaded words hanging in the air between them. Eventually Anna broke away, looking down and turning back into the hall.

'I can imagine,' she answered. 'Hope you get some sleep. We've got a lot of planning to do tomorrow.'

Freddie watched as her silhouette melted into the darkness. If he hadn't been sure before, he certainly was now. Anna was siphoning money from the company accounts. But why? Where was it going? And what exactly did she plan to do next?

CHAPTER TWENTY-ONE

The big black Jaguar pulled up to the building-site entrance and the back window rolled down. Aleksei stared through the wide metal gates at the half-built block of flats inside. The skeleton of the tall building was almost fully erect, the stairwells and partially constructed inner walls visible. Outer walls were not scheduled to be started for another couple of weeks, whilst the site manager dealt with some unexpected gas-pipe issues. Tools and machinery lay abandoned around the site as it was after closing, and a thick metal chain held the bars of the gates together with a heavy-duty combination padlock.

'And you have the code?' Aleksei said to the young man sat next to him.

'I do, boss,' Rohan answered.

'How often do they change it?'

'Never,' he answered, shaking his head. 'There is CCTV around the site, but it's closed circuit.'

'And you can get into this?' Aleksei asked, raising one dark, bushy eyebrow.

'I will have to pick the lock to the security shed, but yes. We can just take it with us so there is nothing for them to see the next morning.'

Aleksei nodded and closed the window, signalling for his driver to continue on.

'It's perfect,' he said, his thick Russian accent curling around his words as he smiled.

Now that the Tylers were back on the scene and Anna Davis had opened up the beginnings of a war between them, they were going to have to be dealt with. This much was obvious.

He had to hand it to her – she had played the game very neatly. He was almost annoyed that he had given her such a perfect opportunity to set this situation up – almost, but not quite. Clever as she thought she was being by handing the brothers a chance to show their strength and eliminate any lingering doubts about their ability to run the central belt, this was a situation that would have come to a head anyway. Aleksei had been around the underworld long enough to know that old reigning kings like the Tylers wouldn't just roll over and accept a newcomer like him when they got out.

He was going to have to face them one way or another. And the sooner the better, before people began to have too much faith in them again. It was why he had started needling Anna with Seamus in the first place. A little flex of his muscles, to remind her that he had no intention of going anywhere.

Having come up with a plan that should solve his Tyler problem and avoid further repercussions for good, he had tasked Rohan with getting a labouring job on a site with the kind of facilities they would need. And as usual, his man had come up trumps. This thought reminded him how glad he was that he had brought Rohan over with him from Russia.

'You've done well, my friend,' he said. Looking out of the window as they passed through the streets of East London, a cold smile spread across Aleksei's face. 'We will wait until the day has ended tomorrow, until Miss Davis's week is up, and then we shall ask to negotiate. They're business minded, from what I hear. A polite invitation should be accepted. We'll see how that first meeting goes, promise something they want and then just when they think they have tamed us, bam!' Aleksei snapped his fingers. 'We will lure them into the trap.'

'It is a good plan,' Rohan said, nodding sagely.

'It is. Simple, quiet and effective.' His dark eyes glinted with hunger as they stared unseeing into the distance. 'And then nothing will be in the way of us and all of Central London. Not even the great Miss Davis. That little cat is about to lose her last life.'

CHAPTER TWENTY-TWO

Anna stared off into space in the booth at The Black Bear where Freddie had asked to meet. She fiddled with the frayed edge of a coaster and bit her lip, the glass of wine in front of her forgotten.

As Freddie slipped into the booth opposite her she jumped, and he lifted an eyebrow in question at her reaction.

'Sorry.' She shook her head. 'I was miles away.'

'You seem tense,' he remarked, shifting over so that Sammy could slide in next to him.

'I'm worried,' she admitted.

'What about?' Freddie asked. He forced his tone and expression to stay neutral, despite his growing suspicions about her.

Lifting her troubled blue eyes to his, she took a deep breath and ran a hand over her forehead and back through her dark shiny hair. 'I've been running something new.' She glanced at Sammy. It wasn't something she had told any of the men because, for once, it was something that was completely unrelated to any of the Tyler businesses.

Freddie tilted his head to one side. 'What sort of something new?'

'Josephine, my madame at The Sinners' Lounge, she's from Hatton Garden. Grew up learning everything there is to know about diamonds,' Anna began. 'She still has a lot of contacts, people wanting to sell on the black market, and connections in Gibraltar who we've struck a deal with.'

'If she has all these connections, what's your involvement?' Freddie asked, frowning with suspicion.

'I put up the capital to buy the diamonds initially and I arranged the logistics,' she replied. 'Josephine didn't have the connections to get the goods across to Europe.'

Freddie was quiet for a moment. Was this something to do with the money she was siphoning from his businesses?

'How are *you* smuggling them across. Damien?' he asked.

Anna blinked. 'I thought Bill told you...' She glanced at Sammy, then back to Freddie. 'We lost the shipping routes. Our main guy on the other end retired and we couldn't replace him. We no longer had safe passage, so I had to find an alternative.'

'What?' Freddie exclaimed loudly. He suddenly remembered where they were and lowered his voice. 'What?' he repeated. This was major – it affected a huge chunk of his business. *Why had he not been told?*

Anna held herself up straighter. 'I had no idea that you didn't know. I struck a new deal with a smuggler called Roman Gains. He has a pleasure fleet down on the coast and regular shuttles from London. I've had him running your products across for a while now. It's a slightly higher cost but much lower risk and just as reliable.'

Freddie's head was whirling. Why hadn't Bill told him all this? The only reason Bill kept information back whilst they were in prison was when he felt he was somehow protecting them, but from what?

'I'm sorry,' Anna continued. 'I thought you knew. I'll update you with all the details and arrange an introduction. But going back to the diamonds, this is who I've arranged to smuggle them over. Only last night was the first run, and...' She trailed off and closed her eyes tiredly. 'I've not heard anything back from them. We should have had word that everything went smoothly first thing this morning.'

'Give it time,' Freddie said, distracted by worries about his own business.

'That's exactly what I was planning to do. Right up until I spoke to Josephine, who told me that Tanya ended up going along for the ride. Now I can't get hold of her and I'm worried sick.'

'What?' Freddie's attention snapped back to Anna immediately. Whatever else was going on, Tanya was family, and hearing that she'd gone missing at sea in the middle of the night on a smuggler's boat was not good news. 'Why the fuck did she go?' he asked, looking up to the heavens in despair.

'God knows, but I'm really worried, Freddie. If they're caught she'll be in deep shit. And aside from that, I don't think she can even swim. A boat is the last place she should be.'

'Fuck.' He bit his lip. 'I'll call Riley, see if she can find out if they were caught.'

'Riley?' Anna asked, surprised. They had given her a wide berth since the brothers went down, at Freddie's request.

'Yes, Riley. It wasn't her who let me down. I've had it looked into and there really was nothing she could have done. She was loyal to a fault, something I greatly value.' His eyes bored into her. 'I can always tell whether someone is or isn't loyal. The disloyal ones always end up tripping themselves up, in the end.' His eyes searched her face for any flicker of fear, but there was none. Just a strong, steady, neutral gaze staring back at him. 'What route did they take?' he asked, switching his attention back to the situation at hand.

Sammy pulled out his phone. 'I could ring Damien, see if there's a boat that can follow the route.'

'I don't know the route,' Anna said flatly. 'I don't know anything other than that they were going to the tip of Spain and then one man was going the rest of the way on land. They were supposed to land back in England before dawn.'

'You sent a shipment of diamonds off with a stranger in the middle of the night to another country, and you didn't even ask the route?' Freddie asked, unable to comprehend how she could do that.

'He's no stranger to me, Freddie,' Anna snapped, angered by the accusation in his tone. 'He's someone I've come to know very well and who I would trust with my life, if it came to it. So yes, I did send them off without needing a breakdown of the exact coordinates of their journey.'

Taking a deep breath and a moment to rein in the stress she was venting, Anna picked up her wine and drank deeply. She didn't notice the way Freddie had frozen in his seat at her outburst, nor the jealousy that had flashed across his face before he carefully masked it again.

Freddie forced himself to take a deep breath too, although his insides felt as though they had turned to ice. It wasn't often in the years he had known and loved her that he'd seen Anna speak so passionately about someone. In fact, he hadn't seen that level of loyalty lash out of her since the times she had defended him against the slander of foes. *This* was the reason Bill hadn't told him about Roman Gains. There was something between them. Something they were keeping quiet.

Pushing the pain that this caused him firmly aside, Freddie began to view her with fresh eyes. She may have kept his firm going and been a good mother to his son, but this wasn't the Anna Davis he knew anymore. That Anna was gone. And all he really knew about the woman in front of him right now was that she was stealing money from his businesses and that her new venture was a secretive affair with a man she seemed to be hiding a relationship with.

Anna swept her long hair back over her shoulder and met his eyes with hers. He tried to read what was behind them, but he couldn't.

'Will you help me find them?' Anna said.

'Of course,' Freddie replied, with a casualness that belied the turmoil inside.

'I'll start making calls,' Sammy offered, standing up and walking out of the pub with a nod to Anna.

'Thank you,' she said to Freddie with a worried smile. She watched him nod and noted how strained he looked himself. His handsome face was drawn and his mouth unusually downturned. 'Are you OK?' she asked. He had been out a matter of days and already challenges were being thrown at him right, left and centre. It must be taking its toll.

'Me? I'm fine. I'm not the one stranded at sea,' he replied, his tone a touch sarcastic.

Anna ignored it. 'If you're worried about tomorrow…'

'Not at all.' He looked up at her. 'If anything, I'm looking forward to this game you've arranged. It's a good plan. I do enjoy a dramatic introduction, especially after a few years locked up in a cage.' He watched Anna flinch at his words and felt a grain of satisfaction settle in his stomach.

He'd spent the last few years feeling terrible for the position he'd left her in and the burden he'd placed on her shoulders. Night after night he'd lain awake wondering if she was crying into her lonely pillow, her heart breaking as his was, for the relationship that had been so cruelly ripped away from them. But now it would seem that was not the case. Anna had thrived. She'd learned much more than he'd realised and her loyalty was as dead as their relationship. That part was the hardest to swallow.

'I've been meaning to talk to you about something,' Anna said, changing the subject, completely oblivious to the nature of the thoughts racing through Freddie's mind, her own too busy worrying about his potential reaction to what she was about to say. 'I've been running things here for a long time now, and over the years this world has become mine too. The things I had to do, the sacrifices I made…' She looked away as she thought back to the naïve, soft person she had been before. 'They changed me. And I can't go back to being who I was before.' Looking up, she held his gaze levelly. 'And I don't want to either. The businesses are yours; I don't expect to continue running things. But I do want to stay involved. I want to stay part of the firm, work alongside you. I think I've earned that. And I think you'll find that I bring a lot to the table too. I have skills and a good business head, and nothing fazes me anymore. Nothing,' she emphasised.

Anna let out a heavy breath, glad to have finally got it off her chest and out in the open. Freddie needed to know how she felt.

He stared at her, taking in all she'd said. So she wanted to stay involved. *Of course she did,* he thought. *How was she going to continue siphoning money if he said no?*

'I'll think about it,' he said. He watched her eyebrows shoot up in surprise and the disappointment at his answer flashed across her face. She had clearly been expecting a different response.

Anna sat back and nodded slowly. 'What I mean by that, Freddie, is that I *won't* walk away,' she said strongly. 'Like I said, I've earned my position here, and I really can't think of any reason why you wouldn't recognise that.' The strength in her voice belied the shaking nerves underneath. She had been hoping Freddie would be reasonable from the start, but if it was a fight he wanted, it was a fight he'd get. 'I haven't worked so hard for you all these years for you to turn me away now.' Her jaw formed a hard line and she lifted her chin a little higher in defiance.

Freddie studied her face. It was so beautiful, her pale skin flawless, her red lips full and inviting, deep blue eyes fringed with long dark lashes. It was so inviting, so soft, no trace of the serpent within. Had he done this to her? Had he created this cold, calculated weapon where there had once been a loyal, loving young woman?

'You're right,' he said eventually. 'It might take some time for us to rub down, but we'll make it work.'

Because after all, he added silently, *one should always keep their enemies close.*

CHAPTER TWENTY-THREE

Anna closed the door to the flat and dropped her keys in the bowl with a sigh. Placing her hands on her hips, she looked around the quiet space, wondering what to do with herself. Usually life was chaotic from the moment she woke until the moment she laid her head back down to sleep. Tonight though, she had found herself at an unusual loose end and she wasn't sure she liked it.

Freddie had taken Ethan out for dinner and a kick around at the park. They were both excited at the thought of spending some proper time together, and she was pleased for the little boy she loved so dearly. She was trying to feel happy for Freddie too, but there was something about the way he'd looked at her earlier in the day that was putting her on edge. He hadn't been overly happy about her wanting to stay in the business, which she had half expected, but the cold, mistrustful look he'd given her as he accepted her argument had sent chills up her spine. What was going on in that head of his? She had no idea anymore.

With Tanya missing – another reason for the stress and worry that pulsed through every inch of her body – and business done for the day, there was nothing to distract her from her unease.

Wandering through to the kitchen, she opened the fridge and pulled out an open bottle of wine, pouring herself a generous measure. She gulped half of it down in one, then refilled it before returning the bottle to the fridge and moving to sit down on the sofa. Taking another deep drink from the glass, Anna pushed her hair back off her face and waited for the alcohol to do its work and release some of the tension in her body.

Now that she was alone, she finally admitted to herself that Freddie's cold response had stirred another reaction in her too. It had caused her heart to hurt. Despite the situation they'd been thrown into and the years that they had been apart, there was still something there between them. Or at least there was on her part. Every time she saw him, every time she smelled his aftershave or saw the crinkle at the corner of his eyes when he smiled at one of the men, it pulled on her heartstrings and reminded her of happier times, when they were not two strangers but one being, together against the world.

But this wasn't healthy. They were not together and too much water had passed under the bridge now to go back. If they were going to make this work, if they were going to work together and both still be in Ethan's life, then she needed to quell these feelings once and for all. Because if the cold way he had looked at her earlier had told her anything, it was that they were not reciprocated.

Pulling her phone out, she dialled Tanya's number for the hundredth time that day. It went straight to voicemail, as it had been doing for the last couple of hours. Either the battery had died or someone had turned it off. Biting the tip of one of her long, polished nails, she wracked her brains for something she could do other than sit and wait for Freddie to get any information.

Eventually she placed another call. It was picked up almost immediately, as she'd known it would be.

'Zack, I need you to see if you can trace a phone. It's off, the battery might have died, but even if you could get a rough area it could be helpful… Yes, I'll text you the number now. It's Tanya's. Doesn't matter the time, if you get anything, call me. Thanks.'

She clicked off the call and texted over the number. Once that was done, she slipped the phone away and sat fiddling with the stem of her glass. Trying to think back to the last time she had been sat on her own with nothing to do, she tutted and sat up.

'This is ridiculous,' she muttered to herself.

Walking to the bathroom, she turned on the shower and went through to her bedroom to undress. She might as well try to unwind while she waited for news; sitting worrying about it wasn't going to find Tanya any quicker. As her thoughts began to turn towards darker possibilities, she firmly stopped them and reminded herself that it had only been a day. It was unusual for Tanya not to be in contact, yes, but it didn't mean the worst had happened. Knowing her wild best friend, she could easily have convinced Roman to stay over there an extra day. She had always wanted to travel somewhere new. If she was having a great time, Tanya may have just forgotten to get in touch. Though that didn't explain why she wasn't answering her phone.

Anna slipped off her dress and kicked it towards the washing basket, then shimmied out of her underwear and picked up the towel that was neatly folded on the chair beside her bed. Wrapping the fluffy bath sheet around herself, she began pinning up her hair in front of the dressing-table mirror.

At first she almost didn't register the noise. It was a block of flats; there was always some creak or bang in the background. The sound of the shower usually masked those though, and as the second creak sounded a little closer, Anna froze and her head snapped round to stare at her closed bedroom door.

The third sound was clearer again, the click of her front door as it shut. Anna swallowed. Someone was in the flat. She stilled her breathing and strained her ears, but there was silence. It couldn't be Freddie – Ethan hadn't long since texted to say they were heading into central to visit the Rainforest Café. It would be hours before they were back and besides, they wouldn't be making such an effort to be quiet.

Picking up her hairbrush to use as a weapon and silently cursing the fact there was nothing better to hand, Anna padded softly over to her bedroom door. She pressed her ear against it and listened harder. It was slight, but she could just make out careful footsteps moving through the hallway towards her. They paused halfway down and then began moving again, ever closer to the bedroom.

Her heart pounding so loudly she could no longer hear, Anna stepped back and pulled the towel tighter around her body. Brandishing the hairbrush, she took a deep breath and readied herself to lunge.

Who the hell was it? A hundred faces flashed through her mind, landing on Aleksei's and pausing there. Had he worked out their plan? Had he decided to head them off first, before they could carry it out? But who could have told him? Surely there was no way he could possibly know?

The doorknob turned and the door began to open inwards. Fear and anger coursed through her body. If it *was* one of Aleksei's men – or even Aleksei himself – she wasn't going down without a fight. She might be in a vulnerable position – she cursed herself one last time for not locking the front door to the flat behind her – but that didn't mean she'd go easily.

As the door widened just enough that light from the hallway beyond filtered through, Anna flew forward with a feral cry, the hairbrush high over her head ready to be smashed down upon whoever was coming for her. She grabbed the doorframe and swiped, narrowly missing the voluminous mass of red hair that ducked out of the way just in time.

'Anna, what the *fuck*!' Tanya screeched, half cowering to the floor, her green eyes wide with alarm.

'Jesus, Tanya!' Anna cried, dropping the hairbrush and holding her hand to her heart as it began to almost painfully slow down. 'You nearly gave me a bloody heart attack!'

'Ditto, you crazy cow!' Tanya stood up, pushing her hair back and taking a long, slow breath. 'Why the hell were you trying to attack me with your hairbrush?'

'Because I thought you were an intruder,' Anna replied indignantly. 'I thought… Oh, it doesn't matter what I thought. What are you doing creeping through the flat like that?'

'I thought Ethan might have been in bed; I didn't want to wake him. And I thought you were in the shower. I was just coming to get your charger.'

'My charger?' Anna's thoughts rushed back to Tanya's phone and then the reason she had been ringing it all day. 'Where have you been anyway? I've been worried sick.'

'Yeah, I figured. That's why I came straight here.' Tanya walked through and sat on the bed. She exhaled heavily as the rest of the tension evaporated from the room. 'I take it you know I went with Roman?'

Anna nodded.

'So we had been on our way for a fair while, I don't know where exactly we were, but the coast guard picked up our trail.'

'Shit.' Anna sat down on the bed facing her.

'Yeah, tell me about it,' Tanya replied with a humourless laugh. 'But I have to hand it to Roman – he knows his stuff. It was touch and go for a while, but he managed to pull us out of there. We ended up having to lie low for a while somewhere off the coast of France. It took us a lot longer to get to Spain, then we had to take a longer route back to avoid the guard. We've just got back and I came straight here.'

'Why didn't you pick up my calls?' Anna asked.

'Roman insisted the phones stay on land, and then they all ran out of battery as we were so long, so none of us had any way to contact you. It was an alibi thing – if we ever got questioned by the police and they tracked our phones' movements, they never left British soil.'

'Fair enough,' Anna conceded. 'Still, Tan, you took a really big risk going with him. You could have been caught,' she added, her tone full of the worry she'd been feeling for her friend all day.

'I know. But you know me.' Tanya grinned. 'I love to live life on the edge. Anyway, all's well that ends well, right? And now I can say I've been to Spain,' she added chirpily.

Anna shook her head and rolled her eyes in despair. 'You'll be the death of me, Tanya Smith.'

'Or the making of you – don't forget that option,' she retorted.

Anna couldn't help but laugh. 'Here,' she said, chucking her charger across the bed to Tanya. 'You have about a million messages, all from me.'

'Well, they ain't going to be from a hot guy, are they? My love life is as dead as the Dead Sea,' she moaned.

'Actually, I read an article recently about the Dead Sea. Apparently it's not completely dead after all – they've found loads of bacteria growing in little pockets around the bottom…' She trailed off, catching the look on Tanya's face. 'But yes, we probably don't want to compare your love life to that. Let's stick with dead. Anyway!' Getting up, Anna repositioned the towel around her torso. 'I need a shower but I'll be quick, so go grab a glass of wine and I'll join you in a minute. I've got lots to talk to you about. I spoke to Freddie.'

'Oh, how'd it go?' Tanya asked as they walked out of the bedroom.

'I'm not really sure,' Anna replied slowly, her forehead creasing into a frown. 'But I think we're going to have an issue and I'm not sure why.' They exchanged a grim look. 'And that doesn't bode well for any of us.'

CHAPTER TWENTY-FOUR

Josephine sat down at her dresser after another long night of randy punters and drunken cads lining up to use her girls. They'd made very good tips tonight, so the girls had left very happy indeed. Pulling her own share out of her bra, where she had stored it earlier, Josephine stuffed it into the prized Chinese vase she kept all her tips in. Peering down into it, she smiled happily. It was getting quite full. Soon she should be able to afford the next step in her transition. She had already obtained a perfectly pert pair of breasts and femininely chiselled cheeks, and the tablets she took every day softened her masculinity more and more. The manhood she was born with still hung between her legs, but this she was able to tape out of the way with no hassle. Plus, it still brought about a lot of enjoyment, so she had made her peace with retaining it for now.

The Adam's apple that bobbed up and down in her neck when she swallowed or laughed, however, was a constant visual reminder of the past life she had shrugged off. This was the next thing on the list.

Staring at herself in the mirror, she smoothed the line of black kohl around her eyes and added a touch more blush to her cheeks. Finishing off with some lip gloss, she smiled as her phone beeped. He was here.

She rushed down to let him in, her heart fluttering as high as a kite. As she opened the door and he stepped inside, she pushed it shut impatiently behind him and wrapped her arms around him in an adoring fashion.

'I missed you,' she murmured between ardent kisses.

'I missed you too, my sweet,' he replied, moving her backward towards the stairs. 'Come on. I have something for you.'

Josephine led the way up to her apartment, the smile of happiness that his presence brought forth never leaving her face. 'You know it's only you I want. Though your gifts are always so thoughtful.'

'I see beautiful things and I think of you,' he replied charmingly.

They reached the small apartment and Josephine set about making them a drink while he made himself comfortable. She loved having him here like this. It was as though, for just a small snippet of time, *she* was the doting wife that he came home to. She would imagine this place to be an opulent mansion where they would host all their couple friends – who would naturally go home at the end of the night talking about how happy and in love this perfect pair were. It was a fantasy, but one she dreamed of every time they were together.

He had been up front with her from the day they met about his family. He'd married young, something his family had pressured him into. And he'd been content for a while, before his deeper desires had kicked in. Sophia was a dutiful wife and a very beautiful woman; Josephine had seen a picture of her once, next to his two adorable children. They had her solemn expression and his dark eyes and hair. Both boys and both still very young. If their happily ever after did come around, it wouldn't be for many years yet, because of this. Ridden with jealousy, Josephine had not looked for photos of his family again.

She watched as he stretched out on the couch and rubbed his head. 'You look tired,' she said, frowning. 'I hope you're not running yourself into the ground.'

'Me? Never,' he replied with a smile. 'And no one else will ever run me into the ground either.'

'Ah,' Josephine said, looking away. 'You're having problems with Sophia.'

'No, not her. She remains her usual, dutiful self.'

Josephine felt the familiar pang of jealousy shoot through her. She knew he had no feelings for the woman and was only stating a fact, but it still galled her that she existed. Perhaps if the ever-dutiful wife would step a toe or two out of line, he would have reason to oust her.

With a deep, long breath, she pushed her resentment aside and tried to focus on the time they had together. As always it would move fast and be over too quickly. She wanted to enjoy and savour every second.

Passing him a drink, she slipped down onto the sofa beside him, twisting sideways so they could face each other as they talked.

'So, what's up then, my love?' she continued. Her eyes roamed his face, from his thick, dark hair, to his heavy brows and down to his full lips. It was a face she could stare at all day.

His gaze narrowed slightly and he bit his lower lip, as though he was wondering whether or not to share something. She leaned in closer and waited.

'How long have you worked here now, huh? In this place?' he asked.

'A couple of years, give or take. Why?' Josephine asked, tilting her head to one side in question. He had never had a problem with it before. In fact, she had already been well settled in here before they even met.

'Do you really want to be here forever? A beautiful princess like you, locked away in this sordid tower, peddling flesh to soulless creatures for the rest of your life?' He paused.

Josephine didn't know how to answer, so instead she just gave him a frown of confusion.

'What if I told you that we could be together properly? My wife's mother is in Slovakia. They would be safe and happy there, if I sent them over. I have the money to set them up comfortably, and you and I can live here, create a proper life for ourselves.'

Josephine's jaw dropped and she blinked rapidly, unsure what to say. This was all she had ever wanted, but why? Why now? Another thought suddenly occurred to her.

'Darling, you know that it isn't just your wife in the way of us being together publicly. My friendship, my *business* with Anna…' She trailed off anxiously.

Aleksei sat forward and grasped both her hands and stared into her eyes, fire in his own. 'The plan I have in mind – the plan I need *you* to help me with, my sweet Jojo – will put an end to all of the issues that lie there once and for all. No more feud, no more Tylers to get in our way. And I know you will do what needs to be done. Because our love is stronger than *anything*. And in the end, it really will be better for everybody.'

Josephine stared back at him in shock, and as his hands tightened around hers, a feeling of dread sank deep into her stomach.

CHAPTER TWENTY-FIVE

Darkness had finally fallen over London in the late hours of the balmy summer evening, and the car they were tailing had started its journey. Just as Anna had said it would, it led them out of the city and into the more desolate countryside beyond. Keeping a safe distance, Freddie, Paul and Bill followed behind in Bill's car.

As they turned onto a narrow road, Bill pulled over to the side and killed the lights. Freddie turned towards him with a look of question.

'The barn where they do the handover for the guns is just up there,' he said, his deep husky voice breaking through the heavy silence.

Sure enough, the car slowed and turned down a narrow dirt track that led off out of sight.

'We just need to wait here. He's never longer than a few minutes, then he carries on around this road in a loop back into the village.'

'And that's where he stops?' Freddie asked.

'Like clockwork,' Bill answered. 'Goes into the newsagent's, buys a few scratch cards and some fags, then carries on.'

'What's the visibility like?' Paul asked, from the back.

'Few houses, usually have their curtains drawn at this time of night. Sleepy little place – nothing much happens. No cameras on the street or outside the shop. One on the till inside, but we ain't going in so that don't matter.'

'Good,' Freddie replied. 'Here he is. Let's go.'

They crawled down the road after the other car, only turning their lights back on when he was a safe distance ahead. Freddie craned his neck, looking for the barn as they passed the entrance to the dirt track, but it was well hidden behind some trees. He made a note to check this out again, once he'd dealt with Aleksei for good.

'Did you look into what happened in Russia yet?' he asked Bill.

Bill pulled a face. 'I have, but I haven't had much luck. Whatever it is, there's no trace of it online, not even within Zack's reach. But then again, all that tells us is that it's nothing to do with the authorities. It seems whatever trouble that forced him out of the country must have been with rival firms. Or that's how it looks anyway.'

'There must be a way of finding out more,' Freddie pressed.

'There is – it just might take time,' Bill replied. The car ahead turned a corner and he sped up a little. 'I know a guy from way back when. We were inside together. He was half Russian, a freelancer like me, but he worked with some of his family over there sometimes. Acted as a go-between for their business interests here in the UK. He's out of the country at the moment but coming back soon, so I'm hoping he might give me something to go on or another connection at least.'

Freddie nodded. This was good – hopefully it would lead them to something useful.

Bill slowed back down as they approached the lights of the small village high street. They watched as, ahead, a lone figure stepped out of the car, locked it and walked into the small newsagent's. Bill pulled into a dead end close by and they all got out of the car.

The brothers each pulled a pair of leather gloves from their pockets and slipped them on, then positioned themselves in the shadows either side of the door, whilst Bill crouched by the bonnet of the other man's car, pretending to search for something on the ground.

'Hey,' the man they'd been following shouted, as he walked out of the shop. 'What are you doing by my car?' Bill didn't answer straight away, and the man walked faster towards him. 'Did you hear me? I said…'

'Oh, he heard you,' Paul answered as he and Freddie sidled up behind him. Bill stood up.

Before the man could react, Paul twisted one of his arms up painfully behind his back and Freddie grabbed the other, jamming a knife up hard against his ribs.

'One sound and I'll gut you like a fish. Got it?' he growled. He waited until the other man nodded. 'Good. Now where are your keys?'

'Oh, Jesus…' He groaned. 'You don't know what you're doing. That's more than just a car…'

'I said *where*' – Freddie pushed the knife up further until a cry of pain escaped the man's lips – 'are the *fucking* keys?'

'Left pocket,' the man gasped. Paul pulled them out and switched places with Bill, swiftly unlocking the car and slipping into the driver's seat. As that car pulled off, Freddie dragged the terrified-looking man back towards Bill's vehicle.

'You're going to take a ride in the back with me, mate,' he said, shoving him in head first.

'You don't know what you've done,' the man groaned as Freddie got in beside him.

'Ah, see that's where you're wrong.' Freddie's eyes glinted dangerously hard in the moonlight as he stared at one of the men who had pushed the crates down upon Seamus. 'You see, I know exactly who you are and what's in the boot of that car. I also know who you work for and that me taking it is bound to piss him off a treat. And I know that when I break every bone in your hand, you'll both know exactly why.'

The man next to him stilled and began to pale as it started to dawn on him what was happening.

'That's right, sunshine. I'm Freddie Tyler. And you're about to wish you'd never set foot in my city…'

CHAPTER TWENTY-SIX

After pulling up to the back door of one of the restaurants he had acquired a few years before, Freddie and Bill got out of the car and met Paul, who was already waiting. Paul flicked away the cigarette he had been smoking and opened the back door of Bill's car. He yanked the other man out by the scruff of his shirt.

On the journey over, Freddie had already secured his wrists with a cable tie and taped his mouth, to make sure he didn't get any ideas about shouting for help when they reached their destination. Not that it would have done him much good anyway. The restaurant was surrounded by shops and industrial units, in an area which at this time of night resembled a ghost town.

Checking down the alley over his shoulder out of habit, Freddie unlocked the back door, punched in the code to the alarm system and led the way through the restaurant to the dingy flat above it.

As they climbed the stairs in silence, he thought back to the last time he had been here. It had been with Tanya's snake of an ex, Tom, the guy who'd teamed up with her mum to kill her and steal her business after a failed attempt to screw the Tylers over. He had been a piece of work and one that Freddie hadn't felt any remorse over. In a double-edged play, he'd actually managed to put Tom in the frame for a crime he'd committed himself against the Mafia. So, after torturing him to a point he could no longer communicate, he'd handed him over as a gift, cementing a good relationship between London and New York and killing two birds with one stone.

Now, here they were again, back to teaching people lessons in the only language most of the underworld responded to. It felt strange to be back here in this capacity. Neither Freddie nor Paul had raised a violent hand to anyone in two and a half years. They hadn't needed to. Their status alone had ensured instant respect inside. Whereas before it was just part of the life they led, now it felt like an almost alien concept. But having stepped out of the strange bubble that was prison life, they were back in the dangerous, feral, challenging world of underground London again. And here there was no room for the weak. There was a very limited amount of time before they had to show their strength to the world again and they knew this. Anna knew it too – it was why she had so strategically set this up.

As his thoughts turned to Anna, the war in his head began to rage again. How could someone who had fought to keep his business going and cared for his son, someone who had shared a life with him for so many years, steal and lie the way she had recently? What game was she playing? What sort of person had she become?

Shaking his head, he pushed all thoughts of her aside once more. He couldn't think about her now; there were more urgent matters at hand.

'Tie him to that chair,' Freddie ordered, pointing to a wooden kitchen chair in the middle of the room. The small flat was musty and covered in dust from years of neglect. It hadn't exactly been a palace to begin with, dark and practically bare save the most basic of furniture, but now it was positively dismal. Clearly no one had had cause to enter since they'd been away.

Freddie wandered aimlessly as Paul and Bill did as he asked, pausing as he reached the bathroom. The bathtub with the strong metal ring screwed into the ceiling above was still there, minus the shower curtain. This had been too drenched in Tom's blood to save in the clean-up. He looked down to his hands and sighed silently. He was getting too old for this.

'Stop fidgeting and shut up,' Paul said behind him. He turned and focused on the job at hand.

'So,' he barked, looking down at the trussed-up man in the chair. 'You broke into our warehouse, waited for Seamus to come in and then pushed a load of heavy crates down on top of him, is that right?'

The man whimpered through the tape that held his mouth shut and his brown eyes pleaded with Freddie. Freddie signalled for the tape to be removed and Paul ripped it off roughly.

'Ouch!' he cried.

'Oh, I wouldn't worry about that. You'll forget all about that in a minute once I get started on your hand,' Freddie replied.

'Please,' he begged. 'You don't understand…'

'I understand perfectly, Eli – that's your name, right? Eli?'

The man nodded, the fear in his face intensifying.

'And that's why there's no point trying to deny any of it. One of my men saw you and your mate coming out of the warehouse that night and identified you. And we already knew about the gun route. Did your boss really think he could push his way onto another firm's turf and keep his business to himself? My brother and I might have been away a while, but that don't mean business wasn't running as usual.'

Taking a step forward he glared down at the man, who was trying not to shake at the thought of what was about to come. 'My firm has been watching you the entire time, keeping tabs on exactly how you do things.'

There was a long silence, and Eli's breath became shorter and louder by the second in the quiet room.

'Now, to be frank,' Freddie continued, 'on top of your cuntish actions, which we are about to address, I also can't believe the audacity your boss had in the first place, setting up shop in our front fucking yard, can you, Paul?' He turned to his brother.

'Can't say I do, Fred,' Paul answered conversationally.

'I mean, how would you like it, eh?' He turned back to Eli. 'If one of us walked into your house one day and just started shitting on your carpet? Because that's basically what it is, isn't it?' He held his arms out with a shrug.

'Wh-what?' Eli stuttered, not quite following.

Freddie suddenly leaned forward, a thunderous expression on his face. 'What it boils down to, mate, is that you fucked with the wrong people and your boss has outstayed his welcome. Not that he ever had an invite to begin with. So, this' – without warning Freddie pulled his arm back and slammed it into Eli's face with force – 'is *your* comeuppance and *his* eviction notice.'

'Argh…' Eli gargled as his head rolled and blood from his split lips slid to the back of his throat. 'You stupid fucks,' he spat, anger suddenly coming to the fore. 'Do you know what he'll do to you for this?'

'He ain't going to do a damn thing,' Freddie replied. 'Because if he don't leave by the time I come looking for him, I'll put him six feet under. And there ain't much he can do from there.'

'He has allies that will come for you,' Eli bluffed. 'He is a very powerful man.'

'Oh, I don't think he does, do you, Paul?' Freddie answered.

'Nah, what we heard was that he had to run away from all these so-called allies and start over somewhere new. I'd bet the only reason they'd have to come here is to help us finish the job.'

Eli's bloody mouth flapped open and shut a couple of times as though he wanted to say something but decided against it.

Opening the small rucksack he had brought in with him, Paul pulled out a hammer and handed it to Freddie. Freddie weighed it in his hand for a second before lifting it high above his head and smashing it down onto one of Eli's bound hands as hard as he could.

The sickening sound of splintering bone filled the air for a split second, before Eli's screams of agony drowned it out. Blood spattered out and Freddie tutted in disgust as it seeped into his suit jacket.

'Ahh, look at that… You spend a few years inside and you forget the little things, like taking off your jacket before you start,' he said to Paul, shaking his head.

'I never liked that suit on you anyway,' Paul replied, wrinkling his nose. 'Not one of your best.'

'Really?' Freddie frowned. 'Oh well.' He shrugged. 'Anyway, how you feeling, Eli?'

The man was sobbing quietly between panicked breaths. 'You're going to pay for this,' he moaned.

'No, you see, it's *you* who owes *us* the payment, Eli. You ever read the Bible? It says in there, *an eye for an eye.* Or in this case, a hand. You fucked up my man's hand, and not only that but a very lucrative deal my firm had arranged on his boxing match. That's something I can't allow, I'm afraid. Now, do you know how many bones there are in a human hand, Eli?'

'What? I don't give a shit, you crazy— Argh!'

Freddie smashed the hammer down once more on the bloody hand and then another two times in quick succession. Eli's screams reached fever pitch.

'Twenty-seven,' Freddie continued, ignoring Eli's response. 'There are twenty-seven bones in the human hand. That's quite a lot when you think about it, really, wouldn't you say, Paul?'

'I would, Fred.' Paul stepped forward to stand behind Eli, firmly securing the chair as he bucked and writhed in pain.

'And you, Eli' – Freddie lifted the hammer again, ignoring the pleas for mercy now spewing out of the other man's mouth – 'managed to break sixteen of them. *Sixteen* little bones that will take months to heal. Bones that will probably never heal properly, not for a boxer anyway. They'll always be a weak spot. How many do you think we've broken of yours so far?'

Peering down to the bloody, swollen mess that was Eli's hand he tried to see what damage had been done.

'I wouldn't say sixteen. Not yet at least.'

'Please, no, no, Freddie, I beg you— Argh!'

Again and again Freddie smashed the hammer down, until Eli began to lose consciousness. At this point he stopped and signalled for them to cut the man loose. Eli came back around and immediately began stuttering his pleas once more.

'Please, no more, please…'

Bill and Paul hoisted him up between them and started back towards the front door of the small flat. 'Where are we going?' Eli's eyes sharpened and began to dart around in panic as he registered the move.

'You're going home, mate,' Freddie answered with a tight smile. 'To your boss. Your personal debt has been paid, but his has not.' His gaze darkened as it bored into Eli's. 'So you're going to pass on a little message…'

CHAPTER TWENTY-SEVEN

From the booth at the back of his strip club where he sat discussing plans with his men, Aleksei barely noticed the front doors swing open. The club was busy, the girls were in full swing and the music was pumping. It was only when one of the girls screamed and a commotion started that Aleksei looked up with a frown.

He clicked his fingers at a passing hostess as his men went to investigate. 'What's going on?' he asked.

'I-I don't know…' she stuttered as he stood up and strode past.

Eli lay in a bloody mess on the floor just inside the door, painfully trying to pull himself to his feet using just one hand.

Aleksei whistled and pointed at two men to go out and deal with whoever had just left him here, whilst two of the others dragged Eli up off the floor and through the gawping crowd to the back. Aleksei started after the men who had gone outside but stopped as they burst back in holding their hands out to the sides and shaking their heads.

'Gone, boss. Whoever it was, they were already halfway round the corner – we didn't catch the plate.'

'*Gavno*,' Aleksei cursed, reverting to his mother tongue in his frustration. 'And his car?' Aleksei gestured towards Eli.

'Not there, boss,' one of them replied, looking at the other worriedly. They knew exactly what was in the car and what the absence of it meant.

After a long, horrified silence, Aleksei stormed through the club to the booth at the back where someone was trying to clean up Eli's mangled hand.

'What happened?' he asked, his tone urgent.

'They ambushed me just after the pick-up. They knew the route, said they'd been watching it for a while.'

'Who?' Aleksei demanded.

'The Tylers,' Eli replied. 'They took me somewhere, tied me up and destroyed my hand.' The sliver of self-pity coloured his tone for only a moment, before he coughed and controlled himself. Weakness was not accepted in their culture. 'They took the guns and sent me back with a message.'

Aleksei felt a deep ball of rage begin to form in the bottom of his stomach. How dare they steal his guns? The damage to Eli's hand, although unfortunate, was understandable. He had expected some sort of retaliation; it was what he had been counting on in order to fire up the feud. But taking his property was another matter. He had orders to fill, a hefty invoice to pay. Oh no, this was not acceptable at all.

'What was the message?' he asked, through gritted teeth.

Eli swallowed. 'My hand was payment for their boxer's. And the guns were part payment for what you owe them for the boxing match.'

'What?' Aleksei roared. He slammed his fist down on the table. 'Those motherfuckers – I do not owe them a penny.' He seethed, blowing a long breath out of his nose. 'Continue.'

'They say the guns account for half, that they expect the other twenty-five thousand to be delivered to them in cash. And then…' Eli paused and licked his lips, knowing his next words would only serve to further anger his boss.

'Go on,' Aleksei said.

'Then they said you have one week to leave their city for good. They say if they come here and you have not left, that we will all be killed and buried where no one will ever find us.'

Having relayed the message, Eli sagged back, giving in to the pain that was beginning to overwhelm him.

Aleksei sat back in his chair slowly, his furious gaze darting around the room as he thought it all through. Around him his men held their breath, exchanging tense looks with one another. Their boss was not a man to mess with, especially at this level. There was going to be hell to pay.

'One week, you say?' he asked finally, his tone low and deadly.

'One week,' Eli confirmed.

Aleksei nodded and looked around at his men. 'Then we shall use this week to get our guns back from those thieving sons of bitches and wipe them off the face of the planet,' he said through gritted teeth.

'What do you suggest?' Rohan asked.

Aleksei licked his lips slowly as he thought it over. 'You will make contact. Tell them I want to meet with them to discuss a negotiation.' Some of the men frowned. 'There will be no negotiation,' he continued strongly. 'But let them think we are being reasonable. We will take one of the brothers and hold them until we get back the guns. Then we kill them,' he said simply.

'I don't think it will be that easy…' Rohan started.

'It will when we have all our men in the shadows, armed. They never travel in packs of more than three or four at a time. It's a stupid overconfidence of theirs,' he scoffed. 'It doesn't matter how much respect you have and how many years you have been around, brute force will always win out.'

'If you are sure,' Rohan said, unconvinced.

'I am,' Aleksei replied, his eyes glinting dangerously.

'Besides,' he added with a dark smile. 'If for some reason this does not work out, I have a backup plan that is absolutely foolproof. One they will never see coming.'

CHAPTER TWENTY-EIGHT

Tanya paced tensely up and down the wide pavement outside Ethan's school waiting for the bell to ring, her arms crossed over her chest as she stared off into the distance, lost in thought.

One of the groups of mothers, all dressed in drab shapeless shades of grey – no doubt the height of Chelsea fashion – were whispering and shooting looks at her, and as she caught the eye of one of them by accident, they all quickly looked away, holding their noses in the air.

Tanya blinked back to the present and shook her head with a small smirk. She would never fit in with the mothers around here. Not that she particularly wanted to. Her tight knee-length burgundy skirt and leopard-print blouse, red lipstick and wild hair probably went against everything they were trying to bring up their precious little darlings to think their world should look like.

The bell rang and she gave a silent sigh of relief that she could walk away from their haughty judgement soon. She had bigger things to worry about than them, that was for sure. Like why Freddie was acting so strangely. It wasn't that she didn't expect him to be different – prison changed people. But Tanya had known Freddie a long time, longer than Anna even. And through all of life's changes, he had always been solidly predictable on one point – his unshakable loyalty to his family and inner circle. So why, after all Anna had done for him whilst he'd been away, would he turn cold on her now? It wasn't like him.

Ethan appeared at the top of the stairs and she grinned, waiting for him to come down, but he didn't move. Instead, his teacher appeared beside him and waved for Tanya to go up.

With a slight frown of concern, Tanya mounted the steps and walked into the large entrance hall to the school, ignoring the vulture-like looks from the previously judging group of mothers. She resisted the urge to turn around and give them something to *really* gossip about.

As the rest of the children filtered past, she put a protective hand on Ethan's shoulder. 'You OK?' she whispered as the teacher finished up another brief conversation ahead.

'Yeah, fine,' he replied.

The teacher turned her attention back to them with a warm smile. 'Why don't you pop into the library, Ethan, just for a moment whilst I talk with your aunt?' she suggested. He did as he was bid and Tanya waited to hear what she was about to say.

Tanya liked Julie – or Miss Andrew, as Ethan referred to her. Miss Andrew was someone who had become a teacher purely for love of the children. She lived for her pupils and had formed an especially close bond with Ethan over the last few years. He had taken to her too, instantly drawn to her kind blue eyes that seemed to be forever smiling, and her rosy cheeks that dimpled when she grinned. She had a caring air about her that most of the other, more austere teachers did not. Which was exactly the sort of person he needed to be around, having started at a new school with a whole new life. She had made his transition a whole lot easier, and for that Tanya and Anna were eternally grateful.

'Sorry to pull you in, Tanya – hope you're not in a rush,' Julie said, pushing her caramel locks back behind her ears and straightening her glasses.

'No, not at all. Everything OK?' Tanya asked.

'Oh yes, in general everything is fine,' Julie enthused. 'Ethan's grades are very good, as always, and he's a pleasure to have around.

It's just…' Julie's pale blue eyes became troubled. 'Is everything OK at home? Nothing has happened, but Ethan seems a little withdrawn at times. He's not quite his usual sunny self. He seems worried about something, but he says he's fine. I was hoping you might be able to shed some light. It's just if I know what's wrong, then I might be able to help him, be there for him.'

'Oh, I see,' Tanya replied, slightly taken aback.

She'd known Ethan had been a little tense about Freddie getting out, but she thought that had been put behind him now. Clearly she was wrong, if his favourite teacher was concerned about him. She tried to think of what she could say.

Well, she thought wryly, *the crime baron dad he knew for five minutes before he was jailed just got out of the nick and is back home living in friction with Ethan's crime baroness stepmother and acting like she's an enemy, but other than that I can't think of a thing, Julie.* She bit her lip. *No, perhaps not.*

'I'm not sure what it could be,' she lied, immediately feeling bad for deceiving such a nice woman. 'But let me talk to him, see if I can find out what's troubling him. I'll let you know if there's anything you need to know.'

'Thank you. And yes, please do,' Julie said, shooting a sympathetic look towards the library doors. 'He's such a lovely little boy; we all want to see him back to his usual sunny self again.'

'I know you do,' Tanya replied with a grateful smile. 'And you will. Thanks for letting me know.'

'Any time,' Julie replied, touching Tanya's elbow to guide her towards the library where Ethan waited patiently. 'Give my love to Anna, won't you?'

'Of course. And ours to Charlotte,' Tanya replied politely. Charlotte was Julie's daughter, her pride and joy. She sometimes came to help out at the school, to spend some extra time with her mother.

'Oh, I will, thank you.' Julie beamed, as she always did when someone referred to her daughter.

'Come on then, mate,' Tanya called to Ethan, who immediately hopped up and walked out with her. Whilst he enjoyed school, he was still like every other child in that he did not want to spend more time there than necessary.

'See you tomorrow,' Julie called after them with a wave as they stepped out into the sunny London afternoon.

As they walked down the road towards the car, Tanya glanced over her shoulder to check they were alone.

'Hey,' she said. 'What's going on, buddy? Miss Andrew says you've been a bit down at school. Do you want to talk about it?'

'I'm fine,' Ethan replied with a shrug.

Tanya noticed his eyes didn't meet hers, and she pulled a grim expression. She unlocked the car and waited until they were both in and on the road before she continued talking.

'Look, Ethan, I know that there have been a lot of changes. And it must take some getting used to. But I thought you and your dad were having a good time lately – or is there something you haven't said?'

'We are having a good time. It's brilliant having him back. I can finally spend time with him like we planned,' Ethan replied. 'It's not that. It's just at home, like… I don't know.' He clamped his mouth shut and his face closed up.

Tanya chewed her top lip as she tried to work out how to get him to talk to her. Clearly the tension between his father and stepmother was affecting him. 'OK. Well, look, you know your dad has all sorts of businesses, don't you? And that Anna and I have been helping to run them?'

'Yeah, 'course,' he replied.

'Sometimes these businesses can be tricky and you know how… well, you know that Dad had to go away, and it was just a lot of mix-up with the business?'

'I know, Tanya,' Ethan said, a touch more irritably this time. 'And it wasn't a mix-up that put him in jail, so you don't need to keep pretending. I know I'm not to talk about it. And I'm not silly – I know our family is different and that other people won't understand.'

Tanya's eyebrows shot up in surprise at how perceptive Ethan was. They had been trying to sugar-coat things without outright lying for years, but he had obviously picked a lot more up than they had realised.

'Well then, good,' she said slowly. 'I'm glad you get it. Anna and your dad are just going through a rough patch right now. There's a lot to sort out and it can be a bit tense, I know. But you mustn't let that worry you, mate.' She reached out and squeezed his hand. 'The important thing is that we're a family and we're all in this together, and we'll all come out the other end of this storm eventually. You've just got to hang in there.'

There was a short silence. 'But what if we don't come out of it together?'

'What do you mean?' Tanya asked, indicating to turn at the lights.

'What if Dad and Anna don't want to be family anymore? Or what if Dad goes away again? He's back doing the things he got arrested for last time…' Ethan trailed off and stared out of the window unhappily.

Tanya's heart went out to him. All she wanted to do was tell him everything would be OK and that there was nothing to worry about, but that wasn't a luxury they could afford. Ethan was only nine years old, but he was part of the underworld's royal family. That came with heavy burdens even for the children, and it was time to help him hold his up.

Hating every word that came out of her mouth, Tanya said what she knew she had to. 'I want to tell you not to worry, but the reality is you're right. Not about your dad and Anna – they love you so much. They'll make it work somehow; I know they will.' She hoped as she said it that she was right. 'But as for his job, yes, there will always be that risk. Your dad is who he is and that's never going to change. What I can tell you, though, is that he is the best of the best at what he does, and that his conviction was a rare occurrence that happened under very specific circumstances. Your dad outsmarts the police ten to one. He has always been one step ahead. That being said' – she took a deep breath and sighed – 'you never know what's around the corner in this life. So you're smart to understand that. But you also need to understand something else.' Stopping at a red light, Tanya turned and locked eyes with him solemnly. 'We can't have people looking too closely at this family and what we do. Not now, not ever.'

'I know that, Tanya,' Ethan said earnestly. 'Like I said, I know not to talk about it.'

'And that's good, babe,' she said encouragingly. 'But it goes beyond that. Even when you're sad and worried, you have to hide it from the rest of the world. You have to put on a smile and crack a joke and let them think that everything's OK. Otherwise they start to ask questions. And that's the last thing we need. That's when the police turn their heads this way. That's when social services take a closer look at your paperwork.'

Seeing his face pale, Tanya hated herself even more. This was the last thing she wanted to put on his thin shoulders, but the boy needed to know. Because that was the harsh reality of being one of the Tylers.

'You can always talk to me about anything. Or if not me, Bill, Sammy, any one of us. But just never outside the circle. OK?'

Ethan nodded and the colour began to return to his cheeks. A car beeped behind them, making Tanya jump. She saw the light had turned green and quickly moved on down the road.

'OK,' Ethan said eventually. 'I'll make sure she's not worried about me again.'

'That's our boy,' Tanya replied, ruffling his hair. 'Now how about we go for ice cream, eh? Up for it?'

Ethan smiled and nodded.

'Good.'

As they drove off, Tanya's heart filled with sadness at her part in stripping away yet another part of Ethan's precious childhood.

CHAPTER TWENTY-NINE

Anna paced up and down in the small office at the back of Club Anya, worriedly biting the end of one of her long, polished fingernails. Roman was due to arrive any minute to discuss the arrangements for the next batch of diamonds and meet Freddie. Except Freddie wasn't here yet.

Rubbing her forehead Anna tried to calm her worries, but they would not be subdued. Things were still tense – more than tense, if she was honest – between her and Freddie. It wasn't that she had expected it to be an easy transition, but the tension without end or visible solution was torture. However long they had been apart, Anna still knew Freddie's moods and expressions better than anyone else. She knew from the way he looked at her, and the aloofness he afforded her at their every encounter, that right now she was viewed as an enemy. And this was a very dangerous position to be in. Every time they spoke she felt like a hunted deer stuck in plain sight of the hunter. Was he going to take a shot? Why was she even the deer in this scenario?

And now she was about to introduce him to Roman. That wasn't going to be fun either.

As she paced, Anna's eye caught the open drawer in her desk, with one of the fake invoices she'd created against her withdrawals just visible through the crack. She quickly walked over and pushed the drawer shut. Had Freddie somehow got wind of what she was doing here? Surely he couldn't have, she decided. He hadn't been anywhere near the accounts for the businesses yet, and nobody else was aware. She'd made sure to keep it a complete secret.

A knock on the door sounded and Carl popped his head round. 'Roman's here – I've put him in one of the VIP booths.'

'Oh,' Anna replied, biting her lip and pulling a face.

'Oh, sorry, did you not want me to put him there?' Carl asked, confused.

'No, no, it's fine,' Anna replied, with a dismissive wave of her hand. 'I'll join him now. Can you bring some drinks over?' She gave Carl a reassuring smile and followed him out.

She hadn't planned on having drinks in the club over this meeting. With everything so fraught, she had figured it might be better to make it a more private and professional affair in the office. But maybe she was overthinking it. Perhaps a drink and a less serious atmosphere would help ease everyone in.

'Roman.' She greeted him with a dazzling smile. 'So good to see you.'

'And you,' he replied, standing up and leaning in to kiss her cheek before they both sat down.

Anna crossed her slim legs to one side and smoothed the skirt of her bright-red fitted dress as she glanced towards the door.

'Freddie's running a little behind, so let's discuss the next package, get that out of the way before he arrives.'

'Sure,' Roman replied, leaning back comfortably into his corner of the rounded booth.

His white shirt was crisp and bright against the smooth dark skin that showed through the top two open buttons. As he saw Anna noticing, he grinned broadly and she looked away.

'So the drop went OK then? All things considered,' Anna said, clearing her throat and focusing on business.

'It did,' Roman replied, sitting forward and lowering his voice slightly. 'We'll have to change the route, but I think we figured out the best way on the journey back, so that won't be a problem.

Your package, the hoody, it was handed over to your contact just fine. I have the payment he sent back to you here.' He tapped his jacket and opened it slightly so that she could see the bulging envelope sticking out the top of the pocket inside.

'Fantastic. We'll pop into the office when we're done here and I'll grab that from you.' Anna glanced at the busy club. 'Best not to do the exchange out here.'

'Of course,' he replied.

Carl arrived with the drinks, a white wine for Anna and a half-full bottle of whisky along with two glasses. 'Here we go,' he said, putting them on the table between them. 'One for Freddie there too.' He glanced at Roman, then smiled at Anna and left them to it.

Roman ran his finger over his glass and then poured himself a measure before picking it up. 'He's very loyal to Freddie, your manager, isn't he?' he asked carefully.

Anna fixed him with a level stare and lifted her chin. 'Carl is loyal to me,' she replied. 'To both Tanya and I. Above anyone.' She reached forward and picked up her wine. 'Though he does get on very well with Freddie, yes.' A small smile played across her mouth. 'It was quite funny, really. Years ago, not long after we opened this place and everyone was still getting to know each other, Freddie was in here one night after closing – there was a group of us – and he challenged Carl to a drinking game. Well, Carl was adamant that he had never been beaten at this particular game.' She shook her head with a smile as she remembered the fun they'd all had that night. 'So naturally they both fought very hard to win. I can't say either of them particularly won, judging by the hangovers the next day, but the lengths they went to that night to outdo each other were absolutely hilarious…'

Freddie walked through the front doors of the club, greeting the bouncers on his way in. They were two of his, hired by Anna through his security company. As he made his way through the busy club towards the office at the back, his attention was caught by the sound of laughter. He would recognise Anna's laugh anywhere.

Twisting round, he searched for the source of the noise and his gaze rested on the pair as they both burst out laughing again. He narrowed his eyes as he observed them. They had drinks in their hands and looked very cosy indeed. Anna chatted animatedly, though about what he couldn't hear. The man opposite her listened intently, his smile matching hers as he laughed a deep, throaty laugh at something she said once more.

This must be the famous Roman Gains, he thought wryly. He studied him for a moment. The man dressed well, his smart tailored suit something Freddie might pick up himself. With a muscular physique and obvious charm, Freddie could see what women saw in him – what Anna must see in him. A painful pang of jealousy shot through him as this thought registered. He swallowed his temper, reminding himself that not only was this no longer his concern, but this man may well be in on the scam Anna was running within his businesses. He needed to keep his head.

Straightening his expression with difficulty, Freddie walked over to the booth.

'Ah, Freddie, there you are. We were just talking about you,' Anna said with a smile, standing to greet him.

'Were you now,' Freddie replied coldly. *So he was the butt of the joke then.*

Anna's smile faltered. 'Yes, I was just telling Roman—'

'Roman Gains,' Freddie cut her off and stepped forward to take the seat Carl had just placed at the table between the two sides of the booth. 'So you're the man I've been hearing so much about.'

Freddie didn't smile nor offer a handshake, which was not lost on Roman. A small smile played across his face and he nodded slightly.

'Freddie Tyler – it's an honour to meet you,' he replied.

'Yeah, I guess it would be,' Freddie replied sharply, his cold gaze not leaving Roman's.

Anna raised her eyebrows at the blatant snub.

'So you've been running mine and my brother's product over from the mainland, I hear,' Freddie continued.

'I have indeed. It's been a well-oiled business arrangement for well over a year now,' Roman replied, showing no reaction to Freddie's hostility.

Anna frowned. 'Where *is* Paul?' she asked, looking around as if expecting him to materialise. 'I thought he was joining us.' With all her worries circling Freddie, she hadn't stopped to give Paul much thought.

'He had some business to attend to, out of town,' Freddie replied without looking at her. 'And how have you been smuggling in the same sort of quantities I was getting on a container?' he asked Roman. 'I thought all you had were a few little beach boats?'

Roman smiled tightly, the action not reaching his eyes. 'I've created a very successful business with a *fleet* of leisure boats. Yes, in the day tourists can hire them out for a price. They're top of the range, so that in itself brings in a decent wedge. But I make my real money through the night, carrying all sorts of things for all sorts of people to all sorts of destinations.' He sat back. 'For any load that's too big for one boat, I send two. If anything, it gives my clients a bit more flexibility than whatever space they've managed to secure on a container. And less risk, with no do-gooder guards doing spot checks.'

'Less of a risk?' Freddie asked, raising one eyebrow in disagreement. 'I could pack ten containers on one of those ships and the coast guards would still wave them on by with a smile. They float straight into the dock in plain sight. What happens when one of yours gets picked up by the coast guard, eh? Tell me that. Then what? You going to take the rap and go down for me, are ya?'

'I protect all my customers, no matter what,' Roman replied seriously.

'Bullshit,' Freddie retorted. 'Not being funny, mate, I'm sure you're serious, but I don't know you from Adam. What's to say you wouldn't roll on me at the first capture? And it *will* happen,' he said strongly. 'Look how close you were with Tanya. The way she tells it, you were inches away.' He shook his head.

'Freddie,' Anna interjected. 'I know this is your first meeting, but Roman has been running this for over a year, like he said. And you might not know him, true, but I do. And I trust him implicitly,' she said.

'Yeah?' Freddie turned a hard stare on her. 'And what value am I supposed to place on *your* trust, exactly?' His tone dripped with sarcasm and Anna blinked, sitting back in shock.

Good, Freddie thought. He wanted her to know that he was on to her. If she began to get uncomfortable, she was likely to start trying to cover her tracks. And the more moves she made out of fear, the more likely she was going to trip and show her hand. He made a mental note to ask Sarah to tail her.

After a long, awkward silence, Freddie turned back to Roman. 'I know tonight's shipment will already be set, so have that delivered as usual, but after that we'll no longer need your services. I'll make sure you're paid up to date.'

'Freddie!' Anna exclaimed, horrified at the turn this meeting had taken. 'What are you doing? We need the shipping routes.' Her eyes grew wide with alarm and they flashed over to Roman, who looked almost as surprised as she did.

Freddie caught the look they shared and his resentment grew. He knew he was being unreasonable, but he couldn't stop himself. For all he knew, this guy was in on Anna's scam, and even if he wasn't, he just couldn't bear the way she looked at him. He stood up and straightened his jacket. 'I'll sort out the route myself. If you'd just asked me at the time, I could have fixed the issue at the other end,' he said, his tone loaded with accusation.

'Freddie, you were inside. Bill and Sammy did everything they could – it was impossible,' Anna argued.

'That was not your call to make,' he shot back, giving her a hard look before turning on his heel and walking out.

Anna stood up to stop him but then pulled herself back, realising it would be pointless. As she watched him go, she felt her stomach churn and an unusual prickle of frustrated tears in her eyes. She blinked rapidly and took a deep breath, placing her hands on her hips as she tried to compose herself. Showing weakness would do her no favours right now.

'Are you OK?' Roman asked.

She took another deep breath and turned back round to face him, forcing a smile. 'I'm fine. I'm so sorry, I don't know what's going on with Freddie right now.'

'Look, let's take this through to your office,' Roman suggested, pointedly looking at the number of curious faces that were staring in their direction.

Anna nodded. 'Yes, good idea.' Ignoring her drink, Anna marched back through to her office and shut the door behind them. She moved to the sofa and sank into it, feeling defeated. No matter what she did, things just seemed to continue spiralling downward between her and Freddie.

Roman took a seat next to her and half turned to face her. 'Look, don't worry about it. If Freddie wants to go his own way, then that's his decision,' he said with a shrug.

Anna frowned and shook her head in frustration. 'Yes, it is, but he's acting rashly and not thinking reasonably. It's not good for the business, and that has always been the most important thing here. And surely you're more bothered than you seem?' She raised a questioning eyebrow. 'This is a huge contract for you.'

'Yes, it is,' he agreed with a nod. 'But the money was never the most important thing for me in this particular case.'

'What do you mean?' Anna asked.

'You say you don't know what's going on with Freddie, but surely you do,' Roman challenged, his dark eyes holding hers intently. 'He can see what's going on between us and it bothers him. Of course it does. He had you and he went away and shit happened,' he stated simply. 'And I bet not a day goes by where he doesn't regret that.'

Anna made a noise of disagreement and shook her head.

'But it did happen,' Roman pressed. 'And you moved on. And I'm sure that taste is pretty sour in his mouth.'

'Roman, you've got it all wrong. You don't know Freddie like I do – it's a much deeper issue than that,' Anna replied.

'Is it?' Roman asked, pulling a face of disbelief. 'I don't think so. The man is miserable now he's out and being faced with the reality of the situation. But *you* have a chance to be happy, to take the leap we both know you've been dancing round.'

Anna's breath caught in her throat as Roman finally brought up the subject she had been avoiding for a while. She swallowed, her heart beginning to race in her chest.

Roman reached forward and took her hand, spurred on when she didn't immediately withdraw. 'We've known each other a long time now. We've laughed and enjoyed ourselves over dinners and drinks – and yes, even business,' he said with a laugh. 'I never thought I'd meet someone I could respect so much as an equal. But I have. And we're a brilliant match, you and I.' He resisted the urge to pull her into him, knowing such a sudden move could break the spell between them.

'Don't think I haven't seen you looking at me too,' he said with a grin. 'I know you've thought about it. Christ, we've been there in the moment and nearly kissed so many times, Anna. If only you'd let yourself go.'

Anna listened to Roman's words with mixed feelings, not knowing how to respond, only knowing that he spoke the truth. There *had* been times – many times – where she could have given in and seen where this could have gone. And he was right about them being a great match too. If she had been in any other position than she was, she would have taken the chance on him a long time ago.

But even after she had been alone for so long she could barely remember being with a man, something had always held her back. Something buried deep within that she had ignored and pushed down and pretended didn't exist – but it did exist. And now she was finally confronted with a decision, she couldn't ignore it any longer.

'Give us a chance, Anna. Give yourself a chance to be happy with me,' Roman said, his deep voice so hypnotic Anna found herself almost leaning in.

As he neared her face and she smelled his sweet, musky smell, she closed her eyes in distress and pulled away.

'Roman, I'm sorry – I can't,' she said strongly, withdrawing her hand from his. 'I'm sorry,' she repeated.

'Come on, Anna,' he replied. 'You're braver than that.' His smile held a challenge, but she just shook her head.

'You don't understand,' she said, standing up and moving to lean back on the desk, away from him.

'You're right, I don't,' he replied with a frustrated sigh.

'We have had those moments, yes,' Anna admitted. 'And there were many times I nearly gave in. But there has always been something stopping me, rightly or wrongly.'

'Freddie,' Roman said flatly.

'Yes.' Anna ran her hands through her hair and closed her eyes for a second. 'I don't think I even fully realised that myself until right now. I thought I was over him, or was at least *getting* over him. But the truth is I haven't. And I never will.' She smiled a sad smile. 'Have you ever been with someone whose soul just seems to merge with yours, and you become this one being and without them you can survive but… you can never be whole?' she asked.

Roman shook his head. 'No, I can't say I have. But what I will say is this, Anna. The man I just met, he don't feel that way for you.'

Anna pulled in a sharp breath as his words hit their mark.

'That man just looked you in the eye and told you he don't even trust you. Do you really want to wait around for that?' he asked, his eyes beseeching. 'Because I tell you now, you wouldn't have to put up with that shit from me.'

'No. I don't want to wait around for him,' she answered. 'I don't even want to feel like this. But the point is, I do. And as unhealthy as that might be, it's just how it is. And if I'm being honest with myself, I can't change that any more than I can change the tides.'

As she finally admitted it out loud, Anna felt a mixture of relief and despair fill her entire body. There would be no more fooling herself to exhausting measures, but there would also be no more hiding from it. What the hell was she going to do now?

The pair stared at each other for a few long moments. Roman watched Anna's dark blue eyes harden over into the mask she wore to fight through each day and her slender neck stretch as her head tilted proudly upward. She was a graceful warrior and a woman who would haunt his desires for a long time. Freddie Tyler clearly had no appreciation for what was right in front of him and this galled Roman more than he'd thought anything could.

With a slow nod of defeat, Roman stood up. 'You're your own worst enemy, Anna Davis,' he said, his tone wounded.

Not knowing what to say, Anna just stared at him solemnly. Stepping forward to drop the money from his pocket on the table, Roman turned and walked out, closing the door behind him.

After he left, Anna didn't move, rooted to the spot as she finally began to process the realisation she had just voiced. How could she still be so hung up on Freddie after all this time? Was it just because their lives were so intertwined? Would she feel differently if she was the other side of the world living a whole new life away from him, or was this truly something so deep that neither time nor space could erase it? Had she just thrown away a real chance of happiness for nothing?

Freddie obviously did not feel the same way; she could practically feel the anger radiating from him whenever she came near. He was rude and cold and clearly wanted her out of the business. Whatever was there before had definitely died for him in prison. And that was fair enough. It wasn't like they were still together. On some unspoken level they had agreed that prison had ended their relationship. The whole plan now was to make things work for Ethan and for the business – that was all. But could she really do that, with all these feelings flying around inside her like an emotional hurricane?

'Fuck,' she suddenly shouted into the empty room. Suddenly everything seemed ten times more complicated than it had just half an hour before. 'Fuck!'

CHAPTER THIRTY

Walking slowly up the garden path towards the front door of Mollie's house, Paul tiredly put the key in the lock, but before he could turn it, the door swung open. Mollie's worried face came into view and he forced a small smile of greeting.

'Alright, Mum?' he said, walking past her into the hallway.

'Where have you been?' Mollie asked in an accusatory tone, but she trailed off as she took in her son's stooped stance and weary face. 'You OK?' she asked, closing the door and following him into the kitchen.

Paul sat down at the table and leaned over on his forearms, staring off into the distance, his mouth downturned in sadness. 'Not really,' he answered honestly. 'I'm trying to be. I know we should be happy we're out and that we have our old lives back, but…' He sighed and shook his head. 'This ain't our old life.' He held his hands out to the sides in helplessness. 'Nothing is how it was. You know, I've just had to go down to the south coast and remind James that he has to keep his mouth shut. *James*,' he repeated, looking up at Mollie. 'The man I shared my life with, who was part of our family. The man who used to come round here to learn your baking recipes. The man who had our whole future planned out, right down to what shoes we'd wear in our old age.'

Mollie sat down next to him, sympathy shining out of her drawn face. Paul shook his head again, still unable to comprehend how things had got to this point.

'He's never looked at me so cold and so… offended. Told me even though we were nothing to each other anymore that surely I knew him well enough to know he'd never grass us out to anyone. And that hurt, Mum. Because right up until that moment, I hadn't realised that I was nothing to him now.'

Clamping his jaw shut, Paul looked away out of the back door to the garden, not trusting his emotions to stay in place if he continued. He sniffed and sat upright.

Mollie nodded and grasped his hand on the table. 'I know, son,' she said quietly. 'For you I guess it's like breaking up all over again, getting out.'

'It is,' Paul admitted.

Mollie sighed, her eyes glazing over as she thought back to the terrible time after Thea's funeral and her boys being sent to prison. It had been difficult for everyone, but Paul and Freddie had not been around to watch how the rest of them had dealt with things and grieved.

'When you first went away,' she said softly, 'James used to turn up here almost every day. With you gone and Thea gone, he didn't know what to do with himself. Anna tried to get him back working on the books, but his heart wasn't in it anymore. He loved you so much that he couldn't seem to comprehend you not being there. I think for a long time he was in denial. I think he expected to wake up one day and find that you'd figured out a way to come home. I mean, we all wanted that, but the rest of us knew it was impossible. James, though, he seemed to hold on to that fantasy like he had an actual hope.' She pulled an expression of pity. 'As time went on and as things got ugly with the business, he finally seemed to snap out of it. Started seeing things for what they were. That was when he started grieving for you, like you're grieving for him now. And that was when he decided he needed a fresh start. So, he did care, Paul. You weren't nothing.'

'Thanks for telling me that,' Paul replied, giving Mollie's hand a squeeze. 'I know I just need to get on with it all now. It just takes a bit of getting used to, I suppose, all these changes. Like Thea…'

He trailed off and looked up at Mollie's face. It was thin and drawn and the rosy light that always used to dance in her eyes had gone, having died the same time his little sister had. Mollie looked a lot older these days, her greying hair now almost white and her clothes hanging loose where she had lost weight.

'Getting used to Thea not being around will be hard on you both, I know,' Mollie said eventually, her bottom lip wobbling. 'It was, um…' Mollie swallowed the lump that had formed in her throat, and tears began to fall down her cheeks as all the pain of losing Thea came back to the fore. 'It was hard, being here every day and not seeing her walk in, or hearing her voice over breakfast in the morning. Still is, really. It doesn't ever go away. It doesn't ever quite seem real either, when you think about it. Like it must have been some horrible mistake. Except it wasn't.' She closed her eyes as the grief washed over her like a wave. 'As a parent you never expect to have to bury your children. Especially good girls like Thea.'

'I'm so sorry that we had to leave you to go through all that on your own, Mum,' Paul said, feeling the guilt flood through him once more.

Mollie had been broken and vulnerable after Thea's death, more so than anyone else. She lived and breathed for her children. It had been their job to look after her, to help her through that difficult time. But they hadn't even made it home from the funeral. Mollie had been forced to get through it alone, with none of her children around to comfort her. It was something neither of her remaining sons would ever forgive themselves for.

'It's not your fault, Paul,' Mollie said, wiping her eyes. 'Nobody could have predicted what happened. I know you'd have been here if you could. And you're here now,' she added with a small smile. 'It's good to have you home. Both of you.'

Paul leaned over and put his forehead to Mollie's, and they sat there in silence for a few moments. With a sniff, Mollie sat up and wiped away the remaining tears.

'Come on – I'll get you a cup of tea and a slice of cake. I made a bunt yesterday; you'll like that.' Mollie stood up and walked over to fill the kettle.

Paul watched her, glad that his presence back in the family home was at least keeping her busy and giving her something to do. He had left home years ago, leaving Thea as the last remaining child for Mollie to cluck over and bake for. But now that she was gone, Paul had decided to come home so that Mollie was no longer alone. Without James, he had no real urge to go back to living in his own place anyway.

'I am surprised though, I have to say…' Mollie called over from the sink.

'What about?' Paul asked.

'That your brother didn't reach out to me at all,' she replied.

Paul frowned. What did she mean by that? He and Freddie had done all they could from where they were – had spoken to her on the phone almost every day.

'I know he's in hiding and I know it's been years since we last spoke…' She sighed sadly. 'But Thea was still his sister. And I'm still his mother. I would have thought Michael might have reached out in some way at least, even if he couldn't be here.'

Paul closed his eyes and exhaled slowly as he realised who his mother meant. She still had no clue that Michael was dead and had been for several years. It hadn't been a lie at first, that their younger brother was in hiding in South America. Michael had committed some terrible wrongs to the worst people he could have, and Freddie had needed to stage Michael's death to get him out of harm's way. They'd given him a chance, a new identity and enough money to start over in Rio. If he'd just stayed there and done what they had asked him to do, he would still be alive. He might have even had a family of his own by now. But he hadn't.

Filled with rage and misplaced blame, Michael had secretly travelled back to England a while later and started a campaign against Freddie, trying to trip him up and get him sent down so that he could step into his older brother's shoes and take London for himself. He couldn't comprehend that the family was protecting him, instead deciding they had shoved him out of their way for their own gain. Becoming more and more unhinged as his plan failed time and again, he'd eventually kidnapped Anna and Tanya, nearly killing Tanya and causing Anna to miscarry the child she was carrying.

It had come to a stand-off, and Anna had been left with no choice but to shoot Michael in order to save herself. It had been a terrible chain of events and one which they had all decided to cover up for Mollie's sake. To this day she never even knew he'd come back, nor that he was buried under his fake identity just an hour down the road.

'He couldn't, Mum,' Paul said gently. 'The people he crossed, they still watch out for any sign of him. It would have been too dangerous for him to contact you. But he knew,' Paul added, trying to give her some comfort. 'We sent word. He would have said goodbye to her in his own way.'

Mollie nodded, clamping her lips together and cutting into the bunt cake she had made for Paul. She stopped herself from commenting on Michael further. She knew they were just protecting him and that this was how it had to be. Every day she sent a prayer up to the heavens for God to keep her youngest son safe and well, and she drew comfort in knowing that even if they couldn't speak, he was OK.

Paul forced a smile as she laid the cake in front of him. 'This looks lovely, Mum. Thanks.'

'Hope you like it. I know it's one of your favourites.' She scuttled off to pour the tea and Paul's smile faded.

Honesty and trust were two of the most important things in life, to both him and Freddie. It was something they insisted on from everyone around them. But however much this meant to them, family meant more. And sometimes to protect those you loved, you had to make a sacrifice. Sometimes to protect your family, you had to tell terrible lies, knowing that you would have to take them to the grave.

CHAPTER THIRTY-ONE

Anna leaned over the kitchen counter and stared off into space as she waited for the oven timer to go off, feeling irritated. There was so much going on and so much she didn't understand that it felt like her whole life was starting to unravel out of her control.

'Anna?' Ethan's voice broke through her thoughts, and she turned to him with a big, fake smile.

The concern and worry on his young face from where he sat at the breakfast bar immediately made her feel guilty. 'Hey, sorry, buddy. I was miles away.'

'I know – your phone's gone off three times and you haven't even looked at it,' he answered.

Anna laughed, realising this was a fair observation. With businesses such as theirs, she had to be reachable at all times. It was unusual for her not to immediately check a message. Tapping the phone, she saw the three messages were from Roman. Her heart dropped. She hadn't spoken with him since their awkward encounter the night before and she wasn't relishing the idea of doing so now. She wasn't sure how they were going to get back onto simple ground again, and that, on top of everything else she had going on right now, was the last thing she needed to add to her worries.

The timer finally went off and she grinned at Ethan, glad of the distraction. 'There we go – dinner's ready. Your favourite: shepherd's pie with sweet potato mash.'

Opening the oven door, she reached for the mitts and pulled the dish out, setting it down on the hob above.

'Thanks, Anna.' Ethan grinned happily. He loved her shepherd's pie, but she didn't always have time to make it and Tanya's attempts were a poor comparison. This was going to be a treat. He waited patiently as she dished him out a generous portion and laid it in front of him. He licked his lips in anticipation.

'So,' Anna started, pulling up a stool on the end next to him and ruffling his light brown hair affectionately. 'How are things at school? I feel like we haven't really talked about school in a while.'

'They're good,' he answered simply, blowing on a hot forkful of shepherd's pie. Deeming it cool enough, he shovelled it in and munched away happily.

Anna smiled, her heart filled with love for this little boy of hers. And he really was *hers*. Of all the people in his life so far, blood relative or not, she had been the only one to truly commit to him as a parent. He was the main reason for everything she did now, the motivation behind every new venture and the push she used to get her through every tired hour. She couldn't imagine life without him. A stab of worry pierced her heart as her mind wandered back towards Freddie and how hateful he was acting towards her right now. If he wanted to, he could take Ethan from her forever. And there would be nothing she could do about it. Her smile slowly dropping, she tried to hide the frown of worry that threatened to replace it. Ethan didn't need to see her worrying right now. He had enough to deal with.

Picking up her phone, now that Ethan was engrossed in his dinner and she wouldn't be getting conversation out of him for a while, she reluctantly clicked into Roman's messages. Taking a deep breath, she read them.

Anna. You and I are in two very different places right now. And I don't blame you. The heart is a fucked-up thing. But I can't do this, whatever it is we do, anymore. I think as far as business goes, it's best we part ways for now. You need to sort your life out and I need to simplify things. I'm sure you understand. No hard feelings. Roman.

'Shhhh—eugh.' Anna stopped herself from cursing just in time and saw Ethan shoot her a cheeky smile of accusation as he chomped his way through dinner. She wrinkled her nose at him and made him laugh, before turning away and opening the fridge.

Pretending to look for something, she pulled a look of sheer exasperation and closed her eyes. If she'd thought dealing with the awkward situation between her and Roman was the last thing she needed, she'd been sorely wrong. *This* was the last thing she needed. They had just got the diamond business off to a good start and now they were left without a transport route. It was a disaster. It wasn't like they could easily replace Roman either – good smugglers that you could trust were horribly hard to come by.

She silently cursed Freddie for kicking off in the club last night. Perhaps if he hadn't done that, Roman wouldn't have made his play and they would all still be carrying on as normal. But even as she thought it, she realised she couldn't blame Freddie, not for this anyway. It had been on the cards for a while. Roman had been gearing up to make a move for a long time. It had just been terrible timing.

Closing her eyes, she sighed and added this problem to the list of all the others.

'Can I have seconds?' Ethan asked, from behind her. Masking her troubled expression, she turned with a bright smile.

'Of course you can, darling,' she answered. 'A growing boy always needs seconds of shepherd's pie.' She blew him a kiss and took his empty plate back over to the dish on the side.

Finding a smuggler was important, but not more important than looking after her son. That was just going to have to wait until tomorrow.

CHAPTER THIRTY-TWO

Josephine stared out of the second-floor window down at the busy Soho street beneath and played absentmindedly with the long string of pearls hanging from her neck. The city buzzed with the boozed-up party crowd of late-night London, glittering dresses and excited conversations flowing through the spaces between bar entrances. But for once Josephine didn't really see it. Her mind was elsewhere, locked in a very dark place.

'Josephine?' A soft voice woke her from her reverie and she turned, quickly fixing a pleasant smile upon her face.

'Yes?' It was Bianca, or Rose, as they had renamed her here at The Sinners' Lounge. Deceptively innocent-looking with flawless pale skin, baby pink cheeks and a rosebud mouth beneath large, adorable eyes, she looked every bit the pure, virtuous virgin that a lot of men craved. In reality she was one of the filthiest girls they had, a lover of her chosen profession and down for pretty much anything. Due to this explosive combination, she was one of their top earners.

'I've got a group that want to threes-up. Back, front and top, same time,' she said.

'It's up to you. You OK with that?' Josephine asked, already knowing her probable answer but needing to check anyway. The safety and comfort of the girls was important.

'Sure, why not?' Rose said. 'I've done orgies before,' she added with a shrug. More money less time.'

'OK. Charge them all three, plus fifty extra for going together. Ask if they want to be watched too, in the viewing room. That's another fifty. I'll make sure your tips reflect it.'

'Will do.' Rose shot her a winning smile and went back to her new clients.

Josephine walked away from the window and over to the bar, pouring herself a neat shot of cherry vodka. As the bittersweet liquid rolled down the back of her throat, she closed her eyes, waiting for it to take the edge off. It wasn't something she usually went for, but lately Tanya had got her into it and she had developed a taste for it. Yet another thing she had picked up from her friends.

Guilt stung her heart like the tip of a red-hot poker as she thought about what Aleksei wanted her to do. She had always known this could come to a terrible clash of loyalties, even when they very first met. She'd known exactly who he was and that he was an enemy to the very firm she worked for. Anna had asked her to do a recce at his club one night, as she was new on the scene and nobody knew who she was. She'd said it would be easy for her to slip in and watch his girls unidentified as a rival, to pick up his techniques and report back.

So one night she had done just that. Dabbing on her favourite fuchsia lipstick and feeling fabulous, she had waltzed in there, ordered a drink and sat back to watch the show. She had been prepared for the odd looks. It probably wasn't often they saw a trans woman in their strip club just chilling on her own. But what she hadn't been prepared for was the way Aleksei had stared at her all night.

At first she had assumed maybe he was offended by her presence. It wouldn't have been the first time she'd experienced such prejudice. But as the evening went on and she watched him out of the corner of her eye, she realised that he was admiring her. Not all the time, not when speaking with his men, but whenever he was alone and no one was watching him. Halfway through the night, a cocktail was sent over, fuchsia to match her lipstick, and a note with his number on. She knew she should have resisted, but curiosity got the better of her, and before she knew it their whirlwind romance had begun.

He had wined and dined her, shown her passion and love and a side of life she had never experienced before. It was real, what they shared, so much more than just some fling. It had finally made her whole. Aleksei had also been honest with her from the start, even more so when he found out who she really was. Rather than be annoyed, he had chuckled and told her he admired her spunk. But he had warned her that his relationship with her would not change his actions towards Anna and the rest of the firm. All she had asked at the time was that he not drag her into any of his battles with them, and he had honoured that – until now.

Now, Aleksei had asked her to get involved in the most terrible way possible. He wanted her to help set up and lure the Tylers into a trap, so they could take them out unopposed.

Such a simple task, Aleksei assured her. Just a few texts. Just assisting in the murder of two men, one of which was the love of her friend's life.

With a deep shaking breath in, Josephine poured herself another cherry vodka and downed this too. Out of the corner of her eye, she caught a hand signal from one of the girls and set about putting a bottle of champagne on ice. Gathering herself, she tried to act normal and push these dark thoughts to the back of her mind.

Hand hovering over the Dom Pérignon, she glanced back over her shoulder and made a quick assessment before picking out the Cristal instead. They only kept the good stuff in stock here. By the time the customers had made it through the vetting process to this point, if champagne was ordered, it was because the girls had ascertained that their pockets were as deep as their lust was strong. They were about to spend a lot of money getting their rocks off – most didn't seem to care what they then spent on drinks. It made good business sense to make sure they only had the best on offer, and therefore the most expensive.

Josephine neatly placed two tall-stemmed glasses on the tray with the champagne and took it over to the table, leaving it ready for the client to open once he'd stopped nuzzling into his companion's voluptuous breasts. Noticing that Rose and her clients had disappeared, Josephine walked down the hallway to the viewing platform hidden behind a red velvet curtain. Two men stood in the dim lighting, their engorged members in their hands, focusing on getting off to the scene in front of them. Through the viewing window, Josephine could see that Rose was well underway with the three excited men. Straddling one of them and rhythmically grinding on top of him, she leaned forward as another grabbed a handful of her hair, guiding himself into her mouth. Josephine flinched as she watched the third man enter Rose roughly from behind, the three of them now filling her from all angles like a trussed-up pig about to be roasted. It looked painful. She was surprised Rose had agreed to it.

Watching the lewd act unfolding in front of her in a strangely detached way, Aleksei's words played through her head once more.

Do you really want to be here forever? A beautiful princess like you, locked away in this sordid tower, peddling flesh to soulless creatures for the rest of your life?

The curtain opened, letting in a little light, and she turned, jumping slightly in guilt as she registered who it was.

'Oh hey, there you are,' Tanya said, glancing through the viewing window. She raised her eyebrows. 'Well, Rose is certainly in full bloom tonight.' Catching the frustrated tut of annoyance coming from one of the viewers trying to reach a climax, she pulled a face at Josephine. 'Better leave them to it. I'll wait for you upstairs – there are some issues on the next shipment that we need to discuss.'

'Yeah, yeah, 'course,' Josephine whispered back, not quite able to shake the feeling of guilt at what had been going through her mind.

As Tanya retreated, she turned back to the men grunting away over Rose one more time. Aleksei was right – she didn't want to be stuck here forever. There was so much more to life than this.

Thinking back over what he had asked her to do, a weight settled in her stomach. There was no way out of this, not now that Aleksei had pulled her in. Whether she liked it or not, she had a role in their whole war now. And no matter what, there would be a winner and a loser. At least Anna and Tanya had no clue of her involvement and so would never suspect she had a hand in it. Seeing the horror in their eyes if they did would have been too much to bear. Taking a deep breath, she made her decision. She knew what she had to do; there had never been a choice – not really. Now she just had to get her head around it.

CHAPTER THIRTY-THREE

Anna knocked twice and let herself into Tanya's flat, then called out to check her best friend had heard her enter.

'Oh hey, how's it going?' Tanya asked, poking her head into the hallway from where she was finishing her make-up in the bedroom. 'You're round early – did I forget we had something on?'

'No, not at all,' Anna replied wearily. 'Just dropped Ethan off and I didn't fancy going back to the flat right now.'

'Oh dear,' Tanya said, pulling a face. 'Things still that bad?'

'Worse,' Anna admitted. 'He's been brooding over something – God knows what – and getting increasingly hostile. If it wasn't for Ethan, for whom he's clearly trying to act as though everything is OK, I think he would have blown at me by now.'

'Why though?' Tanya asked, with a frown of confusion and annoyance. 'He owes you… well, everything.'

Anna shook her head. 'He doesn't owe me anything. I didn't do all I've done to be rewarded. But I really didn't expect to be treated like the enemy and pushed out either.' Anna slipped her heels off and shrugged off the thin jacket she wore over her beige fitted dress.

'Pushed out?' Tanya frowned, abandoning the bronzer and giving her hair one last fluff with her hands before joining Anna at the other end of the hall.

'There seems to be an increasing number of meetings that don't include me,' Anna replied with a sigh. She rubbed her forehead irritably. 'I'm still running a lot of the operations – he hasn't shoved me out completely – but he's certainly making a point.'

Tanya screwed her mouth to one side as they stood together, each thinking it over. 'What could make him turn like this?' she asked.

'Nothing, as far as I'm aware,' Anna answered, but once again a sliver of doubt crept in, and she wondered whether he could have seen the accounts. But how could he have? They only set was on her laptop, and that was kept with her at all times. 'No, nothing,' she repeated firmly.

Tanya shook her head sadly. 'I don't know. It all got worse at this meeting with Roman, right?' She walked through to the kitchen and opened the fridge, pulling out a jug of fresh orange juice. 'Do you think it might all just be down to his feelings about you? I mean… we all know things were heating up between you and Roman.'

'We all know nothing, thank you, Tanya Smith,' Anna said tartly, her cheeks flushing pink.

Tanya held her hands up in surrender and poured them each a glass of juice.

'And no,' Anna continued. 'It's definitely not that. If you'd seen the way Freddie looked at me…' She shook her head and took the offered glass. 'There are no feelings left there, I can assure you. Not on his part, at least.'

Tanya stopped in her tracks and turned around. 'So you're finally admitting that there is on *your* part then?' she asked.

Anna sighed and sat down, pulling her legs up under her on one of Tanya's big, comfy cream sofas. 'I didn't say that.'

'You didn't have to,' Tanya retorted, joining her.

'It doesn't matter how I feel,' Anna said, pulling her dark hair back off her face. 'It's been too long; too much has happened. We've all changed. Whatever I loved in him before, I doubt that's even there anymore. I'm in love with nothing more than a memory.'

'No.' Tanya frowned and shook her head. 'That's not true. Whatever changed either of you, the core things you fell in love with are still there. I mean, the core things I loved about you when I met you are still there,' she continued, when Anna looked unconvinced. 'You know when I found you that night standing awkwardly in that bloody petrol station, you were little more than a bag of nerves with a shitty car.'

Anna couldn't help but grin as she shook her head.

'But even then, despite all you were going through, you had this strength about you,' Tanya continued, smiling as she thought back through the years. 'You were a stubborn cow.' She dodged the swat Anna aimed in her direction. 'And you refused to let life beat you down. And even in your darkest hour, you held your head up high with pride and with a level of class that no amount of money could ever buy. That was what I admired about you.'

Sipping her orange juice, she looked over the rim of the glass at her friend. A hard jaw and eyes that had seen more than they should have in this world stared back at her from a flawless face. She smiled. 'And that's what I still admire about you now. The situation may have changed – you might have adapted – but you're still that same girl. And I think deep down Freddie knows that. And you know the same about him. Nothing could change his heart and all the other things you love about him. Not really.'

Anna looked down at her glass. 'I don't know, Tan. It's just all so complicated.'

'Maybe you should talk it through. Tell him how you feel, see what sort of reaction you get,' Tanya suggested.

Anna barked a humourless laugh. 'Oh sure, that would go down great right now. *Hey, Freddie, I know you're avoiding me and have made it perfectly clear you despise me now, but I think I still fancy you after all these years.*'

'Well, yeah, when you put it like that.' Tanya rolled her eyes. 'Just have a think about it. You guys used to be tighter than the tax man's arsehole. If you can't talk things out now, that really is a sorry state of affairs.'

'Well…' Anna couldn't decide how to respond. 'This orange juice is nice; where did you get it?'

'That little Italian shop round the corner – they squeeze them fresh. And whilst I'll respect that shit subject change, I will just leave you with this. You need to find a way to talk to him and soon. Because it's affecting Ethan.'

'What do you mean?' Anna asked with a frown.

'That teacher he likes at school, Miss Andrew, she collared me when I picked him up the other day. He's been down, worried.' Tanya pulled a grim expression. 'He picks up more than you realise.'

Anna's dark blue eyes became troubled. 'We've both tried to keep our issues away from him.'

'I know you have. But he's a smart boy.' She took another sip of her orange. 'I've talked to him, told him he can talk to any of us in the circle about his worries. But I've also warned him he needs to be careful. That we can't have the police or the social sniffing round. He took it well, I think. He understands the situation.'

Anna nodded. 'Good.' She hated that any of them even had to have that conversation with him, but it was part and parcel of being in their world, of being part of this family. The secrecy they had to uphold made no allowances for age, however much they wished it could. 'I'll talk to Freddie. About Ethan, I mean,' she added, seeing the look on Tanya's face.

'OK. Well, go on then. No time like the present,' Tanya pushed.

Anna blinked. 'Oh, OK then.'

'Go on,' Tanya urged, standing up. 'I need to go figure out which dress I look the hottest in. Because there's a guy who always seems to get his bagel from the bagel shop at the same time I do when I'm down Club Anya and I'm down there today. He's quite tasty, so I wouldn't mind a bite, if you know what I mean.' She winked saucily.

Anna rolled her eyes and moved off the couch and back into the hallway where she had abandoned her shoes. 'Everyone knows what you mean when you talk like that, Tan,' she said drily.

'Well, as long as he don't know what hit him, that's all that matters,' Tanya replied sunnily as she disappeared back into her bedroom.

'The emerald-green Karen Millen you bought last year,' Anna called over her shoulder as she opened the door. 'It brings out your eyes and it's just the right amount of too tight for what you're going for.'

'Thanks!'

Anna shook her head with a grin as she closed the front door behind her and walked up the flight of stairs to her own flat. The further she walked, the more sombre her mood became. Now that Ethan wasn't home, Freddie was not likely to want to talk to her. The atmosphere was so tense when they were in the same room you could cut it with a knife. Once again Anna felt a wave of sorrow that things had come to this. Never in a million years had she thought that she and Freddie would not at least be allies. And now for some reason, they were practically enemies.

Taking a deep breath and ignoring the knot in her stomach, Anna walked back in and, after checking he wasn't in the living area, knocked on his closed bedroom door. There was no answer, and after a considerable pause, she called out and put her ear to the door.

'Freddie? Freddie, are you in there? I need to talk to you. It's about Ethan.'

There was no response. She knocked again but all she heard was silence, the empty sort of silence that is only heard when someone is truly alone. Tentatively, she opened the door a crack and peered in, and when she found the room to be unoccupied let it swing back entirely.

Biting her lip, she felt a wave of disappointment wash over her. Just as she was psyched up to talk to him, he had disappeared. Placing her hands on her hips, she turned around, wondering what to do. Her jaw hardened as she made a decision and marched back out of the flat.

She needed to talk to Freddie about Ethan whether he liked it or not, and besides, it was about time they cleared the air. He couldn't avoid her forever.

CHAPTER THIRTY-FOUR

'Freddie, Paul!' The greeting was coupled with a grin of joy at seeing his old bosses walk through the door into his small Portakabin at the docks.

'Damien, it's good to see you, old friend,' Freddie said warmly, grasping Damien's arm in a familiar handshake.

'I was that glad to get your text, I tell you. It's been boring as old boots around here since you've been gone.'

'Well, we're back now,' Freddie replied, sharing a look with Paul. 'So let's start by getting things back on track.'

They sat down in the two chairs in front of the desk and waited for Damien to sit down behind it.

'Do you want a cuppa?' Damien asked, pointing towards the kettle in the corner.

'Nah, we're alright, mate,' Paul answered. 'We've got another meeting after this in our own cabin. I take it you've got our key?'

'Ah yes, 'course,' Damien said, feeling around his pockets until he located it. He passed it over to Freddie. 'Kept it nice for you, gave it a spruce over now and then to keep it fresh. The pigs made a right mess of it after you was arrested, I tell ya.' He shook his head in disgust. 'Furniture everywhere, paperwork all over the floor. But I sorted it as well as I could without prying into the papers.' He glanced up worriedly at Freddie.

'We know you did, Damien,' Freddie assured him. 'And we appreciate it. You're a loyal man.'

Damien nodded.

'So what happened with the shipments? Anna says someone got retired and couldn't be replaced.'

'That was the base of it, yeah,' Damien said, scratching his head under his flat cap. 'And we did feel his replacement out, but he weren't interested. We had to stop the orders. But...' He trailed off and jammed his mouth shut as if deciding against what he was about to say.

'But what?' Paul prompted.

'Well, if we'd given it some time, just waited a while, I think we could have figured it out. We did still have some contacts, just not the right ones. I was set to get them to work finding a way around the shipping master. But before we could do that, the contract was moved elsewhere. So we didn't get a chance.'

'Given to Roman Gains,' Freddie confirmed.

'Yeah,' Damien said resentfully. 'Him.'

'You don't like him?' Freddie asked.

Damien shook his head. 'No. I don't. He's not given me any specific reason, mind. I just don't trust him. There's something about him...' He shrugged. 'But then maybe that's just that I don't know him. Like you, I have to know someone before I can consider trust.'

Freddie nodded. 'Well, I've taken the contract back. Like you, I don't know him. This means all shipments are on hold until you can get them back across. Do you think you can get it back up and running?'

Damien's eyes gleamed. 'Damn right I can. Especially now. I've been keeping tabs on everything over there, just in case. There's been some moving around within the staff structure. I'm pretty sure I've got a way into at least two containers a week. I just need to make some calls.'

'Good man, get on it. Keep me updated – directly, you understand?' Freddie said, giving him a meaningful look.

'Oh yes,' Damien replied with a broad smile. 'The kings are back.'

Walking over to their own Portakabin, their business with Damien conducted, Freddie breathed in the strange mixture of smells from the river. He'd always loved it down here, watching life on the river go by, listening to the men as they loaded and unloaded ships, the old cobbled stones under his feet a tip of a hat to days gone by. Tucked away from the rest of the city, he could get on with his business undisturbed and unseen from the road above.

He unlocked the door and they walked in to find the cabin as neat and tidy as they had left it – more so, probably, Freddie realised. It had been so long since they'd been here, but it felt like they'd only left it yesterday. It felt strangely like home in a world where even home didn't feel like home anymore.

Paul checked his watch. 'Couple of minutes to go. Will she be here on time? I need to go sort out some extra surveillance with Bill. I'm sure we've got a rogue pill peddler in Ruby Ten.'

'She'll be here. Routinely punctual, that one,' Freddie replied, opening the blinds and letting the bright summer sunshine in. 'I didn't ask you, but did everything go OK with James?' He watched his brother tense and felt sympathy for the position he found himself in. Coming out of prison was like walking out of a time capsule. Paul still loved James, but James had moved on to a whole new life a long time ago. Freddie more than anyone understood exactly how painful that was.

'It went fine,' Paul said gruffly. 'He understands the score.'

'OK. Well…' Freddie trailed off as Paul turned his back and looked out of the window. He clearly didn't want to talk about it. 'That's good,' he finished.

Flicking on the lights, he walked over to his desk and sat down. As he sank into his old, comfortable leather chair, he almost groaned with pleasure. It had seen better days, with the odd tear and grazes of wear, but he couldn't bear to part with it, so it had been sent down to the Portakabin. It didn't matter what it looked like here. The cabin was bare and basic, lacking the opulent décor and trappings of his other offices.

'Here she is,' Paul said.

A knock sounded and Sarah Riley entered, checking over her shoulder one last time. 'Freddie, Paul,' she said with a nod. 'How's it going?' Walking over to the desk, she sat down on one of the chairs in front of it.

Paul joined her and Freddie leaned forward on the desk. 'All good. What's the update?'

Sarah pulled a face. 'It's not as bad as when the task force were watching you, but they are certainly keeping tabs. They're trying to keep up with your burners but luckily failing. The clubs' finances are still under constant review.'

Freddie's interest perked up at hearing this. It was something he may be able to use to his advantage.

'They're checking up on your whereabouts sporadically, but you're not under constant surveillance. They can't afford it now the budget's been cut. Hargreaves is annoyed, but he can't justify putting more funds towards watching you now that you've served your time. It's too close to harassment. You'd do well to report it as such if you catch a tail anywhere.'

Freddie nodded.

'Other than that, there's not much else to feed back. Still nothing on your Russian friend. He's either clean as a whistle, which we know he's not, or he had some hefty sway with the law over there. Not so much as a parking ticket.'

'So I keep hearing. Whatever made him run was nothing to do with that.' Freddie rubbed his chin thoughtfully.

'Listen, there's something I need you to do,' he said, changing the subject.

'What is it?' Sarah asked.

Freddie's eyes darkened as he thought about Anna once more. The secrecy and lies were eating him up inside. Out of everybody around him, he would never have thought she would be the one to turn in a million years. 'I want you to follow someone. I've found dud payments coming out of some of the accounts and going on through a maze of accounts where they get lost. I don't think they can be traced, as they go offshore, but I want to find out why and who else is involved.'

'Who?' Sarah asked with a frown.

'Anna.'

There was a stunned silence, before Sarah opened her mouth to speak again. 'You're joking? *Anna?*'

'I wish I was.' Freddie clenched his jaw.

'That makes no sense,' Sarah said, shaking her head. 'She's got her own money and full access to yours – why would she need to steal it?'

'That's what I need you to find out,' he answered.

'Right.' Sarah sat back, surprised. 'OK, I'll get on it. See what I can find out.'

Freddie nodded. 'Good. That's all.'

Sarah stood up and left, without further ado. As the door swung shut behind her, Paul pulled himself up out of his seat.

'I need to get on too,' he said. 'Unless you need me here?'

'Nah, I'm gonna hole up here today, sort through the paperwork and make some calls. Meet me back here later on though. We need to get in touch with Alfie and catch up with all that side of things. I've been so busy catching up on our inner-city operations, I haven't had a chance to get up to date with our suppliers further afield.'

Alfie Ramone was their new cocaine supplier – or at least new to Freddie and Paul. They had set up the arrangement just before they got sent down, and it had been Anna and Bill who had ironed out the creases and got the operation running smoothly.

'Got it. I'll be back this afternoon.' Picking up his jacket, Paul nodded and left the small Portakabin.

CHAPTER THIRTY-FIVE

As Paul walked up the steep cobbled pathway towards the road above, he saw a familiar figure marching towards him, her stance resolute. His eyebrows shot up in surprise.

'Hi, Paul,' Anna said. 'Is Freddie still down there?'

'Er, yeah…' he answered awkwardly.

'Thanks.' Anna strode on without stopping.

Paul paused, wondering if he should go back, but after a second decided against it. This was a battle he didn't want to be in the middle of. Continuing on, he picked up the pace, moving away from the pair of them as swiftly as he could.

Anna knocked twice and opened the door, walking into an equally surprised-looking Freddie.

'I'm sorry to disturb you down here, but I needed to talk to you,' she said.

'How did you know I was here?' Freddie replied, with a small frown.

'Bill told me you were headed this way.' Anna took a deep breath, trying to ignore her gradually speeding heart rate.

Now that she had finally admitted to herself that she still harboured feelings for Freddie, she couldn't help but feel at odds when she looked at him. His intense hazel-green eyes bored into her, and his chiselled jaw hardened, but instead of feeling deterred it just made her smile sadly. That was a jaw she used to kiss through the long nights when they held each other. Those were the eyes that had seen into her soul, like no other eyes had before. No one could take those memories away, not even Freddie himself.

Closing the door, she walked to the desk and sat down. She bit her lip as she thought over all the things she had practised on the way over, then pushed them aside and decided to cut to the point.

'Freddie, I know things are strained between us right now. Whether that's because we've just changed too much, or because the history we have is always there like the silent elephant in the room, I don't know,' she said honestly. 'But I do know we can't carry on like this.' She pushed her thick, dark hair back over her shoulder self-consciously. 'It's not healthy. Not for the business, not for us and certainly not for Ethan. He's picked up things and he's getting worried. School have started noticing.'

Freddie tensed up at the mention of Ethan. Was she trying to use him to get around him? Was that the ploy here? Or was there something in what she said? Ethan meant the world to him, his only son and one who he constantly felt he needed to make things up to, for the years he wasn't around.

'What do you mean they've started noticing?' he asked, giving her the benefit of the doubt. Whatever else Anna had become, he couldn't fault the care she had given Ethan.

'They mentioned some concerns to Tanya. She smoothed it over, and Ethan's aware he needs to stay off their radar, but I'm worried about him. Because the reality is, his worries are our fault.' She held out her hands in a helpless gesture before dropping them down in her lap. 'So we need to figure stuff out. For his sake if no one else's.'

There was a long silence as Freddie thought it over. He stared at her, wishing for the hundredth time that she hadn't betrayed his trust the way she had. Because trust meant everything in their world. If you didn't have that, you had nothing. As things stood, had she been anyone else, he'd have strung her up in a warehouse and killed her for siphoning money from him. It was only their history and the fact she had maintained his business and his family whilst he was away that had kept her from this fate. And now he didn't know what to do. She was the enemy, and yet still she slept in her bed just two rooms away from his own. Still she came to work every day and ran parts of his business that he hadn't yet caught back up with. Still she mothered his son and resided in a part of his heart that he couldn't quite eject her from. She was the first enemy he had ever come across who he didn't know how to fight. And now here she was, asking for peace, asking them to sort out their differences.

Anna watched the strange mixture of emotions play out behind Freddie's eyes as he stared at her across the desk, and Tanya's words came back to her. Maybe she *should* tell him how she felt. It wouldn't be easy, and part of her thought there was no point, because there was no way back to where they were before, but perhaps her honesty would help Freddie open up to her in return.

Taking a deep breath, she summoned all her courage and tried to put it into words. 'Look, this hasn't been easy for either of us. I know that it hasn't been for me, at least.' She took another deep breath and stared over at him, her expression open. 'I thought that over the years apart, I'd be able to heal and move forward. I thought when you came out we could work together in harmony and put our past behind us. But when the time came, when I saw you at Mollie's…' She momentarily closed her eyes in pain, as all the feelings came flooding back. 'I was right back where I was two years ago, hurting. Because the man I loved – my best friend – was out of reach.'

She swallowed, breaking her gaze away and looking down at her hands, unable to continue under his scrutiny. 'And I've tried to push that aside. Because I know that too much has happened – to both of us. But it's there. And it makes it hard for me every single day.' A wave of emotion swept up her body and brought mist to her eyes. She blinked it away and sniffed, sitting upright and smoothing down the front of her dress as a distraction. 'But for Ethan's sake, at least,' she said, holding her head up, 'I need to stop letting that be so hard that it makes it awkward between us. And I'm hoping that you can do the same. Assuming that you're going through something similar, that is.'

Having gained control of herself, Anna looked over at Freddie again. The pain and anguish she saw in his eyes was mixed with a terrible combination of rage and accusation and she blinked, shocked.

Freddie stared at her, barely able to contain his boiling emotions. He knew that everything she said was one big lie, that she had already moved on with Roman. However hard she had tried to hide it, the chemistry between them was obvious. Which meant that all this was just an act, a merciless act designed to pull on his heartstrings and blind him to her faults so that she could continue whatever she was doing undiscovered. She clearly thought that by acting as though she still loved him, he'd allow his own emotions to come to the fore and forget all his suspicions about her. Because love is blind, right? The timing in itself was obvious – coming just days after he had made it crystal clear he didn't trust her. That she could be so callous and use his feelings against him like this felt like a knife through the heart.

'Get out,' he said, his tone deadly quiet.

'Excuse me?' Anna replied, dropping her jaw in shock.

'You heard me. Get the fuck out of this office now,' he growled. When she didn't move, he finally lost his temper and yelled, 'I said, get out!'

Anna stood up, shocked to the core. Why was he being like this? She had opened herself up, allowed herself to be vulnerable in front of him and this was how he reacted? Blinking and shaking her head, she summoned all her wounded pride and walked to the door with her head held high. Turning back to face him, she frowned in confusion.

'What happened to you?' she asked, her tone full of hurt and accusation.

'You, Anna,' he said with dark feeling. '*You*. Now please leave.'

Not trusting herself not to break down in front of him, she opened the door and left the Portakabin. After opening herself up and being shot down that way, there was no way she was ever going to let him see any of her weaknesses again. As she passed the last of the dockhands and moved onto the part of the pathway hidden from sight, hot tears finally began to flow.

How on earth had they come to this?

*

As Anna reached the road and got in her car, she was too heart-broken to notice the man dressed in black follow her out of the docks and take out his phone to make a call. And as her tyres screeched away, his call connected.

'He's down at the docks,' Rohan said quietly into the phone, watching the car disappear into the distance. 'It is the perfect location, if he is still here after the workers have gone home. Discreet, out of the way… *Da*, I will keep you updated. But be ready. We may be able to finish this tonight for good.'

CHAPTER THIRTY-SIX

Walking down the narrow, cobbled path of the alley, Josephine sidestepped a pile of boxes that had been left for the bin men. As she passed, the small shops that were crammed in all down one side started closing their doors and pulling down the shutters. She was hoping that she had timed this just right and wasn't a few minutes too late. She knew that Thomas shut up shop right on the dot each day. He was religiously habitual.

Reaching the tiny independent chemist, she saw her old friend walking to the door, about to turn the open sign to closed. Holding up her hand in greeting, she waited as he frowned in surprise and then gave her a wide smile. He reached the door and opened it wide, gesturing for her to enter.

'Josephine, it has been too long,' he said in a thin, weedy voice that seemed well matched to his thin, stooped physique. 'To what do I owe this pleasure?'

'Thomas, it's good to see you,' Josephine replied warmly. 'I hope you don't mind me coming now – it's just that I'm hoping to commission you for something off-book.'

Josephine and Thomas went way back. Years ago, when she had begun quietly collecting black-market contacts behind her father's back, she had often gone out for a few drinks to get to know them better. One time, one of these acquaintances had introduced her to Thomas and they had ended up talking all night, soon becoming fast friends. She had been fascinated by him and his stories of the things he could do.

Having grown up with two doctor parents, he had developed an interest in medicine and chemicals. Not wanting to become a doctor himself, he had instead studied to become a chemist and worked hard to open his own business. Along with his qualifications, he had also picked up numerous other skills and a vast knowledge of illegal substances along the way, and these had interested him most of all.

Now, Josephine knew, Thomas made his living by selling prescription drugs by day and illegal substances by night. Not that he was a drug dealer per se; he wasn't at all interested in joining part of a chain with other people. People made him anxious, and for the most part he didn't particularly like them. But what he did enjoy was making small batches of things that people couldn't readily get on London's heaving drug market. And that was exactly why Josephine was here now.

Thomas's eyes lit up at the prospect of a new client, for Josephine hadn't needed to use his services before. 'That sounds interesting, my dear,' he replied. 'Why don't you come through to the back and we can discuss whatever it is you're looking for.'

Locking the door behind her and switching off the main shop lights, Thomas guided Josephine through to the small office behind the shop. Josephine took a seat on a battered old office chair and looked around. The office was outdated and full of old, mismatched furniture, but she couldn't for one second fault the cleanliness. There was not so much as a speck of dust lying around or a sheet of paper out of place. It reminded her that she needed to sort her own office out, which was currently a complete state. As she thought of her work, Anna sprung to mind and at once her heart fell into a pit of guilt.

'So,' Thomas started, sitting down and interlocking his fingers on the desk in between them. 'Tell me what it is you are after and I will tell you if I can help.'

Josephine took a deep breath. 'I've got some hard times ahead of me, Thomas. And I'm really hoping you can help…'

CHAPTER THIRTY-SEVEN

As the light of the summer evening became weaker, Freddie rubbed his eyes and looked up from the mess of papers in front of him to turn on the desk light. Paul frowned down at a book of coded numbers and went over his calculations again.

'Whichever way we look at it, these numbers don't add up against the current ones. We're down about twenty per cent,' he said.

They had been through all the old accounts and filed them back into order after they'd been mixed up by the police in the raid Damien had told them about. Now they were checking the recent figures from the books of their more nefarious businesses against the archived ones from years before. Lines upon lines of data were written throughout these books that could only be deciphered from those in the know. Without the code to break it, the contents would be nothing more than gobbledegook to even the most expert of police teams.

The good thing about these books was that there was only one paper copy – nothing was ever entered into a laptop – and they were kept in a hidden safe in Club CoCo. Not only was Anna unable to keep them on her, she was also probably blissfully unaware that the brothers had them and were going through them with a fine-tooth comb.

'Let me see,' Freddie said, holding his hand out.

Paul passed it over and he flicked through the contents.

'There,' Paul said, pointing to one of the 'total' columns. 'Look at those against the new ones. Either we've lost revenue, or someone isn't entering a portion down, keeping some of it off-book.'

Freddie thought about it. The one thing he could say for sure about Anna was that she was smart. It was one of the things he used to love about her. If she was going to such lengths to hide the money she was taking from the legal businesses, he doubted she would touch these. There would be no paper trail for her to fall back on. It would be too easy for them to spot, and she knew that.

'It's probably down to people losing faith after we went away. That, or fear the Old Bill were going to crack down on our client base as well as us. Twenty per cent is a reasonable amount on those terms, I'd wager,' he responded.

'Maybe.' Paul's expression turned grim. 'But it still ain't good enough. I'll see who's dropped off the radar and pay them a visit.'

'Let me know who we're talking about before you do. I might join you,' Freddie said, running his fingers down the pages of the ledger in front of him.

The writing was small and neat – Thea's handwriting. It was she who had come up with this way of coding things and taught them how to read it. He thought back to the day he had found her in his bedroom, just a kid, her eyes wide and scared as he furiously demanded to know what she was doing. She'd shown him, stubborn bravery shining through her fear, that she'd rearranged his accounts. Instead of one set that needed to be hidden, she'd split them into two, one that could be filed legitimately and would help him hide the rest. From that day she'd slowly taken on all their accounts, eventually growing into her own place in the family business.

Paul glanced over and saw his brother's face. He looked down at the ledger. 'I know,' he said quietly. 'Don't feel the same without her, does it?'

'No,' Freddie said heavily. 'And something tells me it never will.'

There was a long silence as they each thought back to the day of her murder. As the familiar feeling of guilt washed over him, Freddie pushed it back. He could wallow in that later, but for now he had to focus on getting his house in order.

'Let's get back to the club. I want to talk to Sammy – see what we've got coming up at the bookies,' he said, shutting the ledger with care. 'Shove these in the ceiling; we can come back to them tomorrow.'

'Sure thing.' Paul set about doing as he was asked, gathering them up and making sure the ceiling tile was back in its rightful place before they left.

Freddie locked the front door behind them, and the brothers made their way in the falling dusk back up to their cars. The docks were quiet, all the workers having gone home for the night, and the river was peaceful with no strong wind in the air. About to continue their conversation about the bookies, Freddie opened his mouth, then paused as he saw four figures appear on the path up ahead. He squinted, trying to get a better look. As they neared the small crowd of men, Freddie frowned. 'Looks like trouble,' he said to Paul quietly.

One of them carried a hunting knife by his side and another flicked open a Swiss army blade. Whoever they were, they were not here to make friends. Slowing down, Freddie considered what he had back in the cabin, but nothing that could be used as a weapon came to mind. He heard Paul curse under his breath.

'You got anything on you?' he asked.

'No,' Paul said, his tone annoyed. 'You?'

'No,' Freddie replied heavily.

As the gap closed to just a few feet, both parties stopped. The larger-built man in the middle began to speak.

'Well, if it isn't Freddie and Paul Tyler, the kings of Central London,' Aleksei said, his Russian accent thick with sarcasm.

'Ahh, Aleksei,' Freddie replied, as it clicked. 'And what sort of business do you think you have down here on my docks this evening?'

The three distinctly unfriendly men with Aleksei fanned out and Freddie tensed, ready for anything.

'I've come to organise the return of the weapons you stole from me. That wasn't very friendly now,' he chided. 'I have orders to fill, clients waiting.'

'Feel free to pass over their numbers – I'll make sure to leave them very happy customers indeed,' Freddie mocked. 'One hundred per cent off the price.'

Aleksei's eyes flashed with anger. 'You will tell me where you are keeping my guns and then I *might* just let you walk away from here.' The change in his tone as he lied was slight, but not so slight that Freddie didn't pick up on it.

He grinned, the action not reaching his eyes. 'Oh, but come now, that's not true, is it? You wouldn't have come down here with all this muscle, late at night, out of sight, catching me off guard, just to have a chat. No, you want me to hand over the location and then disappear. Well, I'm sorry to disappoint you, but that ain't happening. Not today.'

'Fine. You don't want to play? Don't play. *Poluchit' yego,*' Aleksei shouted, his face reddening in anger.

All at once the three men leaped forward with a roar, and Freddie and Paul fell back. Turning on their heels, they made for the Portakabin in the hope they might find something – anything – to use against the other men.

'Where's the key?' Paul yelled.

Freddie glanced back over his shoulder. The men were hot on their tails. 'Too late,' he replied through gritted teeth. 'Split off.'

Pulling himself up short, Freddie dived in between two towers of empty crates and circled back around, pushing one tower over as he went. As it crashed down, it stalled his opponents and he whirled around wildly, looking for something useful. His gaze landed on a thick cut-off piece of rope with a coiled end, probably once used to tether a boat to the shore. It wasn't much, but it was something. He picked it up, feeling the weight of it in his hands. If he swung it hard enough, the end could do some real damage.

The two men who had followed him were now catching up and he swung wildly in their direction. They yanked themselves back out of the way and Freddie steadied his footing readying himself for their next lunge. Taking his eyes off them for just a second, he glanced over to Paul. He had managed to knock the knife out of the other man's hand and the pair were now going at it with their fists. Aleksei waited patiently on the sidelines, hands in his pockets and a cruel smirk on his face.

Focusing on his own battle, Freddie's eyes darted back and forth between the two men. One of them still had a knife and they were circling around him as though he was a lion they were trying to tame. Thrashing the rope back and forth, Freddie looked for a means of escape. His back was against the wall that ran up to the road above, and the two men blocked his only way out. He growled in frustration, his heart beating hard with adrenaline. There was nothing else for it – he was going to have to fight his way out.

'Come on then, you *cunts*!' he yelled, the veins popping out of his neck as he rushed forward at the one with the knife. Smashing the heavy end of the rope into his face, he knocked him to the ground in one fell swoop, but when he turned, he was met with a fist to the cheek from his second assailant and was momentarily unbalanced. Staggering out of reach, he quickly righted himself and came back at the one who'd just punched him with the rope. It missed and Freddie cast it aside with a roar, leaping forward.

Dodging a left hook, Freddie smashed his fist into the man's stomach and sent him backward with a groan.

'Freddie!' Paul yelled in warning.

About to land another hefty blow, Freddie was caught off guard as someone kicked him in the back of the knee. Falling to the ground, he twisted just in time to see the knife coming towards his chest. He threw himself back and almost got out of range, but not quite. The knife plunged into his flesh just below his shoulder, and he let out a bellow of pain. His assailant pulled the knife back out roughly and paused, waiting for Aleksei's command.

Holding his hand to his injured shoulder and trying hard not to black out from the pain, Freddie pulled himself backward along the cobbled ground, trying to get out of range of another attack. He was in a bad position now. If Aleksei ordered his goon to finish him off, he stood no chance.

Now that Freddie was down, the other man raced over to help his companion fight Paul. Freddie looked on helplessly as he realised that for once they were royally screwed. They had been caught off guard and were outnumbered and out-tooled. Paul threw one of them off with a bear-like roar, but he almost immediately returned and tried to pull him to the ground.

'What is it you English like to say?' Aleksei said, casually strolling over to look down on him. 'Never bring a knife to a gunfight? Well, in this case I guess it was never bring a rope to a knife fight.' He chuckled at his own joke and the man holding the knife next to him laughed along with him.

Freddie looked down at the hand that had been holding his wound and realised it was covered in blood, much like the rest of his shirt. Blood poured out at an alarming rate, alerting him to the fact it was deeper than he'd originally thought. Pressing down, he put on as much pressure as he could, biting his lip to stop himself crying out in pain. Aleksei was already enjoying this enough – he wasn't going to give him anything more to laugh about.

Staring at the knife the other man had dropped a few feet away, he calculated his chances of reaching it before he either passed out or had his throat slit. They weren't good, but he had to try.

'Hey!' A deep voice cut through the air along with the sound of a few pairs of boots running on the cobbles.

'*Chert*,' Aleksei cursed. 'You told me they were alone,' he said, his tone full of rage and accusation as he turned on the man next to him.

'I— They were!' he replied, as surprised as the rest of them.

Damien and two other burly dockhands came into view, one with a baseball bat and Damien flicking up a blade. With the men attacking him momentarily caught off guard, Paul was able to push away and run back towards them.

'Gimme that bat,' he roared. The man holding it threw it over and Paul immediately turned, running back towards their attackers with it held up high, ready to swing down on their heads.

'Retreat,' Aleksei called, already running away. His men swiftly followed, scarpering up the path as fast as their legs would carry them. 'I'll finish you next time, Tyler,' he spat over his shoulder. 'And your brother too.'

Coming to a stop, face red with exertion and anger, Paul threw the bat back to the man who'd given it to him. The dockhands continued chasing the Russians up the path until they were out of sight and Paul hunched down next to Freddie.

'Fred, you alright?'

'I've been fucking better,' Freddie replied through gritted teeth.

'What's the damage? Let me see.' Paul gently pulled Freddie's hand back and ripped the hole in his shirt wider so that he could see how bad it was underneath. 'Jesus,' he muttered.

Damien was the first to return, the others walking behind him. 'What the hell was that?' he asked with a frown.

'Russians,' Paul answered without turning round.

'Ah. That one who set up shop in Soho? I've heard tales of him,' Damien said grimly. He peered over and quickly took off his T-shirt. 'Here, use this. He's going to need pressure on it before he loses too much blood.'

Paul pressed down onto his brother's shoulder and Freddie let out a sound of pain. 'I'm sorry, Fred – has to be done.'

'We need to get him to a hospital,' Damien said.

'No,' the brothers answered in unison.

'I can't go to a hospital,' Freddie continued, his voice strangled. 'We're on probation. It raises too many questions. Just take me home, Paul. Clean me up there.'

Paul nodded grimly. 'Help me get him up to the car,' he instructed the two dockhands. They nodded and pulled Freddie up gently, taking his weight and helping him walk. 'I'm glad you were still here,' he said, turning to Damien. 'I thought they had us for a minute.'

'I'm glad we were here too. We were just going over some new health and safety crap the government sent out, ready to teach the men in the morning.' He looked down at the pool of blood where Freddie had lain with a dry smirk. 'Funnily enough, there's no mention of Russians with knives.'

Paul sighed, looking at the mess on the cobbles. 'Can you have that cleaned up? I'll make sure it's appreciated in your wedge this week.'

''Course. And don't worry about it,' Damien said.

'Thanks.'

As Freddie got to the car, he lost his balance and wavered a little. The men either side of him quickly propped him up.

'I'm fine; it's OK.' He looked up to Paul. 'Just get me home and off these fucking streets.'

CHAPTER THIRTY-EIGHT

Climbing into bed after a long and emotional day, Anna pulled the sheets over her legs and relaxed back into the pillows before picking up the book she had been meaning to start for the last few weeks. Perhaps it would take her mind off things for a while. As she opened the hard cover of *First Blood* by Angela Marsons, she smiled briefly, giving her face a respite from the sad frown lines which had been etched into it all day. It was funny, really, that she enjoyed books like these about headstrong detectives, considering her line of work. Settling back to immerse herself in another world and take her mind off her own troubles for a while, she almost made it through the first paragraph when she heard the key in the lock.

She froze, unsure what to do. She hadn't expected Freddie to be home so early, especially after his earlier outburst. After he had thrown her out of his office so callously, she had assumed he would try to avoid her for as long as possible. Clearly, she was wrong.

Biting her lip, she listened as he moved through the hallway into the kitchen. Her stomach churned and the familiar feeling of hurt and anger rose to the surface. She did not want to speak to him right now. She wasn't sure she'd be able to contain her temper. Hopefully he was going to get a drink and lock himself away in his room, much like any other night that they were here together now. She waited, wondering if perhaps it was just a fleeting visit, if he might go back out any second.

Someone cursed and she frowned. Whoever it was, it didn't sound like Freddie. Low murmurs floated through the door as two men conversed, and her attention sharpened when she heard a groan of pain. Something was wrong.

Thoughts of avoiding Freddie abandoned, she swung her legs over the side of the bed, straightened her thin summer nightie and padded across the room. Hesitating for a moment, she opened the bedroom door and walked through to find out what was going on.

The scene that met her was the last thing she had expected, and her hand flew to her mouth. Her eyes widened in shock as they darted back and forth between Freddie and Paul.

Freddie was laid out on top of the white marble breakfast bar, his blood turning it a strange shade of pink as it seeped from the bloody rag over his wound. Paul was grappling around in the medical bag they kept under the sink, pulling out bandages and seeing what else he could find.

'What happened?' she breathed in horror, glancing over her shoulder to make sure Ethan hadn't woken. He couldn't see this.

'Aleksei and his men jumped us at the docks,' Paul answered gruffly. 'Stabbed him in the shoulder. It's a flesh wound but deep. It needs stitching quickly, before he loses too much more blood.'

'The hospital?' she asked automatically.

'You know he can't go there – not now.'

Anna looked down at Freddie as he grimaced in pain. His face was devoid of colour, his eyes beginning to ring with black, and his lips were as white as a sheet. This worried her even more than all the blood. Their earlier conversation was forgotten for now.

'Right,' she said. 'Move over.'

Pushing past Paul, she reached into the top cupboard and pulled a large bottle of vodka from the back. Standing over Freddie, she took the bloody rag away from his shoulder and pulled back the sodden red shirt.

Looking down into his eyes, she saw a flicker of fear there, before it was replaced by a tired hardness. 'I won't lie,' she said, 'this is going to hurt. But you need to keep quiet for Ethan's sake. Paul, put something in his mouth to bite down on.'

Paul grabbed a nearby tea towel and twisted it up before placing it between Freddie's teeth. Freddie closed his eyes and tensed, waiting for the vodka to hit its mark.

Anna took a deep breath before pouring the clear liquid straight into the wound. Freddie bucked and his neck muscles strained as he threw his head back, but he bit down, and the muffled sounds of agony were as quiet as he could manage.

She wiped around the area with a piece of gauze from the medical bag, and as the blood began to seep out of the clean wound once more she quickly squeezed the two sides of skin together between her fingers. Paul threaded the needle from the medical bag and doused it in the vodka before passing it over to Anna, then watched as her nimble fingers made quick work of the stitches. She worked in silence, her face strangely calm amidst the chaos, and Paul gripped Freddie's hand tightly as he tried to keep still. Freddie's chest rose and fell in quick succession as his heart rate increased with the pain.

'There,' she said quietly as the last stitch pulled together and she tied it off.

Paul pulled the towel out of Freddie's mouth and threw it in the sink. Placing a thick gauze over the wounded area, Anna began winding a bandage around his shoulder tightly. She glanced over at Paul, taking in the bloodstains all down his suit and hands and neck.

'He's going to be fine. I'll finish here; why don't you go jump in the shower – clean up? You can borrow some of Freddie's clothes.'

'OK. I won't be long,' he said, shooting Freddie a look.

He disappeared, and for a few minutes Anna continued cleaning Freddie up in silence. As she worked, he looked up at her, wishing in his weakened state that he could just lean his head on her shoulder and share the weight he carried with her like he used to. Her thick, dark hair tumbled softly down towards him, and her beautiful face was soft and unguarded for once as she worked. He looked away. They could never be like that again. Not now.

'Where did you learn to patch up like that?' he eventually asked.

'You left me in charge of the firm,' she replied quietly. 'Did you really think in two and a half years I wouldn't come across a situation like this? I had to patch our men up a few times when trouble hit. Especially at the beginning. Anyone and everyone tried their luck. It wasn't a fun time.'

Guilt and admiration flooded through him once more – the feelings he used to have when he thought of the situation he'd left Anna in. He'd known from the start she was the right person to leave in charge, however heavy and unfair the burden was. She was so strong, so fearless, she could face anything and come out on top. But that was before he'd realised how mercenary she could be too, stabbing him in the back the moment she had the power to.

As the anger began to rage inside him once more, he sighed, exhausted by the night's challenges and the circus of emotions she roused in him. But more so, he realised, he was exhausted by the games. He couldn't do this anymore. As his thoughts cleared, he made a decision. Looking up at Anna as she placed the last of the tape over his bandages, he let his mask drop and spoke the words he should have said when he first found out.

'I want you gone, Anna,' he said simply. She paused in her tracks. 'I know what you've been doing. Siphoning money from the clubs and parlours, sending them off into a void of offshore companies. Stealing money from my companies and hiding it in plain sight – it's a clever method, I'll give you that. But it's theft from your own, all the same. Theft and complete fucking disloyalty.' He closed his eyes tiredly. 'I don't know what game you're playing, what business venture you've got set up with your boyfriend Roman, but you must know that it's something I can't ignore.'

'What?' Anna replied, aghast. She stepped back.

'If you were anyone else, I'd have strung you up by now. And I think you know that,' he said, his tone hard. 'But you raised my boy, gave him a real mum. And you kept my firm going when I couldn't. I have to credit you for that. So here's what I'm going to suggest.' He swallowed the lump in his throat. 'I don't want to take any more from Ethan than he's already lost. We'll share custody of him. I'll draw a line under what you've done and we'll never speak of it again. But you need to leave by the end of the week. Set up somewhere else, far away from me and far away from my businesses. Because I cannot look at you,' he added, frustration and pain colouring his words. 'I can't see your face staring back at me and reminding me of it all.'

Anna stepped back, her jaw dropping in shock and a mixture of horror and anger rippling through her eyes.

'How *dare* you,' she whispered, her voice trembling with fury. 'How dare you even *think* that of me?'

'I've seen the payments, Anna. I've chased them and come to the brick wall you so carefully constructed,' Freddie replied, painfully pulling himself up into a sitting position. He swayed slightly, the loss of blood making him light-headed.

Anna's drew in a sharp breath. So he *had* found them after all. She narrowed her eyes and stepped back even further.

'You have no clue what you're talking about, you stupid, *stupid* man,' she said in a low growl. 'You see one thing and immediately assume I'm a thief? *Me?* The person who has held everything together all this time?' Anna heard her voice rising and lowered it before she continued. She didn't want to wake Ethan – he couldn't be witness to this. Shaking her head at Freddie, her lip curled up in resentment. 'Firstly, Roman is not – and never was – my boyfriend. We get on, sure. And he's a fun, attractive guy. Maybe if I had been over you, it might have even happened. But it didn't. Because for some *stupid* reason, I'm not. Though this conversation has gone a *long* way towards remedying that,' she added with feeling.

Freddie stared at her across the small kitchen as she spoke. His head was reeling so much from the blood loss and all the events of the evening that he didn't know what to believe anymore. She *would* deny their relationship now – of course she would. It would be the only way to protect Roman. She was smart enough to know that her free pass would not extend to him, once he found proof of Roman's involvement in her little scam. But she sounded so genuine, the conviction and offence in her tone so natural, that even he had to question his position.

'Secondly,' Anna continued, 'you find a few odd payments and instead of asking me about them – *me*, the person who has run all the accounts for two and a half years – you jump to the worst-case scenario? *Really?*' she hissed.

'Don't keep bullshitting me, Anna,' Freddie replied, his own eyes flashing with anger. 'I've been in this game a great deal longer than you. I know there's only one reason someone goes to those lengths to make money disappear.'

'Do you now?' Anna challenged with a bitter laugh. Shooting him an icy glare, she nodded slowly. She opened her mouth to continue and then seemed to change her mind. Closing it again, her jaw formed a hard line and for a moment she stared at him with such strong hatred Freddie wondered whether she was about to fly at him.

Just as the tension became so thick it was almost impossible to bear, Anna suddenly broke it, sweeping past him out into the hallway, past Paul who had silently arrived halfway through their exchange and decided not to get involved, and into her bedroom. The door clicked shut and Freddie turned to face his brother with a grim expression.

Paul raised his eyebrows and walked forward to his brother. 'Here, let me help you,' he said quietly.

Taking Freddie's weight as he eased off the kitchen side, he paused as Freddie got his balance and adjusted to standing up. 'You've lost a lot of blood. You need to eat something sugary and get some sleep.'

Freddie nodded. 'Yeah,' he agreed. Wincing, he caught his breath.

'You OK?' Paul asked, a concerned frown wrinkling his forehead. Freddie didn't look good.

'I will be,' he replied bravely. 'Just get me to bed, will ya?'

As they began to walk slowly from the kitchen, the sound of Anna's door opening stopped them in their tracks. A second later she appeared in the front room, fully dressed, murder in her eyes.

She looked around at the bloody mess all over the kitchen side and floor. Glaring at the two brothers, she pulled herself up to her full height.

'Get this mess cleaned up by the morning so that Ethan doesn't have to see it,' she snapped. 'Because if he does, if that little boy finds this in his home in the morning, so help me God, I'll kill the *both* of you.'

Without waiting for a response, Anna picked up her handbag and keys and swept out of the flat. Too agitated to wait for the lift, she took the stairs down, two at a time.

Replaying the conversation in her head, she felt a surge of anger run through her once more. How could Freddie jump to that conclusion without even asking her about the payments? Surely, after all she had done for him, she deserved the initial benefit of the doubt? If he had come to her, she could have headed this whole thing off. Now, she had to deal with it head-on.

As she reached the underground car park for their building, Anna unlocked her car, the double beep echoing around the enclosed space. Slipping into the driver's seat, she prepared herself for the journey ahead. Freddie's guess was partly right – she *had* moved the money slyly to hide what she was doing and there *was* someone else involved, though it wasn't Roman. His assumptions about Roman were way off.

Now she had to make sure the money was safe and secure, and that nothing – not even Freddie – could get in the way of what she had planned for it.

CHAPTER THIRTY-NINE

Wandering over to the window in her silk dressing gown and bare feet on the cold wooden floor, Josephine stared out at the street below. Her eyes were sunken with hollow rings surrounding them from lack of sleep. She'd tossed and turned all night and had thought perhaps sleep might claim her through exhaustion as the sun came up on a new day, but she'd had no such luck. It was now nearly lunchtime and she'd finally given up on even trying. No matter what she did, she couldn't rest. Her inner demons screamed out at her, over and over, taunting her with the knowledge of what she had to do.

There's no turning back, they screamed. *You have no choice.*

Fingernails picked anxiously at the skin around her other fingernails until they bled, and her lips were sore and chapped from being bitten over and over through the long nights. A fluttering movement pulled her eyes from the street to the gutter running along the roof line under the window. Two birds were taking a bath in a shallow puddle of water, and as she watched, one of them nuzzled into the other's neck. Usually this would delight her, but today she felt nothing but sadness.

'You shouldn't love, little birds,' she murmured. 'Love brings only heartache and pain. It makes you do things you would never do alone. It guilts you.' She touched the window, and at the small sound the birds took flight, disappearing out of view.

Josephine stayed like that, her hand to the window for several minutes, her eyes glazed over as they stared through the gutter, until there was a small knock at the door. She didn't answer but heard it creak open. In exhaustion she closed her eyes. All she wanted was to be left alone, but no one seemed to be taking the hint.

She plastered a fake smile on her face and turned to see who it was. Whatever was going on, she had to at least try to seem normal. It was the only way she was going to get through this without being suspected.

'Thought this might help you feel better,' said Ellie, one of the girls who'd been working here since before Josephine started. She held out a sealed flask and Josephine gave her a questioning look.

'It's chicken soup,' Ellie continued. 'Home-made. You said you thought you were coming down with something, so I thought this might just help…' She trailed off, seeing the confusion on Josephine's face.

'Oh, yes, sorry.' Josephine shook her head and rolled her eyes with a smile. 'I'm so out of it today; I don't know what's wrong with me. Thank you, Ellie,' she said warmly, taking the flask from her. 'This is really nice of you.' She had totally forgotten that had been her excuse the day before for why she looked like death warmed up.

Ellie grinned. 'No probs; me mum used to make it for me when I was ill. There's a bit of a kick to it, just to warn you. It blows off any cold that decides to linger. Enjoy, anyway.' With a wave, she turned around and left the small flat again.

Looking down at the flask, Josephine's eyes began to mist up. She had found a true family here with her girls, after Anna had discovered her on the bridge that night. A family way more accepting and loving that the one she had been born into. That was a gift more priceless than any diamond in the world.

A tear slipped out and landed on the top of the flask, and she closed her eyes, hugging it to her chest. For the first time in her life she had all the love she ever needed, and she couldn't quite believe what she now had to do. She couldn't believe she was about to shatter one of the most important and precious relationships of her life. But the moment Aleksei had declared war on the Tylers and asked her to step up, there had no longer been a choice. The path was laid, and now it was nothing more than a matter of time.

Outside the door, Ellie paused and bit her lip. Pulling her phone out of her pocket, she dialled Tanya's number and walked down the stairs and out of earshot as she waited for the call to be answered.

'Hey, Tanya, it's Ellie. You said to tell you if I noticed anything off with Josephine. Well, there's been a few things…'

*

Freddie pulled himself up the last two steps towards his office in Club CoCo and took a deep breath before walking in.

'Fred, you sure you're up to this?' Paul asked quietly.

'It don't matter whether I am or not,' Freddie replied. 'This needs to be dealt with. I'm not giving that fucking lunatic a chance for another pop – he has to be taken out now. No more messing around and playing games with his guns or his men. That was Anna's tactic and whilst I see the merit' – he shook his head – 'I should have just dealt with this my way from the start.'

Opening the door, the brothers were met by all the men in their inner circle. Bill, Sammy, Seamus, Dean and Simon sat around the room waiting for their bosses to arrive and tell them what was going on. All eyes immediately shot to the sling around Freddie's arm.

'What happened?' Bill asked, with a frown of concern.

'Aleksei and some of his men cornered us at the docks late last night,' Paul replied, watching Freddie warily as he walked around the desk. He was still worried his brother had lost too much blood to be up and about already. But there was no telling Freddie Tyler what to do. He'd be up arguing an hour after they buried his dead body, given the chance.

'What do you mean? How did they know you were even there?' Sammy asked.

'Must have followed one of us,' Freddie said with a shrug. 'There are a lot of people down there in the day – we wouldn't have noticed.'

'Tried fighting them off but we were outnumbered and out-tooled,' Paul continued. 'One of them managed to stab Freddie in the shoulder quite deep.' A sound of outrage rippled through the room. 'Luckily, Damien was in his office with a couple of men – they came out to help and the Russians ran off.'

'Fuck!' Seamus exclaimed. He ran his uninjured hand over his head and stared down at the other bandaged one, wondering how many more of them were going to get hurt before this was over.

'They would have finished the job, if Damien hadn't arrived,' Freddie said quietly, lighting a cigarette. He took a deep drag and then exhaled the smoke slowly. 'It's what Aleksei was gearing up for. Sick fuck would have taken great pleasure in it too.'

'So what are we going to do?' Sammy asked, sitting forward and flexing his hard-earned muscles in anger.

'We're going to end this bullshit,' Freddie said, watching the smoke curl up from his cigarette. 'We're going to smoke those rats out of Soho once and for all, rid this city of that particular strain of vermin.'

He paused to take another drag of his cigarette, savouring the feel of the smoke in his lungs. The wound was hurting more than he wanted to admit, and he covered his grimace of pain with the action of smoking. He couldn't allow himself to think about the pain right now. There was a time to lick wounds and there was a time for action. This was the latter.

'Dean – I want you to go and work out how many fully func-tional handguns we have in the order we stole from them and see what you can do about ammo,' he continued. 'Bill – I need you to get another five to ten of our men together – hard, loyal ones who won't let us down when it comes to *do or die*. Sammy – get your hands on the plans for the building that monstrosity of a strip club is in, and Seamus – I want you to scope the area and stake it out for the next twenty-four hours. Simon – you go with him and take shifts. I want to know all their movements in and out. Stay out of sight.'

Everyone nodded or spoke their agreement, and looking around at the men he trusted most in the world, Freddie felt a renewed hope. This was a dangerous situation, but they'd overcome worse.

'Come back here tomorrow, same time, with all the information. Then we plan a raid.' His eyes darkened. 'And we take back that part of our city for good.'

CHAPTER FORTY

Marching purposefully through the front of his strip club, Aleksei's expression was filled with thunder. One of the girls dressed in a red sequined thong and garter crossed his path, not catching this in time, and he swiped her aside with a roar.

'Get out of my way!'

She landed with a thump against the bar, and after biting her lip to stop herself crying out, she slunk off warily out of his way. Aleksei was well known among the girls for his vicious temper; she certainly wasn't hanging around to find out what had riled him into such a fury.

As he reached the back wall behind the VIP booth he usually sat in with his men, he paused and stared up at a small camera in the corner. Covered from floor to ceiling in padded velvet squares, the wall appeared to be no more than a normal club wall, but as he waited there was a small click and one of the panels pulled back and opened from the inside. He slipped through and it was closed again behind him.

The man who had opened it followed him through the dimly lit, industrial-looking passageway and down a set of metal stairs to the basement underneath. Here, Aleksei flicked a switch and light flickered to life in the vast room, shining weakly over rows of boxes all piled neatly on top of each other.

'Go and find Rohan – tell him I want everybody here after closing tonight. We need to prepare for tomorrow,' he said, reading the labels on the boxes as he searched for what he was looking for.

'Tomorrow?' the man questioned.

'Tomorrow we set our fall-back plan into motion,' Aleksei replied grimly. 'And this plan is one that those slippery snakes will not slither away from.' His lip curled into an ugly snarl. 'This time it will not matter how many people he has with him – they will be crushed into nothing. They should have left my business alone when they had the chance.' His hand balled into a fist down by his side. 'But, of course, we expected that they wouldn't.' He calmed down and opened one of the boxes. 'So this is the game we have to play, to protect our way of life. That is the way of the underworld, whatever country you are in.'

'Yes, boss,' his man replied dutifully. He nodded curtly and left the basement to do as he had been bid.

Fury and resentment bubbled under the surface and Aleksei paced for a moment, trying to calm himself down. He had been *so close* to finishing this once and for all last night. Perhaps if he had not been so cocky he would have got the job done. Freddie had been injured – and badly by the looks of it. If he had just allowed his men to get on with it and finish them quickly, it all would have been over. But his pride had got in the way. He'd told them to push the Tylers into a corner they couldn't escape from and then wait for his signal. He'd wanted to rub it in, to gloat in their faces and see their pain as they realised they had lost, before taking their lives. It would have been the cherry on top, but instead the delay had been his undoing. Now, instead of being fish food at the bottom of the river, the Tylers were getting ready to retaliate. And Aleksei had lost the element of surprise. There was no way they would be going anywhere alone and unarmed now.

Picking up a stick of dynamite from inside the box, Aleksei weighed it in his hand. It was time to set a bigger plan in motion, one that could not fail. He nodded slowly. There was more than enough dynamite here for what he had planned. He just needed to make sure his men were ready and knew exactly what they needed to do. This had to be executed very carefully if it was going to work. And Josephine would need to play her part well too.

He exhaled heavily as his mind moved towards his eccentric lover. He had known all along that she wouldn't find her part in this easy – she had such a large and loving heart. But he also knew that this heart belonged to him, and that breaking down the remaining barriers that kept them apart would give her the motivation she needed. Sending his wife and children away somewhere they would be just as comfortable and finally allowing her to become his leading lady was a small price to pay for what he was getting in return.

Casting his eye over the box one last time, he closed it back up and left the basement. He walked up the stairs to the long hallway once more, ignoring the door back into the club, and instead turned a corner towards the rear fire exit. Next to this was another door which led to his private office. He had instructed Josephine to meet him there, telling her to be careful that nobody saw.

Entering the office, he closed the door behind him, opening his arms as Josephine threw herself into them.

'Oh, Aleksei, I have missed you, my darling,' she said, her deep voice husky with emotion.

'And I, you, my love,' he replied, kissing her briefly. Looking up at her face he frowned. However carefully she had applied her thick make-up, it didn't hide the hollow rings around her eyes or the paleness of her skin. 'What is wrong?' he asked. 'You don't look well.'

Josephine bit her lip, her wide eyes sad and haunted. 'I'm not,' she admitted miserably. 'Darling, please let's reconsider this plan. Don't make me lose somebody I love for something so unimportant as a street address.'

'A street address?' Aleksei repeated with a laugh. 'Is that what you really think this comes down to? Josephine, this is about so much more than that. This is about a way of life, freedom to work wherever we choose and however we choose. If we don't do this here, we will have to fight the same battle somewhere else. There is no free land, not anywhere worthwhile. We have to *take* what we need. And we have done that. Now we have to fight for it. You cannot let me down.' Aleksei felt a flutter of annoyance. This was the last thing he needed. Josephine had to be strong now.

Josephine searched his face for any trace of doubt or weakness but there was none. She cast her gaze down and moved away from him, sitting down heavily on one of the two armchairs at the side of the room.

Aleksei sighed and changed tack. Perhaps he needed to remind her why she was doing this. 'Listen,' he said, crouching down. 'After this is all over we can start our lives properly, with no threat that it could be taken away from us.'

'*Your business* being the part of our lives under threat,' Josephine interjected, with a raised eyebrow.

'Yes, my business, which provides the money we need to live comfortably and in luxury, that provides my men with the money to look after their families, that provides the girls with a job to pay their way,' he said, accusation in his tone. 'My business is what keeps this all going, for everyone.'

Josephine looked down, her cheeks colouring slightly. 'I know that, Aleksei,' she said softly. 'I don't doubt that a lot of people depend on the business. But surely no one will die if you decided to shut down.' She looked up at him. 'We could move somewhere else, start again where no one knows us and just *live* our lives.'

Aleksei shook his head. 'No, Josephine, we are not doing that.'

'Why not?' she challenged.

'Because our lives are here,' he snapped, his anger coming to the fore. 'This is who I am.'

Josephine sat back and pursed her lips. Aleksei sighed and rubbed his forehead.

'Look, this is happening, and I need you to be strong and do what needs to be done. For me – for us,' he stressed. 'And then in just a few more days, it will all be over.' He hunched down in front of her and took her hands in his. 'I have booked the flights for my family. They leave the day after tomorrow. The movers take their things the same day and then the house is ready to make our own. Our life as a proper couple can begin. I have done this all for you. That is how much I love you, Josephine.'

It was true – he had broken the news to his family just the day before that they would soon be departing to start a new life in Slovakia. His wife had cried, not emotional tears for their marriage – it had been nothing more than a friendly arrangement for a long time – but for her children. He had felt bad then, but consoled himself that they were better off away from the grit and the violence of the life he led. In Slovakia they would be placed in private schools where they would make new friends and have the luxury of a fresh start with no criminal element hanging over them.

If he was honest with himself this was overdue. For all of them. He was who he was, and he had been hiding it for too long. With Josephine around and living in this city where people were allowed to be whoever they wanted, he could finally relax and allow himself to breathe. And his wife and children need never know who he really was underneath the pretence, though he suspected his wife had worked it out a while ago and kept it to herself. Everyone would win with this arrangement. Including Josephine.

Josephine looked down into his dark eyes and saw that he spoke the truth. This really was how much he loved her. He loved her enough to force blood onto her hands, then move her into the house he had shared with his wife. She closed her eyes and chided herself. This was not a typical type of love between them, but then there was nothing typical about their relationship at all. And this truly was the maximum capacity that Aleksei had for showing love. She could see that. She cupped his face with her hand and smiled at him sadly.

'I know,' she whispered. Leaning down, she kissed him gently and then rested her forehead against his. 'Thank you.'

Aleksei squeezed her hands. 'So you need to go now. Rest. Because tomorrow night is the night. You need to find a way to take her phone and wait for my signal to send the text. You send a message from Anna to Freddie, asking him to meet her on the fifth floor of the building site, that she wants to show him the building as a potential investment,' he reminded her. 'Once it is sent and you are sure it is delivered, you delete the text, block the number and slip the phone back. She will never know. That is all you have to do, my Jojo. It is just one text. I will take care of the rest. OK?'

Josephine nodded, closing her eyes as two tears fell and rolled down her cheeks. The course of action was set and there was no getting away from it. Aleksei would not be moved on his decision. Tomorrow night she would have blood on her hands and guilt in her heavy, broken heart, for the rest of her life.

CHAPTER FORTY-ONE

Opening the door to her flat above The Sinners' Lounge, Josephine walked in wearily, her conversation with Aleksei still swirling round in her head. She closed the door and dropped the keys back into her pocket before she realised that she wasn't alone. With a small jump, she put her hand to her chest as her unexpected guest placed their glass on the side table with a small thump.

'Oh, my heart, Tanya, you scared me!' she gasped. 'What are you doing here?'

Tanya was sunk back comfortably in the small armchair in the lounge area, one leg crossed over the other, with her hands clasped casually in her lap. She stared up at Josephine, her expression unreadable.

'Sorry to scare you,' she said lightly. 'I did try calling, but when I got here and found you were out, I realised you'd left your phone here too. Which is unlike you,' she added casually.

'Yes, well…' Josephine forced a smile as she hurriedly tried to come up with a logical alibi as to where she'd been. 'I must have forgotten it.'

'But it's right by the door – surely you noticed as you passed?' Tanya pushed.

'Oh, you know me,' Josephine replied with a forced laugh. 'So forgetful.'

Tanya nodded. 'I hate that, when you realise you don't have your phone on you,' she said. 'I'm forever double-checking myself, so I don't end up without it. I think the last time I was without mine was when Roman forced me to leave it on dry land. Though that was of course so that the GPS data wasn't recorded on the phone. Tricky to get that off afterwards, he says.'

'Yes, so I understand,' Josephine replied, her gaze flickering away from Tanya's. She felt her cheeks begin to flush. This was exactly the reason she had left it at home. She didn't want any record of being in Aleksei's club.

Tanya noted the look of guilt flash across her face and hid a frown. Something was going on with Josephine, that much was certain. But what was it?

'Look, are you OK, Josephine?' Tanya asked, cutting to the point. She hated dancing around things and this was no exception. She'd noticed how worried and withdrawn Josephine had been acting lately – it was the reason she had quietly asked the girls to report into her on anything unusual.

Josephine shrugged off her thin jacket and walked over to the sofa, sitting down near Tanya and smiling as though everything was absolutely normal. 'Of course,' she lied. 'I've been fighting off a cold for the last few days, but other than that I'm fine. Why?'

'You just don't seem yourself lately.' Tanya twisted her mouth to one side as she assessed her critically. Gone was the flamboyant spark that usually characterised her friend and in its place sat a heavy burden that seemed to be visibly weighing her down. 'Everything OK with that fella of yours?' she asked.

'Yes, it's fine. Just seen him actually,' Josephine offered, deciding it was best to keep as close to the truth as she could. The more lies you told, the more you had to remember.

'Oh, nice. Do anything fun?' Tanya asked, with a smile.

'Nothing really, just went for a walk down the South Bank, got some fresh air,' she lied.

'Oh, cool,' Tanya responded. 'Did you see that new pop-up? They've changed all those huge flowers to bees. It must be some environmental awareness thing, or something like that. I thought they looked really cool,' Tanya enthused.

'Yes, they looked great,' Josephine agreed with a smile and a nod. She looked down at her watch pointedly. 'I've got to get changed, said I'd relieve Beth so she could take some punters. Was there anything you wanted to go over, with the shipments or anything?' she asked.

'No, no, I just wanted to check up on you – that's all.' Tanya stood up and brushed down her skirt then smiled at Josephine and touched her shoulder affectionately. 'You know I'm always here for you, don't you? If there's anything you want to talk about.'

'Yeah, 'course,' Josephine replied with a shrug. 'We're family, right?'

'We are,' Tanya replied, giving her one last long look. 'OK. Well, I'll catch you later. Keep warm – tell that cold of yours to do one.'

'Will do,' Josephine replied with a forced smile.

Walking out of the flat and down the stairs, Tanya's own smile slowly dropped and a stressed frown replaced it. Waiting until she'd left the building, she pulled out her phone and called Anna. It was time to let her know that something was going on. Josephine keeping her personal life private was one thing, but lying to them and covering her tracks was something else entirely. And that was definitely the case here. Her face had reddened and she'd looked away in guilt when Tanya had mentioned the tracking on mobiles. And then she'd stared her right in the eye as she lied about her whereabouts tonight. Because there were no bees down at the pop-up on the South Bank. There weren't even flowers. That had been last year's display.

The call connected and Tanya glanced back over her shoulder to check she was definitely alone. Her heels tapped out a rhythm on the tarmac of the small car park as she walked, and her lights flashed as she pressed the unlock button on her car key.

'Listen, I think we might have another problem. I'm not sure exactly what yet, but it's Josephine. She's hiding something…'

CHAPTER FORTY-TWO

Freddie's office door slammed open with force, banging back against the wall. He looked up and reached for the gun in the drawer beside him at the same time. Seeing who it was, he exhaled loudly and took his hand off the cold handle.

'Fucking hell, Anna!' he cried. 'I was jumped and stabbed just last night – what you trying to do, give me a fucking heart attack?'

'Maybe a heart attack would wake you up, who knows?' Anna snapped back, not at all deterred by his words.

Freddie sat back and looked at her properly. He had expected her to stay out of his way after he'd finally called her out, or perhaps even be shown the icy front she was so well known for giving her enemies, but he had not expected this. Fury burned in her eyes, and her shoulders were tensed almost in a boxer's stance as she stood in front of him ready to fight.

'What are you doing here?' he asked.

Anna stepped forward and slapped a thick file onto the desk in front of him. 'This is all the paperwork from the other side of that money trail,' she spat. 'Go on – look at it. Open it up.'

Frowning, not sure where she was going with this, he opened the file and began reading.

'These are the details for a company under your mum's name… *your mum?*' he asked, looking up at her with a raised eyebrow. 'Really? I didn't have her pegged as someone you'd be able to draw into doing something like this.'

'Keep reading,' Anna said in a low, deadly voice. The anger in her eyes intensified at Freddie's assumption.

Staring at her for a long moment, Freddie went back to the file and began reading the finer details. The papers were for a consultancy company, the payments all seemingly legitimate and from various sources. She had done a good job in cleaning the money, he had to give her that. But why? The money had been clean in the first place – there was no legitimate reason to hide the source.

Flipping to the next page, his eyes skimmed down to the list of directors. Other than Leslie, Anna's mother, there was only one more. Ethan.

'What is this?' he asked, his tone less certain than it had been before.

'Keep going,' Anna demanded, folding her arms.

Flipping to the next document, Freddie found a legal document naming Leslie and Mollie Ethan's joint legal guardians, should anything happen to Freddie and Anna. As his mind began to connect the dots, Anna stepped forward and swiped the file back out of his hands, snapping it shut.

'When you went away after taking Ethan on, you had a fall-back plan. You had *me*.' She pointed a finger at her chest. 'You knew, no matter what, that I would take care of him and always make sure that he was OK. Because I was above board.' She glared down at him in contempt. 'There was no risk of me going away too, was there? I was the safe bet. But what now, Freddie?' She held her arms out in question. 'You handed one of the largest criminal networks in the country over to me. You turned me into *you*. So what happens to Ethan when we *both* get sent down next time, hmm? Have you thought about that?'

'Of course I have,' Freddie replied. 'We have other family – he'd be looked after.'

'By your mum, of course,' Anna continued. 'But what about money, Freddie? What happens when next time they seize all your businesses – and mine? You were lucky this time,' she reminded him. 'Sarah made sure they couldn't tie enough to the clubs to take them, but you won't always be as lucky. And if they seize everything, there is *nothing* left for our son. *Nothing*,' she repeated strongly. 'And that kept me up nights.'

Anna began pacing irritably, placing her hands on her hips. 'I couldn't sleep, knowing that if it all came crashing down, he would be left with nothing. So I came up with this plan. I lost money as legitimately as possible, every month, through a very lengthy and complicated route, to come back clean into this company. Even if they *tried* to link the two, they couldn't. And it's all for Ethan, an emergency nest egg to fall back on. The only reason my mother is on there is because he's a minor and one of the directors must be an adult. And I picked her because she's the weakest legal link to an adult Tyler who we can trust.'

There was a long silence as Freddie took it all in and realised with horrific clarity just how terribly he'd messed up. His head was reeling and he placed it in his hands, leaning on the desk in front of him.

'Anna, I don't know what to say…'

'I think you've already said more than enough,' Anna cut him off. 'You sat there in our home as I patched you up,' she said accusingly, her voice wobbling, betraying the hurt behind the anger, 'accusing *me* – the person who has held everything you ever cared about together for two and a half years, the person who loved you with everything she had for many more years before that – of stealing from you and screwing you over.' Her bottom lip quivered as the weight of all she had been holding in finally came to the fore.

'*Me*, the person who stood by you in more ways than anyone else ever could. If anything, *you've* betrayed *me*, Freddie. Not the other way around. It was *never* the other way around.' A hot tear escaped and fell unchecked down her face and off her chin.

Every word that came out of Anna's mouth hit Freddie's heart like a white-hot razor. How could he have got it so wrong? What was the matter with him? He closed his eyes. Was this what prison had done to him?

'Anna…' he started.

'Don't,' she snapped putting her hand up to stop him, the pain she felt spilling out in her voice. 'Just don't. I can't.' She shook her head and stepped back with a sniff. 'I need to get this back to my parents' house. It's the only safe place for it; the only place it can't be at all linked to us. Just…' Wiping the tears from her face, she turned away. 'Just please leave me alone.'

As Anna walked out, Freddie felt the world cave in. What the hell had he done? With a groan, he pushed his chair back and stood up. *Of course* she had done this to protect Ethan. *Of course* she hadn't stabbed him in the back. How had his assumptions got so out of control? A thousand memories of all the times Anna had stood by him, had walked through hell by his side, came flooding back.

Walking forward, he tried to think what to do. He needed to do something; he needed to fix this somehow, but how? Could this even *be* fixed anymore? Had he finally gone too far and broken whatever was left between them for good?

CHAPTER FORTY-THREE

Hearing the knock on her front door, Tanya frowned and walked through to see who it was. She wasn't expecting anyone. Peering through the peephole, she sighed and pulled open the door to let Freddie in.

He looked terrible. In fact, she hadn't seen him look this terrible in ages – the last time being when Anna had been kidnapped, years before. His face was drawn and his usually proud, rigid posture was slumped and deflated as though the weight of the world rested upon his shoulders.

Tanya knew why he was here. Anna had been furious – beyond furious – after everything Freddie had said to her last night. She had barely been able to talk through the angry tears as she called Tanya from the car phone on the way to her parents. By now she would have been back and shown Freddie the truth behind the matter. And now, she guessed rightly, he had no idea what to do. Which was why he was at her door, hoping she could tell him how to fix things.

She closed the door and crossed her arms, raising an accusatory eyebrow. 'I'm guessing you've just realised what a twat you've been then,' she said bluntly.

'Yep,' he answered, not even bothering to try to deny it.

'What is *wrong* with you?' she asked, holding her arms out in question. 'Why would you even jump to that conclusion?' As she watched him flounder, unable to answer the question, she tutted and rolled her eyes. 'Oh, come on. Let's have a strong drink and talk.'

Tanya went to the kitchen and pulled out a bottle of whisky, pouring them each a generous measure whilst Freddie slumped down tiredly into an armchair in the lounge. Handing his glass over, Tanya curled up on the sofa nursing hers and waited.

Freddie shot her a grateful look. He and Tanya went back a long way, and for the last few years she had been one of his closest friends. They cared for the same people, thought the same way and both understood the underworld from a unique perspective. They were like two peas in a pod at times. And even now, when she had every right to be pissed off at him, she was still there to listen. He appreciated that more than she knew.

'Before I went away,' he started, 'I was confident that I knew everything, you know? I knew who to trust, I trusted my instincts, I was always a step ahead... And then we got caught out. And I know that's just how it is sometimes. No matter how good you are, the odds are still high. It's the risk we take. But I just wasn't expecting it.' Freddie frowned and took a sip of his whisky. 'And that...' He sighed. 'If I'm honest, that scared the fuck out of me. Not prison itself. The not-seeing-it-coming. Because that meant that my confidence was all just false security.'

'No, Freddie, it wasn't,' Tanya said, shaking her head in disagreement. 'You can't think like that. That capture was a big one, granted. But, mate, it was just bad luck. They got lucky. Look at all the hundreds of times they didn't. You have always been a step ahead, always beaten the odds. You can't let one bit of bad luck make you question everything. Especially the people closest to you.' Tanya shook her head sadly. 'I honestly never thought I'd see the day you turned on Anna. I really didn't.'

'I just don't understand why she didn't tell me,' Freddie replied. 'Why all the secrecy? You're right, I shouldn't have jumped to

the conclusion that I did; I'm not denying that,' he added, 'but I still don't get why it was kept from me. Ethan's my son – I'd do anything for him, to protect what's his.'

'Freddie, you didn't give her a chance,' Tanya shot back. 'Not being funny, but you've been out five minutes. We've all been waiting and allowing you the time to get back up to speed, because there's just so damn much. You've got back in the clubs – great. You've picked up the new routes, the new supplier routines, the new protection clients – brilliant. You've been re-familiarising yourself with everything as you go. But not once have you asked to sit down and go through the accounts yet. When you were ready to do that, Anna was going to explain it all. But she wasn't going to just throw the whole lot at you at once, was she? *Oh, here's your kingdom, here's everything that's happened in the last few years, off you trot!*

Tanya pulled a face, showing him just how ridiculous the idea was, and Freddie sighed heavily.

'I guess not,' he said.

'She was never hiding anything from you,' Tanya continued. 'She was just waiting for the right time. And now you've gone and royally fucked it all up.'

'Yeah, alright, Tan,' Freddie replied sharply. 'I'm more than aware of that, thank you.'

'So what are you going to do?' she asked.

Freddie shook his head. 'I honestly don't know.'

There was a long silence. Freddie stared off into the distance and Tanya watched him, biting her lip as she wondered whether to voice what she was thinking. Pushing her long red hair back over her shoulder, she decided to go for it.

'Freddie, she still loves you, you know. She tried to tell you, but…' She trailed off.

'I know,' Freddie groaned, rubbing his face. 'I thought it was a game; I thought she was playing me.'

'Oh for fuck's sake,' Tanya snapped. 'Prison really did do a number on you, didn't it? Anna playing *you*? Jesus.' She shook her head.

'Well, I realise that now,' Freddie responded. He thought back to Anna's words, to how much it must have taken her to talk about it after the way he had treated her, and he felt his insides twist up in guilt. 'I need to talk to her,' he said finally.

'You can try, but I'm not sure it will help,' Tanya said honestly. 'She would have forgiven a lot of things, Freddie, and I think she even would have tried to get back on track if you'd felt the same. But this time you might have finally gone too far. I've never seen her so angry, and, well, heartbroken.'

Freddie nodded. Downing his whisky, he pulled himself forward and stood up. 'Thanks for the drink. I've got to go.'

However pressing the issue with Anna was, he also had a raid to plan, and he needed to focus on it. There was going to be a lot of firepower in the stand-off, however well they executed it, and no doubt casualties. They had to be on top form.

'I *will* deal with this, OK? I'll sort it out. I just need to deal with Aleksei first.'

Tanya nodded. 'Do you need anything from me and Anna?' she asked. 'Whatever the situation is between you, we're still on the same side when it comes to business, you know,' she added, seeing the look on his face.

Smoothing his jacket, Freddie pulled himself upright and forced his head back in the game. 'All I want is for you two to steer clear of CoCo and Aleksei's little corner tonight. It's going to get ugly.' Striding through to the hall, he called back over his shoulder, 'We're going to sort these Russian fuckers out once and for all. And then maybe we can all get back to working out what normal life is again.'

CHAPTER FORTY-FOUR

The next day, Anna strode into Club Anya dressed to kill and with an expression to match. Carl caught sight of her and blinked, unsure what had put his boss in such a fierce mood. He frowned and put down the bottle of rum he'd been holding.

'Hey, you OK?' he asked.

Anna's murderous glare swept round towards him and he almost stepped back. Blinking, Anna adjusted her expression and gave him a tight, apologetic smile.

'Sorry, got a lot on my mind.'

'Clearly,' Carl answered. 'Do you want to talk about it?' He had become close over the years with both Anna and Tanya and at times stepped into the role of agony uncle, though more so with Tanya. Tanya liked to share her woes, talk them out across the bar, seek advice when she was troubled. Anna on the other hand rarely opened up, but he always offered anyway, so that she knew he was there.

'No, I'm fine. Thanks, Carl,' she replied.

He nodded. It was the answer he'd expected. 'Let me know if you want a drink. You going to the office? Seamus is in there, waiting for you.'

'Seamus?' Anna repeated with a frown.

'Yeah, said he had to tell you something urgently.'

'Thanks, Carl,' she replied, already walking towards the office.

It wasn't that it was strange, Seamus seeking her out here – he often had over the last few years whilst she'd been his boss. But now Freddie was back, and given the power games he'd been playing with her, Seamus, along with most of the others, seemed to seek her out a lot less. She hadn't been expecting him here at all tonight.

Opening the door, she found him perched tensely on the edge of the sofa. He stood up immediately, nodding to her in respect. She smiled, the first genuine smile she'd given out all day. She and Seamus had always had a good relationship from when he'd first joined Freddie as little more than a boy. Not many people had known how to help her, when life got tough. She wasn't one for talking about her feelings like Tanya, or drinking her sorrows into oblivion like many she knew. But Seamus had understood. He'd helped her get over some of the hardest times in her life by channelling all her damage and her rage into boxing. He'd seen her struggle and had shown her the path he always took when things were hard, being much the same way himself. She would be forever grateful to him for that.

'Seamus,' she greeted him. 'Is everything OK?' She gestured for him to sit back down and took her own seat behind the desk.

'I'm not sure, to be honest,' he answered, taking his place on the edge of the sofa once more. His brow furrowed into a frown. 'I've been watching Aleksei's place in preparation for the raid tonight.'

Anna nodded. She knew all about the plans to take Aleksei out tonight. What she wasn't sure about was why Seamus was here talking to her about it. She and Tanya had been kept out of it all. This sort of thing, she had to agree, was Freddie's territory. 'But while I was there, I saw something strange. And I thought it best to come to you,' he said carefully.

'What was it?' Anna asked, frowning.

'Your friend Josephine, that manages your whorehouse...'

Seamus exhaled heavily. 'She was there last night, late.'

'Where?' Anna asked, sure she was misunderstanding him.

'At Aleksei's club,' Seamus confirmed grimly. 'She didn't know I was there – I was in the car, out of sight down the road. She was all wrapped up, trying to hide herself, but she turned my way and it was definitely her. She, well…' He tried to figure out how to word it. 'I'd recognise her anywhere. She stands out.'

Anna sat back in her chair, shocked. She stared at Seamus, unsure how to respond to that for a moment. 'You're sure?' she asked eventually.

'Positive,' he replied.

Wiping her hand down her face, Anna tried to process this. Of the truth in Seamus's words she had no doubt. She trusted him implicitly. He was also one of the most black and white people she knew. If he wasn't sure, if he even had a sliver of doubt, he would not have come to her with this.

She cast her mind back to Tanya's call. They already knew Josephine was hiding something – they just hadn't known what.

'How long was she there?' she asked.

'Not long, perhaps an hour. She went down the side alley to the back door. It must have been to get in there, because the alley is a dead end. Aleksei got there about half an hour after she arrived, then she left half an hour or so after that. She seemed upset when she left, but that's all I can tell you.'

Anna nodded. 'Who else knows about this?'

'Just me. I thought it best to talk to you first, seeing as she's one of yours,' he answered.

'Good. Can you do me a favour? Can you keep this between us, just for now?' Anna asked, her eyes pleading with him to agree. Although they all worked together now, Freddie was once again Seamus's boss and therefore his loyalty was supposed to lie there before anyone else. But this wasn't asking him to go against that, as such – she was just asking him to keep quiet. She needed time to figure this out, and if needed, to deal with it herself. Josephine was her responsibility.

Seamus thought on it for a moment, obviously weighing up his duties in his mind. In the end he nodded. 'So long as this doesn't affect anything else, I'll leave it with you,' he said carefully.

'Thank you. I will deal with this,' she promised, her eyes growing hard. 'I just need to work out exactly what we're dealing with first.'

CHAPTER FORTY-FIVE

Her nerves jangling so hard she was sure they could be heard, Josephine nodded almost imperceptibly at the man watching her from just inside an alleyway further down the busy Soho street. Aleksei told her he had placed him there for her protection, in case something went wrong and she was caught out. She turned into Club Anya and smiled a tight greeting at the bouncers as she passed. She was on her way to see Anna, just as Aleksei had planned out for her.

Inside, the club was still quiet as the day had not yet turned into evening, open to those who were in the market for a quiet drink but not yet geared up for the entertainment ahead. Carl caught her eye and smiled, walking to the end of the bar towards her.

'Hello, Josephine, I haven't seen you in ages. Fancy an Irish Car Bomb? Just trialling some variations before a hen party we've got booked tonight. I could use another guinea pig,' he said with a warm smile. His own cheeks were already rosy, suggesting he had been trialling the variations for a while already.

'I can't,' Josephine said, trying to force the strain out of her voice. 'I really need to talk to Anna.' She glanced at the office. 'Is she here?' It was an unnecessary question – she already knew Anna was here from Aleksei – but she didn't want to look suspicious.

'No worries,' Carl said in his easy way. 'Yes, she's back there.' He glanced at the door himself with a serious expression. 'Here, take this with you.' Opening the fridge, he grabbed a bottle of wine and handed it to her. 'She's probably about to come out for a top-up. She's not, er…' He scratched the back of his neck as he searched for the right words. 'I think it's been a bit of a bad day.' He glanced at Josephine and frowned. 'You don't look too happy yourself – everything OK?'

'Oh, I'm fine,' Josephine lied, quickly giving him a large, fake smile. 'Just tired.'

'You work too hard, that's your problem, Josephine,' Carl said with a grin. He handed her a fresh glass. 'Here, have one with her. You never seem to stop, you don't. Maybe you need a break, a good night out or something away from work.' He looked back to the office door. 'Perhaps you should take Anna and all. I don't know, you girls…' He shook his head. 'You all work yourself to the bone.'

'Well, you'd know a thing or two about that yourself,' Josephine replied, trying to sound jovial. She thanked him for the wine and went off to find Anna.

Knocking on the door, she waited for the invitation before opening it.

'Hi, how are you, my dear?' she said, shutting the door behind her.

'Oh, hello, Josephine,' Anna said, looking up from the papers she had been staring at for the last hour. She tried to smile but the action was forced. 'How lovely to see you.' She tried to keep her voice neutral, not wanting to alert Josephine to the fact they were on to her just yet. 'I'm fine. How are you?'

Josephine placed the bottle down on the desk and her glass next to Anna's empty one. As she leaned forward, she clocked Anna's handbag on the floor by her feet. It was open and her purse and phone were visible sitting at the top – the phone that Aleksei had told her to send the text to Freddie from. 'I'm very well, thank you. I have something to show you.'

Reaching into her voluminous floating dress, Josephine pulled out a small folded paper packet. Carefully opening it, she tipped it up and the diamonds trickled into her open hand.

Anna leaned forward to take a closer look, with interest on her face. 'They're beautiful,' she breathed. 'Is that…' She squinted and pulled the desk lamp closer.

'It is, yes. Two almost flawless yellow diamonds,' Josephine replied with a grin. 'In fact, having scaled them, I can confirm that they fall in the *fancy vivid* range, meaning' – she licked her lips excitedly – 'we'll get almost twice as much for them. These are fantastic specimens.'

Anna sighed heavily. 'These are amazing but they're going to have to wait until we find another route for them. Roman… Well, Tanya told you that he's decided not to work with us anymore, hasn't she?'

'Yes, she did, but she didn't elaborate,' Josephine replied. 'What happened? Why did he pull out?' she asked.

'Personal reasons,' Anna replied, pursing her lips. 'Anyway, don't worry about it. We'll figure it out. Just take them back to the safe for now and we'll sort them out later, OK?'

'Oh, yeah, actually I was thinking maybe you could keep these in your safe here for now,' Josephine replied, looking away. 'I have some things to do – it will save me running back. Do you mind?' It wasn't entirely true, but with the dangerous task she had ahead of her, Josephine wanted to make sure Anna had the diamonds. Who knew what would happen if things went wrong… She shook her head slightly, pushing away the thought.

'No, not at all,' Anna replied with narrowed eyes, picking them up and resealing them in the packet with care. What was Josephine playing at? Why did she want to keep the diamonds here? With all that she already knew about Josephine's connection to Aleksei, she had to treat any and all unusual behaviour as suspicious.

Standing up, she opened the small safe they kept in the office and slipped them inside, before sitting back down at the desk. She sighed tiredly and Josephine noticed the strain starting to show behind her eyes and in her unusually downturned mouth.

She bit her lip, wondering whether to ask what was wrong. Of course, she already knew what was going on between her and Freddie – everyone did – but for once, with her own problems, she wasn't sure she had any energy left to deal with someone else's.

Picking up the wine bottle, she untwisted the cap and leaned over the desk to pour them each a glass. 'Here,' she said, 'let's have one of these to celebrate the yellow diamonds and commiserate the loss of their transport.'

Stretching across the desk to hand Anna her glass, Josephine suddenly went over on one of her heels, staggering to the side as she righted herself and spilling the wine all down the front of Anna's dress. Immediately Anna leaped to her feet in shock, trying to wipe herself down. She was drenched.

'Oh my goodness!' Josephine exclaimed in horror. 'I am so sorry, Anna. Oh, Christ on a bike, I can't believe I've just done that.' She grabbed a tissue from the box Anna kept on the desk and tried, unsuccessfully, to help Anna clean herself up.

'Don't worry,' Anna replied, trying rather unsuccessfully to hide her irritation. 'It happens.'

'It does with me – I'm a right clumsy fool, I tell you. Oh, I'm so sorry – your lovely dress,' Josephine replied with a look of guilt and a tut of annoyance at herself. 'Go stand under the dryer in the ladies for a minute – that should dry you out at least.'

'Yes, I think I might have to,' Anna said resentfully, looking down at her sodden front. Leaving Josephine alone in her office was the last thing she wanted to do right now. But then again, she reasoned, there wasn't exactly much she could get up to in there for the couple of minutes she'd be away. And until she had decided what to do, she didn't want to start acting any differently than normal. With a tight smile, Anna left to go and dry herself off.

As the door closed shut quietly, Josephine breathed out a long, heavy breath. Turning back to the desk, she sat down and her eyes travelled to the phone poking out of the handbag once more. Going back over the instructions Aleksei had given her in her mind one last time, her jaw formed a hard line, her expression resolute.

CHAPTER FORTY-SIX

Freddie walked into Club CoCo and looked around at the sea of customers who were already gearing up for the evening. Tension gathered in his shoulders as he scanned their faces, half expecting to see one or more of Aleksei's men lying in wait.

One man stared back at him from a far table, where he sat alone drinking a pint of Guinness. Freddie frowned, trying to place him. He didn't think he was one of the Russians; he looked more like a local, a guy having a quiet drink, perhaps around fifty. But looks could be deceiving. And he seemed a bit out of place here. The man smiled slightly and nodded. His frown deepening, Freddie walked to the bar where his manager Gavin sat at the end working on the rotas.

'Hey, that guy over there, the one in the corner in the check shirt,' he said, turning his back to the man in question and leaning in over the bar to talk quietly. 'You seen him in here before?'

Gavin shifted slightly in his seat to look without being too obvious. 'Yeah, he's a regular, been coming the last couple of months. Bit of a loner, but no trouble. Comes in for a pint or two, then leaves. Sometimes chats to the staff if we're quiet. Why?' he asked. 'Is something wrong?'

'Nah, not at all,' Freddie said, standing back up. 'Just wondered. Thanks.' He tapped Gavin on the back and walked off upstairs to the office.

Shaking his head, he tried to get his focus back in the game. He was all over the place, seeing enemies in every corner. First

Anna and now just a regular customer who enjoyed a quiet pint. Hopefully once Aleksei was dealt with he could start getting back to normal. Because if he'd learned anything from his brief time back on the outside, it was that he was totally out of sync with the world. And that was dangerous. He couldn't hope to run a criminal empire and not get caught again without thinking straight.

Walking into the office, he greeted everyone who was already there waiting. Paul was half sitting, half leaning on the desk and his face was troubled as he nodded at something Bill said. The others sat in silence, waiting for the meeting to begin.

'What's wrong?' Freddie asked Paul as he took his seat behind the desk.

Paul exhaled heavily. 'Bill's source came through. We know why Aleksei was forced to leave Russia.'

'Well, that's good, isn't it?' Freddie replied. 'If it comes to it, it's something we can use against him, right? Use to push him into a corner and force him out. If he's got a threat over his head so serious he had to flee the country, knowing what it is right now is more valuable than fucking gold.'

No one spoke immediately and Freddie frowned, confused as to why they didn't seem happy about this. Holding a threat over Aleksei could be the key to getting this sorted for good. Tonight was going to be dangerous and violent, of that there was no doubt. Things had gone too far for it to be any other way. But if they ended up at a stand-off with Aleksei himself, this could be a make-or-break piece of information.

Bill cleared his throat. 'The other mobs Aleksei was involved with back in Russia, two of them ran some sort of neo-Nazi organisations. They had a habit of setting fire to anyone they caught in the business who didn't fall into their rigid lines of what was acceptable. Burned them to death at the stake, so I'm told. There was a third firm whose head wasn't quite so hardcore but leaned the same way.'

Bill's gaze flickered to Paul and back. 'This one caught Aleksei in an – er… awkward position, with another man. He did some digging, found out Aleksei had some private preferences that he hid from the rest of the world. Understandably, considering the views of his peers,' he added, pulling a face. 'Apparently, this guy had always wanted a piece of Aleksei's patch and he used this information to get it. He had photos, names, dates, the lot. Told Aleksei to disappear without a trace and never return or he'd hand it over to the others.'

'Oh,' Freddie said, raising his eyebrows in surprise. 'Right.'

There was a long silence as everyone waited to see what Freddie was going to say. He shook his head slowly.

'Aleksei is a lot of things and he has a lot to pay for,' he said. 'But I won't use that. Bury it.'

'Fred?' Dean piped up. 'I know it's bad, but if it's just the threat—'

'Dean, I have never made a threat that I'm not prepared to carry out in an instant,' Freddie said, cutting him off sharply. 'Never.' His hazel-green eyes turned cold as they bored into him. 'The minute you start making empty threats is the minute this world no longer takes you seriously. And I'm not going to threaten a man with handing him over to people who will burn him alive for nothing more than his sexual preferences. No matter who they are. We're organised criminals, not fucking savages. When we take him out, it will be for the right reasons.'

Paul and the others all nodded. Dean turned crimson and hung his head a little. 'Sorry, Fred,' he replied curtly.

Freddie pulled out his cigarettes and lit one. So this was why Aleksei had needed to flee so suddenly, leaving all his businesses and status behind him. It had never made sense before, when there was no legal barrier for him. But now it did. Moving here like he had, he had kept his life, his family and a good smattering of his men and girls too. He had made the best of a bad situation.

Freddie understood that completely. It was the same thing he would have done, if he had found himself in that position.

Still, that didn't change the fact that it was their ground he had stolen and it needed to be taken back. And it didn't change the fact Aleksei had tried to kill them either. For *that*, he would pay.

'Bury that information, Bill. And I don't want it discussed again outside of this room, got it?' He looked around at everyone as they nodded, blowing out a long plume of smoke. 'Good. Now as for our grievances with that Russian cunt,' he said, his tone hardening, 'he needs to go. Tonight is going to be dangerous on a few levels. Firstly, we're going in with a lot of firepower. We have the element of surprise on our side, granted, but they have a fucking arsenal at their disposal in there, and once they realise what's happening, they're going to be raining bullets back at us. We need to be accurate and quick.' He took another long drag. 'I've got bulletproof vests for all of you in the motor, but they don't cover everything. Once it starts, you need to find a position that covers you as much as possible.'

Looking around at his men, he wondered not for the first time if he was doing the right thing. The chances were that some of them would at least be hurt, if not killed. But there was no other way to get the Russians out, and now that Aleksei had turned it into a murder race, they were running out of time to get this sorted for good.

Seamus was looking slightly pale but had a brave face on, as he always did. Sammy and Bill didn't look ruffled in the slightest, but he knew underneath their calm exterior they were worried. They had been around too long and understood too much not to be worried about something like this. Dean and Simon looked as though they were gearing up for a fight, ready as always to jump into the fray without pause. Freddie exchanged a look with Paul. They had a loyal group of men in their inner circle.

'On top of this, we have to be aware of time. I've organised a staged brawl at Heaven Sent, between the girls. They'll make it look good and Sarah will make sure all the Soho units are dispatched there to deal with it so that they're out of our way when we raid Aleksei's.'

Simon chuckled. 'Nice.'

'They're going to keep it wild for as long as possible, and we'll bail out the girls who get arrested in the morning. But this does only buy us a window, not the whole night. When people start reporting shots fired, they'll be sent back our way quickly. Now I can't stress to you enough the importance of not getting caught.'

He and Paul exchanged a grim look. 'You all know the protocol if you do, but this is one you really don't want to be collared on. They know you work for us. You won't talk, I know, but they'll do whatever they can to force you to – and that means, with something as serious as gun charges, they'll slam you away for a very, *very* long time.'

The room fell into a sombre silence as everyone thought this over.

'So no matter what,' Paul continued, 'you get the fuck out of there and away. We calculated that we have ten minutes from the first shot, to stay on the safe side. You need to be gone by then. Even if we aren't done.'

Freddie's phone pinged, indicating that he had a new message and he picked it up to see who it was. Anna. Skimming the text, he frowned slightly and slipped it into his pocket.

'I've got to go out for a bit. Paul will sort you out with the vest and the plan of action for when we arrive. We meet back here ready to go in two hours. Got it?'

He stood up and shrugged his arms into his jacket, nodding as everyone voiced their agreement.

'Right. See you then.'

Marching out of the office, Freddie felt his insides twist anxiously. Anna wanted to meet up to talk. But was this going to be a good talk – or the one where she told him where to go for good?

CHAPTER FORTY-SEVEN

Josephine jumped as the sirens on a police car were turned on as it passed right beside her. She put her hand to her chest to calm her racing heart. Already she felt like a hunted criminal and nothing had even happened yet. Closing her eyes, she swallowed and breathed out slowly, before continuing on down a quiet, dimly lit side street.

It was at the bottom of this road, the building site in which Aleksei was setting his trap. As she walked, her heels tapping loudly on the pavement the only sound around her, the dark carcass of the half-constructed building loomed up ahead. The sun had just about set and the street lights began to sputter to life, one by one. She had to admit, he had picked the site well for what he had planned. There was hardly anything around, other than another building site and some derelict homes that were scheduled to be torn down. No one would be around to see a thing.

As she approached the entrance, she saw the two men Aleksei had left guarding the front in their car. They nodded to her as she passed through the unlocked gates, without question. Letting them swing shut behind her, Josephine swallowed, looking up to where a dim light shone out from the fourth floor.

She trod on the roughly poured cement stairs, clinging tightly to the flask she held in her hand and holding the wall in the absence of a stair rail, and made her way up to where she had seen the light. The wind rushed through the building, with no outer walls and very few inner walls to stop its path, and she pushed the strands of hair that escaped her high, intricate updo, behind her ears. The sound of the sledgehammer reached her before she caught sight of Aleksei swinging it at the cement pillar in the centre of the floor, near a lantern torch and mess of tools, wires and technology on the floor.

'Hello, my love,' she said, approaching with caution.

Aleksei turned, surprised to see her there. 'Jojo! This is no place for you – what are you doing here?' he asked.

Josephine smiled. 'I was curious,' she replied. 'I wanted to see it for myself before it all goes down. And,' she admitted, 'I just needed to see you. I feel so anxious and pained.' She put her fist to her chest, where a knot of worry seemed to have lodged itself. 'I just needed to hear you tell me it's going to be OK.'

Aleksei sighed and pulled her into his arms, putting his forehead to hers in comfort. She felt tense under his grip, and he stroked her head soothingly. 'It is all going to be OK,' he said. 'This is for the greater good of everyone.' He pulled back and gave her a reassuring smile. 'You need to go home now.'

Josephine nodded, smiling sadly at him. 'I know. I just wanted to see you.' Her gaze wandered to the sledgehammer and she tilted her head to the side. 'What are you doing up here anyway?'

'Well—' Aleksei turned to show her. 'The dynamite charges have all been buried in the pillars on the ground and first floors. This should ensure the building starts to collapse. There is only the cement skeleton right now, no walls to hinder its fall, but there are ways to help the collapse along on the higher levels. Cracking the cement in the pillars up here now will mean they break down quicker when the charges go off.' He shrugged. 'It makes it more efficient. And, of course, quicker. Chances are they will not feel a thing,' he added to be kind. In truth, he didn't care how slowly they died, but he knew that Josephine did, with her soft heart.

She nodded, her expression sombre. 'So how does it all get set off? I mean, you will be far away, won't you?' she asked, biting her lip anxiously.

'Of course, my sweet Jojo,' he replied, laughing fondly. 'You do not need to be worried about me. I have the charges hooked up to an electrical wire. At the end of it is a detonator. This is linked to the wireless remote you see there.' He pointed at a small handheld remote on the ground with the rest of his tools. 'I then press the button from a safe distance, where I shall be watching to make sure it works, and then I shall leave. There will be no trace that we were even here.'

Josephine stared at the remote for a moment, her expression still worried. Eventually she turned back to Aleksei with a wobbly smile. 'As long as you're OK, that's all that matters. Anyway, look, I made you some soup. I know you won't have time to think of food tonight. I guess it's probably not your biggest priority right now, but' – she shrugged – 'it kept me busy for a while.'

'That is sweet of you; thank you, my love,' Aleksei replied with a fond smile. She was playing the dutiful wife already, clearly looking forward to the future he had promised her.

'It's an old recipe my grandmother used to make; it's the first time I've tried it. You'll have to tell me if you like it,' she said with a tired smile.

'I will do that,' he replied. 'Now come, my Jojo, go home. Your part is done.'

'Yes, of course,' she said, leaning down to place the flask of soup by the rest of his things on the floor. Straightening up, she stared at him for a moment, then stepped forward and hugged him tight, kissing his neck and nuzzling into it. 'I love you so very much, my Aleksei. So, so much.'

'I know that; I love you too,' he said, gently prising her off him. 'Come on now – go and relax and I will see you later, OK?'

Women had always been a mystery to Aleksei, but especially Josephine. Her emotions ranged wildly and crazily. And strangely, unlike the others, it was something he loved about her. But he still could never understand what drove a woman's moods.

Josephine leaned in and kissed him one last time. 'Yes, OK. I'll see you later.' Touching his face, she turned and walked away, back the way she came.

Staring after her for a moment, Aleksei shook his head. She was an enigma, his Josephine. As he looked down to the flask of soup she had left, his eye was drawn to the pile of tools he had been working with.

With a frown that deepened with each passing second, he looked back up to the empty entrance to the stairwell. The remote to the detonator was gone.

CHAPTER FORTY-EIGHT

Freddie paused as he reached the building and closed his eyes for a second, pinching the bridge of his nose. Life had been one big whirlwind since coming out of prison and everything seemed to be spiralling downward out of his control; even the things that were of his own doing. And the biggest of these issues was his relationship with Anna.

Aleksei he could deal with. He had spent his whole life dealing with men like him, in one form or another. That came with the territory. It was dangerous, sure, and it had to be executed perfectly if they were going to come out of this on the right side. But it could be done. Anna, on the other hand... He had wronged her in a way he had never been so stupid as to wrong anyone close to him before. Never, in all his years at the top of this game, had he so badly misjudged a situation. The friends and family surrounding him had all earned their place. They had been there for him, had his back and shown true loyalty, Anna included. Yet he had turned on her at the first unexplained piece of information he'd found. He'd treated her like an outsider, with distrust and disdain. And he had no idea how he was going to be able to put that right.

With a deep breath, Freddie rolled his shoulders back and walked into the club with purpose. Not stopping, he walked straight through to the back, knocked on the office door and walked in.

Anna looked up from her desk as he entered, tired rings around her eyes as she pulled together the last of the papers in front of her. She didn't smile or offer any greeting. Freddie supposed that was fair enough. He didn't exactly deserve a red-carpet welcome after what he'd accused her of. Sitting down on the seat opposite her, he unbuttoned his jacket and waited.

After a long, tense silence, Anna began to talk. 'I've collated all of the above-board accounts into a simple spreadsheet and written up a handover, which is all on here.' She tapped the closed laptop beside her. 'I've included all of the updates you haven't yet got to for the legitimate companies as well.'

Freddie frowned. *Why was she writing up handovers?*

'The other set of accounts should be fairly clear; I used your own codes throughout and there's nothing new that shouldn't be self-explanatory, though if you need to question anything, Tanya is up to speed.'

'Tanya? Why would I need to talk to Tanya about the accounts?' Freddie asked, a stone sinking in his stomach as he began to realise what Anna was doing.

'You've sacked Roman,' Anna continued, ignoring his question. 'So as far as shipping is concerned, you've already taken that back under your own control. The parlours, protection and drugs have been run by your men alongside me over the last few years, so there's nothing they can't tell you about any of the changes there, and everything else you're already up to speed on. The flat is half yours.' For the first time since she began talking, she looked at him properly, and Freddie saw her eyes harden. 'But we cannot go on as we have been, both living there. It's not fair on us and it's not fair on Ethan.'

'Anna—' Freddie tried to interject, shaking his head with a frown, but she cut him off.

'If that means we have to sell, then so be it. But I would rather buy you out. I have the money available – from my own businesses, not taken from yours,' she added in a sharp, sarcastic tone. 'And I would like, if you will agree, to continue living there with Ethan.' Seeing the look of shock on Freddie's face, Anna tried to soften her tone. 'I'm not trying to play games. I'm not Jules,' she said, referring to Ethan's birth mother. 'But Ethan has been through a lot in his short years and right now he's settled. That is his home and I am the only stable parent he has ever known.'

Freddie sat back, recoiling from the sting in Anna's words. He watched as she looked down and saw she took no pleasure in saying that to him. He swallowed the retort that immediately sprang to mind and tried to push aside the pain that her comment brought. Anna was right, whether he liked it or not.

'That isn't your fault,' she continued. 'But it is the current situation. I'm just trying to be realistic. If you decide to take him, I won't stand in your way,' she said, her voice cracking. 'He's your son by blood, and I'm only his stepmother.' She stopped to swallow the lump in her throat. It killed her to say this, but she knew she had no choice. She just had to pray that Freddie would see reason and let Ethan stay where he was settled and secure. 'I'm not trying to be selfish, and I'm not trying to keep him from you. But I love him dearly and I want what's best for him.'

'Anna…' Freddie bent forward and rubbed his hands over his head in stress. 'We don't have to do this.' He watched as her expression began to close off. 'Look, please,' he beseeched. 'I fucked up. Big time. And I can't begin to work out how I'm going to make that up to you. But just give me a chance,' he asked. He held her stare levelly.

Anna watched him, saw the truth behind his eyes, glimpsed the real Freddie for the first time since he had come out of prison and felt the familiar tug in her heart as her gaze met with his. Breaking eye contact, she cast her eyes down and mentally pulled herself back.

A glimpse of who he used to be wasn't enough. She had no idea who he was anymore, and after all this time bending over backward to protect him, watch over his businesses, raise his son and be there no matter how hard and terrifying it was, she couldn't do it anymore. Not after he'd turned on her the way he had. What was to say he wouldn't do it again? She no longer trusted in the unshakeable bond she'd thought they once had. And her heart was too fragile to keep being broken by the same situation over and over again.

She had thought that the heartbreak of losing him was the worst thing she would ever go through. Then she'd thought the pain of the cold rejection he'd given her when she'd tried to open up about her feelings was the last time it would happen. But then he had called her out as an enemy, making up reasons in the shadows. *That* had been the last straw.

They would always be bound by Ethan, but other than that she needed a clean break. It was time to walk away and at least try to start getting over him.

'My mind is made up, Freddie,' she said tiredly, standing up. 'I can't do this anymore. Let me know what you decide with regards to the flat and Ethan.' She walked to the door and opened it, then looked back over her shoulder. 'Everything you need for the business is there. Collect it together and see yourself out. As of now, I'm no longer anything to do with it.'

Forcing herself through the door, Anna held her head high and strode out through the club and onto the street. Without stopping to acknowledge the bouncers, she turned and carried on walking, quickly losing herself in the crowd of people in the busy area.

Finally letting the tears fall – now that she was just an anonymous woman walking through a busy city – she let the heartache flow out of the tightly locked box she usually forced it into. There was so much going on, so much at stake, that it felt like there was a hurricane raging around her head.

Ethan meant more to her than anyone. The lost, neglected, scared little boy who had come to them just a few years before needing to be loved had become her son in all but blood. The bond that had formed between them when she finally took him under her wing was stronger than anything she'd ever felt. Being his mother had changed her in ways she never knew she could change.

And she had worked so hard for the business over the last few years, had thought she had carved herself out a permanent place in the underworld. She had evolved there, incredibly so, hardened to such a point that she no longer fitted into the normal world. But the price to stay in the game was too high. Because it meant staying near Freddie, seeing him each day, a man she still loved with all of her dark heart but who had let her down badly and who she no longer knew or trusted to have her back when the chips fell. And that was integral, in this way of life. Without that – without trusting those around you – you had nothing.

Wiping the tears off her cheek, she pushed forward, walking towards the bridge she always went to when she needed to clear her head. No matter what happened, the bridge was always there – the bridge would never let her down.

There was a lot still to do tonight, but right now she had to just press pause for a few minutes and try to come to terms with her decision. What was done was done. It was time to forge a new path, a new life that no longer included, or depended on, Freddie Tyler.

CHAPTER FORTY-NINE

A while later, Anna stepped out of the cab onto the dark, dimly lit street and paid the driver. As he drove off, she made her way to the corner of the side street where Tanya had said to meet her. As she passed the last darkened doorway of a dreary-looking computer shop, she jumped as Tanya walked out from the shadows.

'Christ, you nearly gave me a heart attack,' she whispered.

'Sorry, just thought I'd best stay out of sight until you got here,' Tanya answered.

'So tell me what's happened so far,' Anna said urgently.

'She got here and went up that road there,' Tanya said, gesturing towards the entrance to the side road. 'She nodded to the two men in the car opposite the entrance to a building site, then went in. I couldn't get close enough to check without showing myself, but I'm guessing they're Aleksei's men.'

Anna formed a grim expression. 'What the hell is she doing?' she muttered.

Tanya sighed heavily, 'I'm guessing he's the married guy she's been keeping so secret.'

Anna raised a sceptical eyebrow.

'Well, think about it,' Tanya pressed. 'It's the only logical explanation. She's our friend, she's practically family. I can't see her doing something like this for any other reason.'

'I guess that would make the most sense. But what is *this* exactly?' Anna asked.

Tanya shook her head slowly, 'I really don't know.'

Anna nodded, her jaw forming a hard line. 'Well, all we know for sure is that Aleksei is the enemy. He's already tried to kill Freddie and Paul – he even made an attempt on Seamus. So buddying up to him in any way is flat-out treachery.' She moved to the mouth of the road and peered down it.

The building site ran from the other side of the street, all the way down the road to the other end where the entrance and the car with Aleksei's men sat. A makeshift wall had been erected all the way around, blocking the view of whatever lay within and showing no other obvious entrance. Reaching into her pocket, Anna pulled out a small handgun.

Tanya gasped and clapped her hand to her mouth. 'What the fuck are you doing with that?' she exclaimed in a horrified whisper.

'Honestly, I'm not entirely sure yet. But I figured it was best to come prepared,' she replied.

Anna's face displayed a resolute calmness that she didn't feel inside. On the inside, her heart was hammering against her chest at the thought of walking into an unknown situation with no backup other than a gun, which she wasn't exactly relishing the thought of using. But it had to be done. Josephine was *her* responsibility, no one else's. And if Josephine was betraying them all, then it was she who had to deal with it. As a boss in the darkness of the underworld, you couldn't choose which parts of the jobs to take responsibility for and which to shy away from.

It hadn't been hard to get the gun. She knew about the shipment of guns Freddie had taken from Aleksei – she had arranged the whole thing. She just didn't know where it was. But Seamus did. He had gone and taken one from the pile for her, assuring her that there were more than enough for Freddie's plans that night, and that one less wouldn't make any difference.

Checking it was loaded and that the safety was securely on, Anna placed it back in her pocket, then, biting her lip, she turned to Tanya.

'Listen, Tan, I want you to stay here…'

'What?' Tanya exclaimed. 'No way!'

'Yes,' Anna insisted. 'I need you to be on lookout. As far as we know those men down there are Aleksei's. If they leave the car and come inside, I need to know. If more turn up, or even if Aleksei himself turns up, I need eyes out here. Right now, other than Josephine, we have no idea who or what is in there.' Her eyes pleaded with Tanya to listen to reason.

Tanya ran her hand through her long red hair, agitated. 'I really don't think you should be going in there on your own,' she argued.

'Well, that's what's happening,' Anna replied forcefully. If she ended up in trouble, the last thing she wanted was to drag Tanya into it with her. 'Look' – she softened her tone a little – 'I have the advantage at the moment. Josephine won't be expecting me to be in there. It's also dark and it's a building site. There will be loads of places to hide. I just need to find out what she's doing.'

'Eugh, for fuck's sake, Anna,' Tanya hissed. She knew she wasn't going to win this one. At times, Anna could be the most stubborn person she'd ever met. 'Well, you keep your phone in your hand,' she demanded. 'And if I call you, you pick up. Because it will be to warn you. You got that?'

'Loud and clear,' Anna replied.

'Well…' Tanya sighed, annoyed. 'How are you going to get in?' she asked, looking over towards the building site.

'I'm going to have to climb over one of the boundary walls,' Anna replied, squinting to see how high they were. They weren't too high. 'Unless we can break through it somehow. Doesn't look that sturdy.'

'Doesn't look it, but it is. That's plywood slotted in between fence posts that are dug deep. You've got no chance,' Tanya answered.

Anna glanced at her with a raised eyebrow.

'What?' she continued. 'I dated a builder for over a year. What do you think he had to talk about for all that time? It weren't the status of the stock market, I can tell you that much.'

'OK, well, you'll have to give me a leg-up round the side. They won't see us from the car there,' Anna replied. 'Come on.'

Careful not to look suspicious as they crossed the road, they moved as quickly as they could down the side of the site until they were sure they were well out of view. Tanya stopped and crouched down slightly, lacing her fingers together and offering them out to Anna as a boost.

Anna placed her foot firmly in Tanya's grasp, suddenly wishing she'd had time to change into her gym gear before coming over. But there had been no time. Tanya pulled a face as she too clocked Anna's heels.

'Well, it's too late now,' Anna muttered in answer. Hoisting herself up, Anna peered over the edge and looked around. A few feet to the left there were a stack of boxes piled up against the wall. 'Let me down a sec,' she whispered to Tanya, who was grunting slightly with the effort of holding Anna up.

'Christ, you weigh more than you look,' she complained, rubbing her hands.

Anna walked down to where she'd seen the boxes. 'Help me up here,' she said. 'I can get down easily the other side. If you can stay here, do, as it's where I'll come back out.'

'OK.' With another grunt, Tanya pushed Anna back up again, this time further to help tip her over the edge.

Anna grabbed the top of the wooden wall surrounding the site and pulled herself up, hooking her other leg over with some difficulty in her restrictive skirt. Taking the rest of her weight, she hesitated on the top for a moment, locking eyes with Tanya, before disappearing over the edge into the darkness beyond.

CHAPTER FIFTY

Josephine moved down the darkened stairwell as quickly as she dared, unable to see the rough edges and building-site debris that was scattered everywhere. She squinted as she went, wishing she'd thought to bring a torch of some sort. A clattering sounded somewhere to her right as she reached the second floor and she froze, her eyes wide with fright as she stared into the dark abyss. With a small shudder, she turned to start down the next flight and screamed out in terror as she was met with a shadowy figure blocking her way.

'Oh my life, Aleksei! You nearly gave me a heart attack in this creepy place.' Josephine put her hand to her chest and stepped back slightly.

Aleksei didn't move and his unreadable expression didn't change. 'Why did you come here, Josephine?' he asked, his voice calm and deadly in the silence.

Her breath caught in her throat as she sensed the underlying tension and her heart rate began to rise again. 'You know why. I told you,' she answered brightly. 'I just wanted to see you and hear you tell me everything was going to be OK.'

Aleksei still didn't move, and Josephine realised with a sinking feeling of fear that he wasn't buying it. Somehow he knew. She took a deep breath and began walking slowly around him in a wide arc.

'Come on – let's go outside if you're done. I don't like it in here; it's too dark and messy.' She looked pointedly at all the piles of rubbish and equipment that the men who worked there had left lying around.

'Where is the remote for the detonator, Josephine?' Aleksei asked.

'What?' Josephine feigned ignorance as she tried to work out how to wriggle out of the corner she was in, but her tone sounded fake even to her.

'The remote,' Aleksei repeated. 'I don't understand why you would take it. What game are you playing, Jojo?' He stepped towards her and she stepped back, further into the building.

Her heart was now beating wildly against her chest as she began to panic. The look in Aleksei's eye had already left her with no doubt that he wasn't buying her casual innocence for even a moment. She was in deep shit. Casting her eyes down and attempting to look contrite, she tried a different tactic.

'Oh, Aleksei, I just can't bear the thought of all this murder. It's eating me up, especially now that I'm involved. Can we not just sit down and talk this through? Please, my love, for me?' She forced a wobbly smile, trying to appeal to his love for her.

'Josephine,' he groaned, rubbing his face in annoyance. 'We have been through this and I do not want to have to go over it again. This is the way things are. You have done your part, and now it is time I do mine. I do not have time for you to have cold feet.'

Josephine nodded, her head still bowed. 'Perhaps we can just talk it through though, one last time. Let's go sit back upstairs and talk it out. And you can eat your soup. You must be hungry after all the physical work you've been doing today.' Her eyes flickered up to Aleksei's face and down again.

There was a short pause and Josephine waited, her whole body tensed. She cursed herself for taking the remote. It had been a stupid move.

Aleksei narrowed his eyes. 'Fine. Let's go upstairs and talk. And then we can get on. Yes?'

'Yes, of course. Thank you,' Josephine replied, letting him guide her back up the stairs.

They reached the floor Aleksei had been working on, and he bent down and picked up the flask before twisting off the lid. He pulled it to his nose. 'Mmm,' he murmured in appreciation. 'It smells good.'

Josephine nodded with a smile and cast her eyes away. Her anxiety was beginning to overwhelm her and now all she wanted to do was go home.

'Here, you have some first,' Aleksei continued, holding the flask out with a sudden hard glint in his eye.

Josephine blinked as she turned back to him, shocked. 'Me? Oh, I've already eaten,' she lied. 'I'm not hungry. It's all yours.'

'I insist,' Aleksei replied, holding her gaze and raising one cold eyebrow in challenge.

Josephine swallowed and felt her cheeks begin to burn. She hoped it was too dark for him to notice. 'I really don't feel like it; I had some earlier. Please, just try some and let me know what you think.' She cursed herself silently as she heard the frightened wobble in her voice. His expression was growing darker by the second. She must have given herself away somehow.

Suddenly Aleksei leaped forward and grasped the back of her neck, pushing the open flask towards her face as she let it out a terrified yelp. 'I said, *I insist*,' he snarled. 'Eat it. *Now!*'

'No!' Josephine screamed, twisting away and knocking the flask out of his hand in terror.

As it clattered to the floor, the soup seeping out into a puddle, there was a heavy silence. Josephine's eyes widened with horror as she realised she had all but confirmed that the soup was poisoned. In truth, it wasn't even her grandmother's recipe. She had hated her grandmother. It was just a tin of Campbell's, but she had added something extra, something that she didn't dare put to her own mouth.

Aleksei seemed to swell up with rage in front of her eyes. He looked at her, shaking his head in disbelief.

'You poisoned it,' he accused.

Looking at the shocked sense of betrayal playing out on his face between angry contortions, Josephine's shoulders dropped along with the pretence.

'Aleksei, I love you so very much, for all that you are. But that doesn't mean I don't *see* all that you are. You're so hungry for war and power, and you don't care who you have to trample over to get it. And I accepted that – I knew that before I had even met you,' Josephine said honestly. She held her arms out in an open shrug before they dropped to her sides. 'But then you pulled me into your games. You made me part of what you were doing and you gave me no choice.' The tears began to fall down her face. 'I know how you work. I know that if I refused, you'd just kill me too.'

'What?' Aleksei cried, outraged. 'I would *never* have done that to you,' he said, taking a step towards her.

Josephine stepped back. This was no more than a game now – she had set the stakes and she needed to keep a careful distance between them.

'Don't lie, Aleksei. Not now,' she said softly, shaking her head. 'We both know I'm right. So I couldn't refuse you. But I also couldn't betray the only family who have ever loved me.'

'Family,' Aleksei scoffed. 'They are not your *family*, Josephine; they are just people who pay you to do the work they can't be bothered to do themselves,' he spat. 'And you would *kill me* for them? Is that what they told you to do?'

'No.' Josephine shook her head. 'They don't know any of this. And they would never ask me to kill you, Aleksei, or anyone else for that matter. That's the big difference between them and you.' She took a deep breath, seeing the murder set into his eyes, the resolution that she now had to be dealt with. 'I love you, my darling,' she said emotionally between tears. 'More than you know. But I will not become your puppet. And if I have to choose between protecting those who protect me and helping those who try to force me to hurt people I love, I choose them.'

'Well,' Aleksei said, shaking with rage. 'That was a very bad decision. But I can promise you it is the last bad decision you will ever make.'

As he lunged towards her, Josephine picked up her long skirt and ran like the wind into the darkness of the room beyond.

CHAPTER FIFTY-ONE

Freddie, Paul and eleven more of their closest and most loyal men sat silently in the dark in the back of a van Bill had stolen for the occasion. No one talked or joked, the way they often did before a job. This time the danger was much higher and there were a lot more elements involved that were out of their control. Freddie spoke to Bill through the metal grate separating the back from the front seats.

'Where are we on the cameras?' he asked.

'I've got the dampener ready to go. We should wait until the last minute, because once I set it off, the signal will die on all the cameras in the street, including the ones in their club. It could tip them off that something's up,' he replied. 'Once we start I'll keep it on until we're well away. None of us should show up on anything.'

'Good. Well…' Freddie glanced back at the group of men. 'Still keep your balaclavas up just in case. We don't need any witness statements describing things like the shit tattoo you got on your neck in Scarborough when you were sixteen.'

Dean snorted and nudged Simon with his shoulder.

'Yeah, alright,' Simon responded irritably. 'Like the one on your arse is any better.'

There was a small wave of laughter and Dean crossed his arms moodily.

Freddie's phone vibrated and he looked down at the message on the screen. It was from Sarah. She was in the station, checking off all units as they left to go and deal with the brawl he had arranged at Heaven Sent. He read the one-word text.

Go.

'It's time,' Freddie said with a grim expression. 'Everyone ready?' He watched as everyone nodded. 'Remember, no more than ten minutes from the first shot, no matter what. Check your watches. You get out here and into this van, OK? After ten minutes this van leaves, just after Bill comes in. If you're late for some reason, you get the fuck out of here and go underground any way you can. Then you meet at the rendezvous point. Got it?'

'Got it, yep,' they all replied in quiet chorus.

Checking once more that his gun was loaded and ready to go, Freddie pulled the balaclava down over his face. Locking eyes with Paul – who looked as grim as he felt – he sent a silent prayer up to the heavens that this would not go completely tits up and then banged on the metal grate twice. Bill pulled the van off and down the road, stopping right outside the front door of the club.

'Go!' Freddie yelled.

He yanked open the door and all the men save for Bill steamed forward, jumping out of the van and in through the front door of the club. As they fanned out and people began to stare at the large group of masked men, Freddie pointed his gun to the roof and let off a single shot.

'Everybody out,' he roared.

Immediately all the customers who had been gearing up for a good night began to run for the door, Freddie's men shouting and pushing them on their way, pointing their guns at anyone who paused. The strippers swiftly ran out the back, scared but not entirely terrified. They had been working for Aleksei for a long time – this wasn't their first rodeo. The barmen held up their hands and shuffled out of the building as they realised that the masked men were not interested in them at all.

As all this was happening, Freddie clocked the group of men in the booth at the rear of the room. One of them disappeared out the back, probably to collect backup, and the others leaped forward towards Freddie and his men, pulling out their own guns.

'They're tooled,' Freddie shouted out just as the first shot was fired from the other side.

His head spun round to see if it had hit anyone, but luckily it hadn't. He shot back and missed the shooter by inches. Everyone on both sides ducked down behind whatever furniture they could as the Russians began shouting at each other in their own language. Freddie wished he could understand what they were saying. One thing was for sure though: they had definitely taken them by surprise.

From where he was crouched behind a table that had been knocked over in the initial panic, Freddie saw that he was just a couple of feet from the end of the bar. If he could get behind it, he could sneak up much closer to the Russians without being seen.

'Where's Aleksei?' he shouted across the room. A shot was fired back and hit the wall behind him.

'Preparing your funeral, you English pig,' came the retort.

Freddie locked gazes with Paul across the room and signed as best he could, asking him to cause a distraction. Paul nodded and whispered to Sammy, who was next to him. Carefully peering round the bottom of the stage where they had ducked, they began firing. Following suit, Seamus and some of the others that side of the room joined in, and as the Russian fire and attention was drawn away from him, Freddie made the leap into the bar.

As he landed on his knees there, he winced. His shoulder was far from healed and he had unstrapped it for the occasion. Gritting his teeth, he tried to ignore the throbbing that came from the wound. Now was no time to think about that – he couldn't lose focus for even a moment. Crawling forward down the bar – careful not to make any noise big enough to draw attention to himself – Freddie checked his watch. It had been nearly four minutes already. He gritted his teeth and sped up. If he could get behind them, it might offer him an opportunity.

The sound of the back door opening made Freddie freeze for a moment. He was close but he couldn't see what was going on. If he put his head up to look it would give away his location.

'Two more,' Sammy yelled across the room, clearly for his benefit. He did a quick calculation. There had been seven of them in total, though one had left, so two coming back made that eight men now. Freddie's men outnumbered them.

'Move forward,' Paul shouted.

Another wave of bullets fired off and Freddie crawled the rest of the length of the bar. As he reached the end, he peered around. He was near two of them – and even had a clean shot on one of them.

'Come on then, you fuckers,' this man shouted, taking aim and sending off another round of shots. There was a cry of pain from one of his own men as it hit its mark and in anger Freddie took aim and shot the man responsible in the back.

Immediately three of the men closest to him turned and began firing back. Freddie pulled back behind the bar and winced as the sound of splitting wood made him realise his position was more precarious than he'd realised. Glass and spirits rained down on him as bullets smashed through the optics hanging above him. Reaching around, he let off another few shots in the right general direction, but he didn't dare risk looking to aim.

Taking a few deep breaths and pulling a shard of glass out of his arm, Freddie gritted his teeth and geared himself up for the next stage. If he didn't move soon, they'd come to him, and on his own as he was, he was a dead man.

'Paul,' he yelled urgently. 'Get in there.'

'Move, come on, move forward,' Paul's deep voice boomed out around the room.

With feral cries, Freddie heard his men rush in, guns still being shot from both sides. Within seconds they were upon the Russians and were fighting with their fists. Hearing this, Freddie stood with a quick turn and dived into the fray. Someone threw a well-aimed punch and he took it on the chin. Snapping his head back without pause, he landed one straight back on his attacker, then, turning again, Freddie smashed the heel of his gun into another man's head, hearing the sickening crunch of metal on bone before he went down.

As he fought, Freddie tried to quickly assess who was still with him. He knew at least one of his men had been hit, most likely more. The man he had shot lay lifeless on his side, as did another further down the room. Outnumbering the Russians by twelve to eight, it didn't take long to beat them into submission. Paul came into view, dragging one man by the scruff of his neck and threw him down into the middle of the circle their firm had formed around Aleksei's men.

Wiping blood from the corner of his mouth with his sleeve, Freddie stepped forward and kicked the nearest of these men hard. He checked his watch. They only had two minutes left.

'Where's Aleksei?' he asked sternly. When there was no answer he kicked out again, savagely. 'I *said,* where is Aleksei?' he repeated in a more aggressive tone.

'He is not here,' one of them finally answered, his head lolling around as he tried to stay conscious. 'If he was you'd have known by now. We don't know where he is – he comes and goes.'

Freddie nodded as frustration built up inside him. He believed Aleksei was not on-site. If he was here, he'd have called a hell of a lot more backup than this for a start. These guys were clearly just the B team, the ones who had been left to watch the club for the night.

Signalling to his team to wind up and leave, he turned towards the two members of his team who lay together on the floor near the door. It was Simon and another man Bill had roped in who usually worked in their protection team, called Dave. They were both clearly injured but still alert and alive, which was the main thing.

Freddie ground his teeth and quietly seethed as he walked away from the group of Russians on the floor. Leaving right now, just when they had overtaken them, was agonisingly frustrating. He really wanted to inflict some more damage here, perhaps torture one of the men until he got information he could actually use, but time was running out. They had to get out of here if they were going to ensure there were no arrests and no links back to them.

'Help me get these out,' he called, pulling Simon up and hooking his arm across his shoulders. Several others came forward and they swiftly moved the two injured men back towards the door.

'Where the fuck is Aleksei?' Freddie murmured to Paul.

With a shake of his head, Paul shrugged. 'I don't know. He should be here.'

As they reached the door, it swung open and Bill walked in with a small machine gun in his arms, his expression grim.

'Fuck me, that's heavy duty,' Simon said, bravely trying to ignore the pain of the bullet in his leg. Freddie pushed him towards the van without comment and gave Paul a nod. Hanging back, Paul stood beside Bill and waited.

As the last of their men slipped past, Bill aimed the gun high above the heads of the pile of men they had left on the floor. He pulled the trigger and wove the gun from side to side until all the lights and remaining bottles smashed into tiny fragments and the walls were littered with holes. He continued on, methodically spattering the room until no piece of furniture was left unbroken.

Stepping forward after Bill finally stopped, Paul waited for the dust to settle. He wanted them to be able to see the thunder in his eyes as he delivered their final warning.

'This is no longer Aleksei's property or his turf, and as such you are no longer welcome,' he said loudly, his voice hard and strong. 'You tell him from us, if any one of you are caught in Central London again, it will be your last day on this earth. You have twelve hours to vacate for good. Because this area belongs to the Tylers,' he roared. 'It always has and it always fucking will.'

CHAPTER FIFTY-TWO

Running through the darkness, Josephine's heart was beating so hard against her chest she was sure it was going to burst through at any moment. She was terrified – terrified of Aleksei catching her, terrified of losing her way in this darkness and terrified that at any moment she was going to accidentally run straight off the edge and fall to her death. Tears began to sting her eyes as she realised her odds of getting out of this situation were slim at best.

It was supposed to have been a simple, cut and dry operation. She'd laced the soup with the Ricin her chemist friend Thomas had made for her, meaning that even a mouthful of the soup should have ended Aleksei's life. Thomas had told her that even an amount the size of a grain of sand would have done the job. She'd poured a whole tablespoon in. If only she hadn't taken the damn remote, it would all have been OK. That had been stupid. But she'd wanted to be sure that even if he didn't drink the soup until later, he wouldn't find another way to lure the Tylers here and still carry out his plan.

Gathering her long, flowing skirt up tighter, she wished she had dressed more practically. She loved her dramatic outfits, but they were cumbersome, and tonight this one was slowing her down. At least she had chosen to wear fairly sensible shoes though, she reasoned, trying to find a positive.

Twisting around, she looked back through the darkness, trying to see how close Aleksei was behind her, but there was nothing but empty space and walls. She slowed to a stop, forcing herself to breathe more quietly so that she could listen. Cocking her head to one side, she strained her ears but all that reached them was an eerie silence.

Looking around fearfully, she tried to work out where he was. She felt like a deer being hunted in the woods, and if she knew anything at all about Aleksei it was that he was a stealthy hunter. He had often told her with pride about the hunts they would go on back in Russia, that he knew the secret to luring one's prey to where you wanted them.

Pushing on, she moved at a slower pace, being careful not to make a sound. He could be anywhere. He could be watching her right now, waiting for her to walk into the perfect trap. Tears filled her eyes as terror threatened to overwhelm her. Wiping these away angrily, she mentally slapped herself. Self-pity wouldn't get her anywhere. She needed to think.

The next room was empty – three black holes leading off where doors should have been. A pile of rubble filled one corner and a stray strand of moonlight shone on the floor just outside the last exit. It appeared to lead into another hallway, to another stairwell. This must have been how Aleksei had got down to the next floor before her earlier. The wind picked up and sent a chill down her spine, and she froze as she thought she heard a noise. Pushing forward, she decided to try the stairwell. He could be lying in wait for her, knowing this to be the natural route she would try, but then again maybe not. Perhaps he was still behind her, creeping up slowly, knowing that she'd pause as she pondered what was best to do. She needed to keep moving.

Reaching the end of the room, she peered around the edge of the partially built wall, expecting Aleksei to jump out at her at any moment, but the hallway was empty.

Holding one hand to her chest against the painful panic that was building up there, she glided over to the top of the stairs and began to descend. Reaching the third floor, she held her breath and looked around quickly, searching in the darkness for any sign of him. Still there was nothing.

Perhaps he was still by the other staircase, lying in wait, assuming that she would circle around and try to make her way back. Hoping this was the case, she set off down to the next level, faster this time. All she wanted to do was get out of this place. After that, she wasn't sure. There was only one official exit from the building site, the gate she had come in through. He may already even be there, waiting for her to run towards him. She'd run towards the back, she decided. There had to be some way of scaling the wall to get out.

Reaching the second floor, her eyes darted around again, swiftly checking that he wasn't lurking in the shadows. She was so concerned with whether or not he was on that level, she almost didn't see him crouching on the stairs leading downward. With a yelp, she pulled herself back as he lunged towards her once more. Just escaping the tips of his fingers as he reached out to grab her, she set off running through the building. This time he followed her, the loud thumps of his heavy footsteps echoing around the concrete shell.

'Give me the remote, Josephine,' he shouted furiously. 'If you give me that I will let you go.'

Picking up the pace, Josephine tried to widen the gap between them. For a few short seconds it seemed to be working – her legs were longer than Aleksei's. But then with a cry of horror, she tripped and began to fall. Grabbing out at thin air, her hand connected with a wall, and with difficulty she managed to right herself again. It seemed this was a case of too little too late however, as just as she pushed back off again, something suddenly stopped her in her tracks.

Aleksei wrapped his hand around the long skirt that flowed out behind her like a cloud and yanked her back – hard. With a resounding thud, Josephine tumbled to the ground and Aleksei!

immediately jumped on top of her so she couldn't get away. Wrapping his hands around her neck, he began to squeeze, murder in his eyes as he stared down at her, his face almost purple with rage.

'Where is the remote? Give it to me right now, you treacherous slut,' he roared.

'No, I won't,' Josephine replied with difficulty. 'Aleksei,' she begged, her voice turning to little more than a squeak under his tight grip. 'Please…'

As his hands tightened further, Josephine grappled with him, trying and failing to get him off her. She bucked and writhed, but he was too heavy and too hell-bent on killing her to be pushed off. Pulling at his arms, she scratched so hard with her nails that she drew blood, but still his vice-like grip did not falter. She tried pulling her body along the floor and managed to move a few inches, but it still made no difference.

As the oxygen withdrawal began to affect her body, spots started to blur her vision and the fight began to leave her. In this moment time seemed to pause, and Josephine looked back on all the moments that had led her to this. She couldn't believe that after all she had been through, this was how she was going to die. Would they ever find her body? Would he still let the charges go off in order to bury her, even after he realised Freddie was never coming?

As the walls began to close in, something snapped inside, like a light switching on in the dark. Her natural instinct for survival kicked in and her body refused to give up. Letting go of his hands where she had been trying to prise them off her neck, she reached out trying to find something – anything – that would get him off her. As her fingers touched the pile of rubble and registered what it was, she gripped a large chunk of cement and, with all the force she could muster in her dying body, smashed it over Aleksei's head.

The hands that had been choking her to death suddenly released her as the shock of the pain set in, and she drew in a loud and painful breath. Aleksei paused, swaying above her for a moment before, with a feral cry of rage, his hands tightened again.

'You think you can kill me?' he roared, spittle flying from his mouth onto her face as he shook with adrenaline and rage. 'You think you can kill me?' he repeated, hysteria beginning to tinge his voice. 'I will be the one killing you, Josephine,' he screamed, blood pouring down his cheek and over one eye from the wound she had inflicted on his forehead. 'You will never take another breath.'

Josephine stopped struggling, spots blurring her vision once more as she finally gave in to the darkness which was trying to claim her.

As she began to drift away there was a loud bang that seemed to echo off the walls, which brought her consciousness back around. Aleksei's fingers released her neck, and she automatically gulped air back into her oxygen-starved lungs, the action painful in her now raw throat.

Aleksei fell forward on top of her and she quickly pushed him off, still in fight mode, still unsure what was happening. He didn't put up a fight, his body slack and unmoving. She blinked, staring into his face next to hers on the floor for a moment, realising that his eyes were still open but now dead and unseeing. He was dead.

Looking up into the room as she tried to lift herself into a sitting position, she froze. Just a few feet away from them in the shadows stood Anna, with cold murder still blazing in her eyes and the gun she'd just killed Aleksei with pointed directly at Josephine's head.

CHAPTER FIFTY-THREE

An hour later the three women sat in silence around a small table in the bar area of The Sinners' Lounge, Anna's gun still where she had laid it as an open threat whilst Josephine was talking, filling them in on everything from start to finish. She had stopped talking five minutes ago, having come to the end of her very detailed tale. She hadn't bothered holding anything back, glad to finally get everything off her chest, even the bad parts.

It was luckily past closing time and therefore had been empty when they'd arrived. As Mondays were the slowest night of the week, they shut a few hours earlier than usual, for which they were all thankful tonight.

Josephine's clothes were ripped and covered in a mixture of building-site dust from the floor and Aleksei's blood. Her hair was all over the place, half of it having fallen out of her high bun in her struggle with Aleksei. Black rings were smudged around her eyes and streaks marked her cheeks where her heavy make-up had come off as she'd cried. As she stooped, defeated by the night's events, she looked more broken than ever before.

Anna stared at her, still trying to sort through the mountain of information Josephine had just relayed to them. She was a traitor, that much was certain. She'd been seeing their greatest enemy behind their backs for a long time; sneaking around and living a double life, whilst being part of a family where trust and loyalty was everything.

Tanya poured neat cherry vodka into the three glasses in front of them. They'd already had a couple, but it wasn't taking the edge off for anyone. She downed hers immediately before running her hands through her hair in despair, the stress visible on her face. She crossed her arms and waited. This was a huge shock for both of them, but for once she had no loud comments to express. The situation was too serious, and the decision as to which route they were going to take was down to Anna.

Tanya and Anna had always been equal as business partners and still were – as far as their clubs were concerned. But there had been a subtle shift in power with regards to everything else since Freddie went away. It had been Anna he had handed the reins to, not her. And therefore when it came to situations like this, it had to be Anna who led the way.

Anna ran her hand down her face and shifted in her seat. 'How long were you considering doing what Aleksei had asked you to do, before you changed your mind?' she finally asked.

'I never considered it for a moment,' Josephine replied, her eyes begging them to see that she was telling the truth. 'From the moment he said it, I was horrified at the thought. I knew I could never do it.'

'What, kill someone?' Anna asked sceptically. 'But you tried to kill Aleksei, so we all know you're not above that.' She watched Josephine flinch and fresh tears appear in her eyes at the harsh words, but she felt no flicker of remorse.

'No, not kill someone. Betray you. I knew I could never betray you. You are the family I never had. I told him, in the end, that this was why I could never have done it. I loved you both, but he would have me kill someone important to me. Whereas you would not. That isn't love.' She shook her head. 'If he loved me the right way, he would never have asked me to do that. I couldn't do it. But I knew he wouldn't stop.' The tears began to fall and she bowed her head as sobs rocked her body.' I knew he wouldn't stop trying, and I knew if I failed him, I would be next. So, you see' – she pulled her head up and miserably wiped away the tears of pain – 'I didn't just plan to kill him for you. I killed him to save myself too. I was doomed either way. This seemed the lesser of two evils.'

Tanya exchanged a long look with Anna, and Anna closed her eyes in stress. There was another long silence, and for a while all that could be heard in the large room was the ticking of the grandfather clock in the corner.

'In our line of work,' Anna eventually began, staring down at the glass she held loosely in front of her on the table, 'in our *family*,' she added, 'trust is more important than anything else. It has to be. It's the only thing that keeps us out here in the world instead of behind bars, or dead by the hand of an enemy.' She exhaled heavily. 'The rules have been in place for generations and they're cut and dry. If someone close to you betrays you, they pay with their life.'

Josephine let out a sob and Tanya closed her eyes in grief. She wanted to beg Anna to reconsider, but she knew that what she said was the truth. If Freddie was here, it would have already been done.

'However,' Anna continued, 'the fact that you made a play against Aleksei – that you tried to take him out to protect us, in the end…' She let out a long, slow breath, shaking her head. 'That makes this situation not so black and white.'

Josephine held her breath, hardly daring to hope that she might be off the hook. As she sat there, the desperation clear on her unhappy face, Anna was reminded of the woman she'd saved on the bridge that night. This had been a colossal fuck-up, of that there was no doubt. But the one thing she had always loved about Josephine was her good heart. And that had shone through this mess, in the end. Even despite having to let go of a man she loved. 'You've already suffered for your mistakes with Aleksei,' she said eventually.' And I'm betting that's something that's never going to leave you.' Her gaze was still cold as she looked Josephine in the eye. It was going to take a long time to forgive her for this. But she wanted to try. 'I think it's best that we bury this whole situation and start again. But,' she continued curtly as Josephine began blubbering incoherent gratitudes, 'you will be watched *very* closely going forward, Josephine. And if you betray us again, in any way, I will have no more mercy for you.'

'Thank you, Anna, thank you,' Josephine uttered in between sobs. 'You all mean the world to me.'

Anna nodded. 'I really hope we do,' she said, her voice slightly hoarse with emotion as the betrayal she felt began to truly set in. No matter how much time passed, and although she understood it to a degree – love made you do things you wouldn't usually do – she wasn't sure she would ever forgive Josephine for not coming to her with this before everything got so terribly messed up.

Tanya sat forward, wiping away a tear from her own eye at the sorry unfolding of events. 'What are we going to do about Freddie?' she asked.

'What do you mean?' Anna replied.

'If he finds out, he won't be so lenient. The rules are very straightforward, where he's concerned. I don't think even you'd be able to save her from that.'

Anna thought about it for a few moments. 'The only people who know of you having any involvement with Aleksei are us and Seamus,' she said slowly. 'I trust Seamus to keep this to himself; he's loyal to a fault and never goes back on his word.'

She bit her lip. She might be at odds with Freddie herself right now, but even so, she was still deeply loyal where business was concerned. It was ingrained into the very fabric of her being. But looking at Josephine's frightened face and having already made up her mind to move on from this, she knew she couldn't allow Freddie to change that.

Looking at Tanya, she pulled a grim expression and nodded. 'We'll cover this up and keep it between us. Freddie can never know. We'll sort out an alibi and Josephine' – she glanced at the dark purple bruises all around her neck – 'you need to cover up, act normal and keep your head down for a while. Do you understand?'

'I do – thank you, Anna,' Josephine breathed.

'We had a girls' night in at mine tonight,' Tanya said. 'We had pizza and cocktails and watched *Dirty Dancing*. Just so we have our stories straight, if anyone questions where we were. We were never anywhere near a building site. Got it?' They both nodded. 'Good.' She stood up, sighing tiredly. 'Not that they're likely to find anything in the rubble anyway,' she added. Josephine looked down.

After Anna and Josephine had reappeared at the boundary wall together and relayed a swift, short version of events, they had been ready to run, but Tanya had stopped them, pointing out that they couldn't just leave Aleksei there. Their DNA, the bullet and all sorts of other evidence would be all over the scene, leading the police straight to them once his body was found by workers the next day. That was the point at which Josephine had realised she still had the detonator. They'd set off the charges, watching with horror as the building collapsed in a catastrophic display in front of them. As the dust began to settle, the three women had fled into the night.

'Hopefully they put it down to some sort of accident, but even if they don't, there shouldn't be any evidence that we were there. Aleksei was already there setting up for his own plans, which means the cameras were most certainly down, and even if they found his body, they won't be able to get any DNA from you guys out of all that rubble. Let's go home,' she said, turning to Anna. 'It's stupidly late and we need to clean ourselves up and try to forget about all this.' She glanced at Josephine.

Josephine wouldn't forget. She would mourn and grieve for the love she'd lost and forever question if things could have been different. That was the curse of taking on the sort of burden she had. Anna would likely not forget it either, having been the one to take Aleksei's life. But something told Tanya she would be OK this time. The Anna that stood up next to her now was not the fragile bird with a broken wing she'd first met, nor was she the emotional wreck she'd been when she'd been forced to take Michael's life, years before. This Anna was a stronger, harder, colder model. This way of life had given her that invisible suit of armour to protect her in times such as these. And so Tanya believed she would come through it, fighting, moving forward and with more strength than ever.

Touching Josephine on the shoulder, she gave her a tired half-smile. 'Get some rest,' she said, before walking out.

Anna straightened her skirt, now rumpled from the evening's antics, and picked up the gun from the table.

'Can I ask you something?' Josephine said tentatively.

'Go ahead,' Anna replied, her tone emotionless.

'After you shot Aleksei' – she swallowed the pain that rose with her words – 'you had the gun aimed at my head. You cocked it. If Tanya hadn't called' – her voice trembled slightly – 'would you have shot me too?'

There was a long silence as Anna's dark blue eyes bored into Josephine's, her gaze troubled and sombre. Eventually she spoke.

'I'd like to tell you no. But the truth is that I honestly don't know, Josephine. And I don't think I ever will.'

CHAPTER FIFTY-FOUR

The next morning Freddie leaned over the breakfast bar in his pyjama bottoms, re-dressing his shoulder wound as he listened intently to the news on the radio. The reports of the shooting had gone national, but so far no one seemed to have any clues as to who was responsible. Two bodies had been found at the scene – the ones who had died in the shoot-out – but nobody else had come forward, no witnesses other than a few of the customers who had run out at the beginning. This was unusual, but Freddie guessed that most of the men who were in the strip club that night didn't particularly want their wives finding out, and so had stayed staunchly quiet.

A voice Freddie knew well came on, as Sarah Riley was interviewed as the DCI in charge of the scene.

'As yet we have no definitive leads. It's a difficult scene to asses, as there are hundreds, if not thousands of people's DNA all around and the attackers left nothing behind. The bullet casings are common and untraceable, meaning this was most likely a professional firm. We can confirm that the club was owned by a known Russian mobster who seems to have gone into hiding, so it is possible that this was an inter-firm disagreement.'

Freddie smiled. She was good. Sowing the seeds now that this was probably just the Russians falling out with themselves was a good ploy. It was the most logical option, or at least it would be for the tired coppers who really couldn't be bothered to deal with a case like this. They already had a hundred other cases to solve, so pushing this under the rug would be the most attractive option. Or so Freddie hoped anyway.

Anna walked into the room and grabbed her keys, not making eye contact as she attempted to avoid him. She was fully dressed and obviously ready to go out for the day, though her carefully applied make-up could not hide the stress in her frown or the hollow rings of exhaustion under her eyes. He felt guilt flood through him, knowing that her sleepless night would have been down to him. Ethan had stayed over at Mollie's the night before, a tactical move on their part in case anything went wrong, and so she had no need to do the school run today. She could have stayed in bed and slept in, so she was clearly only leaving the flat this early just to put some distance between them.

'Anna, wait,' he called as she went to leave.

She stopped and half turned back, still not looking up at him.

He took a deep breath. This was his one chance to change things, to stop this terrible path they were both rolling down.

He had crept in sometime in the early hours of the morning after the raid and seeing to the injured men – luckily both just had flesh wounds. He should have been exhausted – he *was* exhausted – but instead of falling into the deep sleep his body craved, he found himself staring at the ceiling and thinking back over all their years together. This couldn't be the end for them, not now. He had thought it was, when his time in prison separated them. He had even come to terms with it, despite the ache in his heart, and thought perhaps time would fade what they had. But when he had come out and seen her that day at his mother's house, he'd realised that his feelings for her hadn't diminished at all. Not even slightly.

He'd been angry at her since then, dreaming up this stupid idea that she'd double-crossed him. It had helped mask how he really felt. Perhaps that had been why he'd been so certain, despite not really having any hard evidence. Maybe being angry with her had just been easier than loving her. But now that he knew what a fool he'd been, he could no longer escape the fact that nothing had changed for him. He still loved her and he still wanted to make things right. If there was even a slight chance, he had to try.

'Anna, I know that you don't want to hear anything I have to say, but you need to. I need you to just hear me out, and if you still want to leave, I won't stop you.'

Anna sighed tiredly and rubbed her forehead in distress. Freddie was right – she didn't want to hear it. She'd been through enough, and it was time to call it a day. But for all the years they had shared, she guessed she could give him one more minute of her time so that he could offload his guilt before she walked away. And that was surely all it was at this point. Reluctantly she walked to the sofa and sat down.

'Thanks. Look, Anna, I have no excuse for what I've done to you since I got out. Literally nothing can even explain how I came to such a ridiculous conclusion.' He shook his head, still unable to explain it even to himself. 'I think maybe…' He paused, reluctant to be so open but knowing he needed to be. 'I think maybe subconsciously it was easier to see you as an enemy than someone I loved and couldn't have.'

Anna pulled a face and shook her head. 'That's not love, Freddie,' she said tiredly. 'You don't do that to someone you love.'

'That's where you're wrong, Anna. Because I *do* love you. I always have,' he admitted. 'And while I was inside—' He pulled a grim expression, remembering the strange half life they led in there. 'While I was inside it was like time somehow stopped. I mean, it stretched on for an eternity, but at the same time, nothing ever really changed. So when I got out, I was still at the same point in my life as I had been before I went away. I hadn't learned to deal with life – normal life I mean – without you by my side.'

Anna felt tears prickle up in her eyes and one slowly rolled down her face. It had been a long, difficult night and to come back to dealing with this whole emotional mess with Freddie was just too much to bear. She stared straight ahead at the wall, not trusting herself to look at him without breaking down.

'I didn't know how to handle it,' Freddie continued. 'So, I guess my mind just sort of jumped on the first opportunity to cope. In the worst way, and I am so sorry for that. Because the last thing I have ever wanted to do is hurt you.'

Walking forward out of the kitchen, Freddie moved closer, hoping this wouldn't push her away. He bit his bottom lip and stared out of the window for a moment, trying to find the right words but knowing that they may well no longer exist.

'Do you remember the first time we found out who each other was?' He watched as she frowned, confused. 'It was in the warehouse. One of Tony's men had taken you, and we came to get you out. I pulled that fucking bag off your head, and even though you were the one who had been taken and who he planned to kill – the sadistic fuck...' he added. 'Despite the fact you were in the worst position possible, you were worried for *me*. You wanted *me* to get out, so I wouldn't get hurt.' He grinned, shaking his head at the memory.

Even through her tears, Anna couldn't help but smile slightly too. After all these years she could finally look back and see the funny side of that situation.

'I think I was already in love with you before then,' Freddie continued. 'Because I'd fallen for the person you were inside, no matter what else that came with. And if I remember rightly, you'd fallen pretty hard for me too.' He watched for her reaction and saw the corner of her mouth twitch as she stubbornly hid the smile that wanted to escape. 'And even though you found out who I really was that night, that I am *this*,' he said, pointing at his shoulder, 'that I am violence and everything that makes up the dark side of this city, you still loved me anyway.'

'That was a long time ago, Freddie,' Anna replied quietly.

'It was,' he agreed. 'But the point is, we change as people, all the time. Sometimes in big ways, sometimes small. But no matter how much you change or grow' – he risked kneeling down on the floor beside her, opening himself up for better or worse – 'I have always loved you. And I always will.'

Anna's hands began to shake in her lap as her heart reached out towards Freddie. She so desperately wanted to forget the pain he'd caused her and the hardships of the last two and a half years, but was this enough? Could they ever get over that? She closed her eyes, but the sight of him kneeling beside her – his face more open than she had ever seen it, his bare torso battered and bruised from the life he led – seemed to be etched into her eyelids.

'You came to my office and you told me you still have feelings too, so I know they're there, Anna. I know you feel the same. And yes, I pushed you away when I shouldn't have. But I'm here now. I know we can't just go back to how things were.' He reached out for her shaking hands. 'But please, just give us a chance to start again.'

The tears began to flow freely from Anna's eyes as the situation overwhelmed her. For a moment Freddie thought he had finally pushed her too far.

'It's been so long, Freddie,' she said in an emotional voice through the tears. Everything she had resting on her shoulders suddenly seemed so much heavier than before, as her defences began to break down. As her emotions began to tumble out, one on top of the other, she suddenly yearned to be held by him, to not have to be the strong one just for a few moments. She turned to him. 'It's been so long and it has been just… *so* shit without you. Without the real you.'

Reaching forward, she wrapped her arms around him and slid to the floor where he was still kneeling. Freddie pulled her close to him, savouring her warmth and inhaling the sweet scent of her hair as she cried. For what seemed like an age they just sat there, locked in an embrace that had been years coming. Eventually she pulled back, and before she could say anything or change her mind, he pulled her in for a kiss. As their lips met, Anna let go of the last of her resolve, and the parts of each of them that had been missing for so long finally fell back into place.

CHAPTER FIFTY-FIVE

One week later, Freddie and Paul sat at the desk in the office at Club CoCo as Anna talked them through the paperwork she had spread out in front of them. It was the new lease agreement for the building Aleksei's strip club had been in. Since the night of the shooting, it had been completely abandoned, and after doing some digging, they'd found that Aleksei had taken it over by force, never paying a single penny of rent to the owners.

'… and the rental price is an absolute steal for the area. After Tanya got in there and made out it was almost untouchable, being an area rough enough for guns and murder, they couldn't drop it quick enough. I think the owner is just desperate for someone to cover the mortgage on it, to be honest,' she said.

'Good,' Freddie replied with a nod. 'And the paperwork is under your name?'

'Mine and Tanya's – there's no official link to you. But obviously we're going into this one together, the four of us,' she confirmed, referring to herself and Tanya, Freddie and Paul.

'Equal partners,' Freddie confirmed, his eyes meeting hers warmly. 'Joining forces really is the best idea I've ever had.'

'*Your* idea?' Anna retorted, her eyebrows shooting up.

Freddie laughed. 'OK, let's call it a mutual agreement then.'

Anna's eyes glinted with amusement as she shook her head at him. After they had agreed to start over, they had sat down and ironed out every part of their lives together. She'd wanted to be crystal clear on where everyone stood. It was so important to get it right, for Ethan's sake as well as their own. Now that Freddie was thinking straight again and was starting to truly see the value she had added with her unique way of thinking, he realised that keeping her in the business — to help develop things and to advise — was the best decision all round. Tanya too had proved to be more involved than he'd realised at first, and so it was agreed that they had each more than earned their positions in the inner circle. This was going to be their first official joint venture, and they were all excited to get started.

'And you think a restaurant still?' Paul piped up.

'I do. We need another laundry, especially with all the new things we have going on between us. It would do us good,' she answered in a practical tone. 'But Tanya and I were thinking, why don't we make it sort of an experience restaurant?'

'What do you mean?' Freddie asked.

'Well, you've heard of Circus — they have food and circus entertainment. Others, including our own, have food and burlesque. Why not create somewhere where there are completely different acts or forms of entertainment each week. It would keep things fresh, bring old customers back in for totally different experiences each time.'

'That's not a bad idea actually,' Paul replied, looking at Freddie to see what he thought.

'It's a blinding idea,' he agreed. 'We'll be full every night once word gets out.' He smiled at Anna, reminded once more of what a genius his other half was. And how lucky he was that he could once more call her that. 'Keep going this way, Anna, we'll all have so much legitimate money we'll have to go straight.'

There was a short silence and then all at once the three of them burst out laughing.

'Good one,' Paul replied, between laughs.

'Ah, Freddie, you do have a sense of humour,' Anna continued. Standing up and smoothing down her cherry-red body-con dress, she pushed back her dark hair back with a grin. 'Come on then – we'd better not keep the others waiting. We promised them a good celebration, and Ethan's only with your mum for a few more hours.'

Anna led the way out of the office, and Freddie and Paul followed. As they walked, Freddie turned to Paul with a small frown.

'Still no word from anywhere at all about Aleksei?' he asked.

'Not a dicky bird – it's fucking bizarre, to be honest,' Paul replied, pulling a face of disbelief. 'Not one person in the underworld has heard a thing.'

'Someone must be hiding him,' Freddie mused. 'But who?'

'No idea,' Paul replied as they headed over towards the VIP area. 'We'll just have to keep looking and be ready for when he surfaces.'

'We certainly will,' replied Freddie darkly. He had a world of torture planned for that Russian snake when he finally did reappear.

Anna cast her eyes down as she listened to their conversation. She'd kept up with the news surrounding the collapse of the building and knew it was an ongoing investigation, but so far the body that lay under the rubble had not been discovered and she doubted it ever would be. Once they gave up trying to work out what had happened, they would get industrial machines in to clear the site and start again. No one would be any the wiser.

They reached the VIP area and found their group already celebrating in one of the booths. Plastering on a smile, Freddie greeted Tanya as she skipped over with two glasses of champagne, the green sequins on her dress shining in the light. She did a small twirl as she saw their eyes being drawn to it.

'Do you like it? I fancied a bit of glitz tonight,' she said happily, passing them each a glass.

'It's very beautiful,' Freddie said graciously. 'And very you.'

'I totally agree,' she replied. 'I think I might have even *been* a sequin in a former life you know.' And with that, she glided back off to talk to Carl.

Freddie took a sip of his champagne and looked at the people around them. All their most loyal men were there, joking and laughing. Even Simon, who was drinking through the pain and sitting on a pile of cushions due to the wound on his thigh. Anna and Tanya had always been part of the family of course, but somehow they felt even closer, even more bonded now that they were officially part of the firm. Carl was there, talking animatedly to Josephine about some of his latest drink creations. Freddie didn't know Josephine very well, but he accepted that Anna had bought her into the fold and trusted her. That, now more than ever, was enough for him. If Anna trusted her, he would give her the benefit of the doubt too.

The only person missing was Thea. Her absence was like a gaping void in this loving, loyal group of people. The familiar ache stabbed at his heart as he thought of her and he turned to Paul with a sad smile. He seemed sombre too and Freddie wondered if he was also missing their sister.

'She'd have loved the idea of the restaurant,' Freddie said quietly.

'Yeah, she would,' Paul replied without pause, answering his brother's silent question.

Freddie leaned to the side and nudged Paul as a show of reassurance, and then took a long, deep breath. 'Right,' he said, straightening his suit jacket. 'Come on then. Let's enjoy ourselves. Everything else can wait until tomorrow.'

Stepping forward, Freddie wound his arm around Anna's waist and joined her conversation with Sammy and Seamus. Paul made his way over to Bill and his wife Amy, and they greeted him with a warm smile.

Anna locked eyes with Josephine across the room and gave her a small nod with a smile that didn't quite reach her eyes. Josephine returned it respectfully. Tanya caught the exchange, and as Anna cast her eyes away from Josephine, they shared a loaded look. The secrets they had buried under the rubble would stay between the three of them for eternity. It had to, if Josephine was to stay safe and if the new era of peace they had forged in the firm was to continue. Turning away, Anna accepted a glass of champagne and smiled, rejoining the conversation.

Nobody noticed the man sitting a few tables away, the regular with his pint of Guinness, who always drank alone but caused no trouble. And why would they? He didn't stand out and had been careful not to draw attention to himself. He wasn't ready to be noticed by Freddie and Paul, the infamous Tyler brothers. At least not yet anyway. But soon, very soon.

With a strange half-smile at the brothers' backs, he picked up his coat and left. He'd seen enough for now. Their 'not so chance' meeting could wait for another day.

A LETTER FROM EMMA

Dear Readers,

For those of you who have just joined the Tyler family saga, I really hope you've enjoyed it and welcome aboard! And for those who have been through this journey with me since the beginning – wow. Just wow. I can't believe I'm writing this at the back of the sixth book in the series!

If you liked this book and want to hear about my next one, sign up here. Your email address will never be shared and you can unsubscribe at any point.

www.bookouture.com/emma-tallon

When I look back at how far our characters have come, it really amazes me. Mainly because I don't even plan half of their development. They just seem to evolve, book on book, underneath my fingers. It's like they truly do have a mind of their own. I love looking back on who they were, to who they are at this point, Anna, I think, has come the farthest. Although her stubborn nature and her inner strength has never changed, she has grown so much from that broken young woman we first read about in *Runaway Girl*.

I really enjoyed writing this instalment, especially Josephine's character. She is so flamboyant and at times utterly ridiculous, but in the best way. She's someone I'd love to go and grab a drink with, just so that I could sit and listen to her and soak up some of her sparkling energy – that is, when she's not feeling glum about having to kill off someone she loves.

There is another new character in this book who you may have picked up on. She only appeared in one scene, but it's one that will remain close to my heart: Julie Andrew, Ethan's favourite teacher. I was contacted part way through writing this book by a friend of the real Julie, who was a big fan of the series and who I learned, through this friend and members of her close family, was a truly beautiful soul. Sadly, Julie passed away towards the end of last year, from cancer.

I never met Julie in person, but each and every one of my readers mean a lot to me and so my heart broke for Julie and her family and friends. Back before she died, Julie wanted to know if the book would be out in time for her to read it. It wasn't, so instead I spoke to Julie through video message and I created a space for her in this novel, where she will live on forever. Between these pages she will never die but instead will live on as a character people love. Cancer is an evil that none of us can control, but although it's taken her life, it will never take her memory. So do me one small favour: if you take anything forward with you from this book, take her. Take Julie with you, the kind woman with the golden hair and the smiling blue eyes.

Thank you all again from the bottom of my heart, and I'll catch up with you again in the next book!

With love,
Emma Xx

emmatallonofficial

EmmaEsj

@my.author.life

www.emmatallon.com

ACKNOWLEDGEMENTS

To all my readers, thank you so much for reading my books and for the priceless support you continue to show me through this series. I appreciate it more than you know. Without you, my stories and I wouldn't be anywhere. Except, perhaps, still stuck in my log cabin office at the end of my garden where no one ever sees us.

To Helen, thank you for being the best editor in the world. Thank you also for being a good sport and such a fun person to be on this journey with. Writing full-time can be isolating at times, so the jokes and banter we share between edits are truly cherished.

To my family, my loving husband, my beautiful boy and my growing bump, thank you for being the motivation I use each day to work so hard and to push through every challenge. You are the reason I create worlds and work long into the nights as I approach deadlines even when I ache for bed. You make me want to give you the world, and you give me the strength to do what needs to be done to achieve that.

And finally, to my Bookouture family, thank you for being the best, most crazy, dysfunctional, wonderfully supportive and hilarious work family I could have ever hoped to be part of. Never change, you beautiful people.

Lightning Source UK Ltd.
Milton Keynes UK
UKHW011913071022
410079UK0000B/354